More Praise for

LADY BE GOOD

"*Lady Be Good* is a fascinating, endlessly entertaining romp set during the 1950s through the eyes of a clever, complicated socialite. Funny and incisive, richly detailed, and full of unexpected twists, this novel is a delight from the first page to the last."

—Anton DiSclafani, author of *The After Party*

"Brock uses descriptions of the glamour of 1950s New York, South Beach, and Havana to add sparkle to this quick-paced period novel about a spoiled heiress who slowly learns to see beyond her own privilege."

—*Library Journal*

"An exciting romp through 1950s Manhattan, Miami, and Havana . . . a spellbinding story complete with captivating characters, sweet romance, and fascinating female friendships."

—*Bustle*

"Satisfying and heartwarming . . . a solid choice for historical fiction fans interested in the 1950s as well as readers who enjoy tales of women becoming empowered, taking control of their lives, and learning true friendship."

—*Booklist*

LADY BE GOOD

A NOVEL

AMBER BROCK

B\D\W\Y

BROADWAY BOOKS

NEW YORK

Copyright © 2018 by Amber Leah Brock Player
Reading Group Guide copyright © 2019 by
Penguin Random House LLC
Excerpt from *A Fine Imitation* copyright © 2016
by Amber Leah Brock Player

All rights reserved.
Published in the United States by Broadway Books,
an imprint of the Crown Publishing Group, a division
of Penguin Random House LLC, New York.
broadwaybooks.com

Broadway Books and its logo, B \ D \ W \ Y, are registered
trademarks of Penguin Random House LLC.

Extra Libris and the accompanying colophon are trademarks
of Penguin Random House LLC.

Originally published in hardcover in the United States by
Crown, an imprint of the Crown Publishing Group, a division
of Penguin Random House LLC, New York, in 2018.

Library of Congress Cataloging-in-Publication Data is available
upon request.

ISBN 978-1-5247-6041-0
Ebook ISBN 978-1-5247-6042-7

Printed in the United States of America

Cover design by Elena Giavaldi
Cover photographs: (pool water) Pattern Image/Shutterstock;
(woman) H. Armstrong Roberts

10 9 8 7 6 5 4 3 2 1

First Paperback Edition

To
Tom
and
Sandra

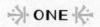

ONE

NEW YORK CITY
NOVEMBER 1953

Kitty Tessler sat at the long wooden bar in the Palm on a chilly Friday evening, steadily losing confidence that her date deserved the seat next to her. Raymond had seemed like a true catch, the perfect fit for her meticulous plans. About five minutes after they ordered their drinks, however, he had begun flicking his gaze over Kitty's shoulder with a frequency that suggested a fugitive searching the crowd for a plainclothes policeman. Perhaps a change of scenery would still his wandering eye.

She waited until he paused the stream of names he'd been dropping since her rear hit the bar stool. "Raymond, don't you think we ought to get a table?"

"Oh. Oh, sure. Right."

Another glance over her shoulder. *Who is he looking for?*

"Not to rush you." She flashed him a coy smile. "Don't want you to think I get too hungry for dinner at eight."

His brow furrowed in confusion, and she swallowed a sigh. "Never mind," she said. "Why don't I get our drinks?"

"I can't let a lady pay," he said.

"It's on my father. He has a tab here." She motioned for the bartender.

"What? Nicky Tessler has an open account at the Palm?"

Kitty turned her full attention on him. No one she knew would dare to call her father "Nicky." "Is that so hard to believe?"

"That's usually based on a certain . . . status. At a place like this, you understand." He sipped his drink, unaware of the approaching storm.

"I see. And what kind of status would you say my father has?"

"Don't get me wrong. He's done well for himself. But it's not like he runs in *my* father's circles."

"And remind me, where is your father spinning these days?"

Raymond straightened his tie. "Well, he's a partner at Dunham and Lowe, for starters."

"That's right . . . aren't they the ones who bungled that big corruption case that was all over the papers a few months ago?"

He squirmed on his bar stool. She pressed on. "That's right. Your father was the lead lawyer on the matter. The papers really made it sound for a while there like he was awfully tied up in the whole situation. Thank goodness there wasn't more of a scandal. It sure went away quietly."

He scowled. "Hold on just a minute. You don't know the first thing about it."

"Now, now. I'm saying it's a good thing. He avoided losing any of that stellar reputation." She turned to smile at the now-waiting bartender. "Won't you be a dear and put my drink on my father's account? Nicolas Tessler is the name. In fact . . ." Kitty glanced around and raised her voice. "A round of champagne for everyone in the bar. Something French and old." She pointed a manicured finger at Raymond. "For everyone but Raymond here. He can't stay."

His lips were a thin, tight line. He fumbled with his wallet, threw a five on the bar, and walked out without another word. She folded the bill. When the bartender returned with a sparkling glass of bubbly,

Kitty handed him the five. "This is for you. And I'll get Raymond's martini on my tab. Poor fellow. Had a sudden upset stomach."

The bartender nodded, then shot her a knowing look. "I'm surprised to see Mr. Leighton here on a Friday. You must be a friend of his girlfriend Carol's. Is she coming in with him on Saturday, as usual?"

Kitty loved a chatty bartender. "Oh, yes. She and I are dear friends. And I'll tell you what—the next time they come in, will you put Carol's first drink on my tab? Compliments of Kitty Tessler. She'll be so delighted."

The bartender winked and held the bottle aloft. "All right," he said. "This young lady is buying champagne for anyone who wants it."

A cheer went up from a few patrons, who crowded around to claim their glasses. Kitty stewed. She had known Raymond was flawed. None of them were perfect, after all. But she'd held out hope he would prove a viable candidate anyway. All he had proven was that he was the same as the other men she'd gone out with lately: appropriately wealthy and connected, yet all with some disqualifying factor she couldn't ignore.

A meaty hand landed on her shoulder, making her jump.

"Didn't mean to scare you," the man said. Kitty scanned him. Hideous sweater vest, shoes not shined, greasy grin.

"You don't scare me," she said, turning back to the bar.

"Hey, that's good, that's good." Ignoring all signs that he shouldn't, he took the seat beside her. He stuck out a hand. "Joe Carlo."

"I'm not looking for company at the moment, Mr. Carlo. I hope you understand."

"Ah, yeah, I saw that guy leave. You had him pretty hot under the collar. But he obviously didn't know how to talk to a classy lady like you. I'm glad you let him have it."

Kitty turned her head so her eye roll wouldn't be obvious. "Listen, you seem like a nice guy, but I'm not—"

"I noticed you recognized my name when I introduced myself. I won't leave you guessing. Yes, I am that Carlo. The Muffler King is my uncle."

The confession signaled the final curtain on Kitty's doomed evening. She downed her glass of champagne.

"Oh, look at the time. I'd better go." She hurried out. Sharing a drink with Joe Carlo, already an unappealing prospect, would only make her situation more impossible than it already was. She would never find the kind of man she needed to propel her into the social stratosphere if someone she knew caught her consorting with the Muffler King's nephew.

She took a cab back to the Vanguard Hotel, barely seeing the city as it whizzed by outside the car's window. Her mental list of acceptable mates was growing shorter with each disappointing Friday night. It wasn't really about money. She had money. Even guys like the Muffler Prince had money. She needed the warm, cocooning protection of good breeding. And that kind of security could never be hers until she had a venerable and appropriately Anglo-Saxon name attached to her own. The trouble was, only a thimbleful of New Yorkers had the right lineage to counterbalance Kitty's own pedigree. Even more troubling was the fact that the children of those respected families had an irritating tendency to marry each other. Though she moved in their social world, the dismissive way people like Raymond still said her father's name was a constant reminder of how far the Tesslers still had to climb.

The cab pulled up to the curb in front of the Vanguard. Kitty considered going into the club on the first floor, but her mood was too sour. Instead, she took the elevator up to the top-level suite that she and her father called home.

The suite was a unique space. The diamond-shaped living room offered double the view of the area surrounding the hotel through two sliding-glass doors that led to a triangular balcony. If Kitty leaned over the point of the triangle, she could see down to Herald Square. She rarely went out onto the balcony these days, since they'd parked the bar cart in front of the windows. Nothing like a glittering view of city lights while mixing a drink. The door leading to her room and bathroom was on the wall just to the left of the balcony, while her father's bedroom door was mirrored on the other side of the room. Thick, cream-colored rugs and a brocade couch with heavy pillows satisfied Nicolas Tessler's preference for a classic look. The chaise longue had been Kitty's choice, since she liked to have her feet up when she rested. He'd also given in to her request for a television, though he hated the clunky box.

A clattering of claws on the wooden floor meant Kitty's little dog, Loco, had heard the key turn in the lock. She bent down, and the cocker spaniel leapt into her arms. Kitty laughed as she stood up.

"Oof. You're gaining some weight, pretty girl. Time for that diet. Nothing but cottage cheese and lettuce for you from now on." The dog licked Kitty's face until she set the wriggling bundle of enthusiasm on the couch.

Fresh start tomorrow, Kitty thought, going into her bedroom to change.

The phone rang the next morning just as Kitty returned to the suite from taking Loco out. She launched herself at it, hoping it might be a last-minute invitation for a Saturday night date. Not that she could accept under those conditions, but she liked knowing she was in demand. Instead of a potential beau, it was her father's secretary, Miss Jones, on the other end of the line.

"Miss Tessler, your father would like to meet with you immediately. Should I tell him you'll be in his office at ten?" Miss Jones had a stuffy voice that always made Kitty think of a dour schoolmarm.

Kitty glanced at the clock. Nine forty-five. Not nearly enough time. "You can tell him that, but it won't be true," she said, her tone falsely sweet. "I'm taking Loco to the groomer's, and then I have a hair appointment. I can see him at three o'clock."

"I would recommend you reschedule your appointment. Your father said the matter is urgent."

"Oh, it will be fine, Miss Jones. I'm sure it can wait a few hours, whatever it is." Kitty plunked the receiver back into its cradle with Miss Jones's now-tinny voice protesting all the way down. Loco's appointment was real, but Kitty's was fictional. Still, if her father was in the kind of mood that had him using his secretary to schedule a meeting with his daughter, Kitty needed to brace herself. She decided to treat herself to lunch at the Colony. Sitting among the well-dressed ladies always made her feel more composed, and it allowed her to dream of the day when she'd at last be able to walk into the Colony Club across the street.

When she returned to the penthouse, feeling refreshed, she chose her outfit with care. The combination of a white button-down blouse with a Peter Pan collar and the fluffy skirt with large purple pansies would give her the sweet, girlish air most likely to soften her father's heart, especially after keeping him waiting. Properly dressed, she went down to the first floor of the hotel late in the afternoon. It would have been near the end of another businessman's workday, but her father was just hitting his stride by three o'clock.

As soon as Kitty entered the office, she could feel the heat of her father's glare. She kept her own expression cool, dropping into a maroon armchair and sliding off her shoes before the secretary even had the door closed. Her father leaned across his enormous mahogany desk as she rooted around in her beaded handbag for her cigarette case and lighter.

"You can't smoke in here," he said, his face beginning to redden.

Kitty pointed. "Then why is there an ashtray?"

"That's for people more important than you. People I can't say no to."

She pulled the crystal dish closer and lit up anyway. "May I ask why we're meeting in your office? You must really be trying to scare me this time."

"Maybe I am." Her father watched the pale gray tendrils of smoke as they wafted toward him. He ran a hand across his slicked-back hair. Kitty could remember when it was solid black, like ink. Now it had threads of silver. Every few weeks, her roots reminded her that her hair was the same pitch black without dye. *Thank God for blond in the bottle*, she thought, pulling on one of the platinum curls that framed her face.

"If you haven't scared me once in twenty-five years, it's going to be hard to start now," she said.

"Oh, I think this will do it." He slid a long piece of paper across the desk to her. "Do you know what this is?"

The Palm's logo topped a long list of numbers. Kitty's throat tightened. "It looks like a bill."

"It sure does. It looks like a very high bill. It's also something else. Can you guess what else?"

She smelled the trap, so she shook her head wordlessly.

"It's also the last straw. This nonsense ends here and now. You seem to have no interest in making a life for yourself, so I'm giving you a push."

"I just wanted to have a little fun, Papa. I won't do it again."

"Doing this again is not the problem. It's all the times you've done this before. You've had too much fun, but that's partly my fault." His brow wrinkled. "Maybe mostly mine. I keep paying these bills, after all. But now I've got the solution."

"You're making it all sound so dire. It's not like I've been running wild."

"Believe me, I know the mistakes I've made with you. But after what happened in January . . ."

She dropped her gaze to the gold geometric patterns in the rug under her chair, but looking away didn't help. She still saw her father, only in her mind he was thin and sweating against the crisp linens of the hospital bed. Her papa, the tough, sophisticated businessman, being fed oatmeal by a nurse in a starched cap. He hated oatmeal. Kitty squeezed her eyes shut for a moment, and the image evaporated.

"I'm fine now. I am. Never felt healthier. But an episode like that makes a man evaluate. And something like this?" He tapped the bill with his finger. "Something like this makes him certain. You've had enough fun. It's time to get serious about your future."

Kitty leaned against the back of the chair and smiled, hoping she looked more languid than she felt. "We both know you're going to live forever, Papa."

"The fact is I'm not going to live forever." His sharp tone wiped the smile from her face. "I need to be sure you're settled when I go. You need someone to take care of you."

She fanned the lingering smoke in front of her and stubbed out her cigarette. "Is that all? I'm planning to get married at some point."

"No, that's not all. I've got to consider what happens to everything I'm responsible for. Everything I've built. You're my only child, only real living family. Everything will be yours, and you'll need someone to help you."

Kitty shrugged. "What, do you think Andre will quit? He'll never leave."

"Exactly." Her father pressed his palms together and was quiet for a long moment. "I think you should consider Andre, Katarina."

She frowned. "Consider keeping him on? Why wouldn't I? He's the hardest-working man I know, second to you."

"No." He sighed. "Consider marrying him."

A cold shock ran to the tips of Kitty's fingers. Andre, built like a tank from her grandfather's beloved Mother Russia. Andre, with all the smooth sophistication of a bear in the woods. She saw herself, a kerchief smushing her golden curls, ladling out borscht for the rest of her life. "Papa. No."

Her father's jaw set at the word. "Yes. It solves my problem, and you don't have any problems to solve, so you don't get a say. That way I know you and my properties are taken care of. You need to start seeing Andre socially."

Kitty folded her arms across her chest. "Or what?"

Her father's eyes widened. "One way or another, these hotels and clubs are going to take care of you. If you won't accept Andre, you'll learn the business the way I did. You'll work your way up, starting with cleaning toilets."

"You're not serious."

"It's time for you to settle down. Andre is a perfect fit. He's only a few years older than you, he's a good man, and he's from a respectable family. And he's been working for me for years. It's not like you have any other serious prospects from that tennis club set you run with."

Considering the previous evening's events, the remark stung. "I've been seeing a few men. What if someone does come along? Before anything happens with Andre?"

"If you find someone else, someone who can take care of you and my business, then I'll think about it. Like I say, none of these Rhode Island fellas."

"Why not? They've got money."

"Sure, but they don't value it. The minute I'm in a box in the dirt, they'll turn around and liquidate everything. Gamble with your legacy in the stock market, and where does that get you? Plenty of their set loved the stock market until about twenty years ago. Then . . ." Her father sent his hand down in a swan dive and let it pound on the desk.

"You don't know they'd put the money in the stock market."

"I do! That's what they all advised me to do when your grandfather died. He came here with—"

"I know, I know. He came here with seven dollars and a gold ring stuck in a bar of soap," she said. She felt like she'd heard the story more than she'd heard her own name spoken aloud.

"That's right. And he turned that ring into a men's clothing store through nothing but hard work. And I turned the money he left me into everything." Her father gestured to the ink drawings of his hotels and nightclubs that hung in lacquered frames on the wood-paneled walls around him. "Into everything that made your life possible, little girl. So, yes, this time you're going to listen. You're going to do what I say. One way or another, these hotels are your future. You can be Andre's wife, and be set up, or you can start as a maid. Whatever suits you best."

Kitty pursed her lips, considering the two equally unattractive options. "What would that accomplish exactly? Why would you want me working as a maid? To humiliate me?"

Her father held up a hand. "There's no shame in earning your way. It's what I did. Learned the business from the inside, and it only took me ten years. If you really won't consider Andre, you'll have to prove you can handle the hard work of running these places. But wouldn't it be easier to marry a man you can trust to do the work for you? You'd make a better wife than a manager, we both know that."

Flames shot through her, out to the tips of her fingers. Kitty hated not having an answer, but she couldn't think of a solution that would satisfy both her and her father. She suppressed the urge to toss the crystal ashtray at her father's head and smiled instead. "Sure, Papa. I'll think about it."

"No thinking about it. I want you to promise me you'll make some time for Andre." Her father tilted his head, and his tone softened. "Go out with him. I'm sure he likes you. I won't tell him about the Palm."

Internally, Kitty shuddered. "Fine. I promise." It was the only way to be done with the conversation.

Her father let out a relieved *whoosh*. "Good. Good."

Kitty gave him the Broadway-footlights smile, the one that never failed. "So I can go? Hen's coming over in a little while."

"You can go." Her father's mouth eased from its tight line, and his eyes sparkled. Her smile had hit the bull's-eye yet again. He stood and held out his arms, and she swooped around the desk to hug him.

"You girls don't get into too much trouble, all right?" he called as she went to retrieve her shoes.

"Never."

Kitty pulled the door closed behind her and padded in stocking feet down the corridor toward the elevator. She had some thinking to do before her best friend, Henrietta, came by that afternoon. No way was she going to let Andre start squiring her around town. He'd chase off the real game, the boys who wore light suits to the shore every summer

and whose families owned polo ponies. Andre was the dictionary definition of solid, but he could never give her the life she was after. She
had started to wonder, however, who could. All the men who had the
social cachet she'd need were already involved with other women. As
Raymond had proven, most of them were still all too willing to take her
out. Fewer were willing to ditch their appropriate society match for a
girl like Kitty.

She stepped off the elevator and opened the door to the penthouse,
a space she was used to inhabiting alone given her father's long hours.
When Kitty was very young, before her mother died, her father was
home much more. Then again, in those days, the critical pieces of
Nicolas Tessler's empire were all located in New York. The Vanguard
Hotel, his first, was the only hotel he'd owned when Kitty was born.
They still lived there, surrounded by furnishings her father had picked
out himself before the hotel opened, down to the plush hand towels
in each bathroom. Her father liked the old-world look, a European
grandeur that set the standard in the newer properties of his growing
empire. The Vanguard had its thick Persian rugs and lamps on low
mahogany tables in the hallways. The Maxima, his second property
near Madison Square Park, had green marble in the lobby and sparkling chandeliers. Kitty would have preferred a more modern décor,
but when she'd suggested refreshing the interiors, her father insisted
people wanted the glamour of a bygone era. In her opinion, the present day had glamour enough for anyone with good taste, but her father
stuck by his polished woods and embroidered curtains. When he'd
expanded to Miami, he'd had to concede somewhat to the pastels and
stucco that ruled South Beach. Still, he'd chosen plain white wood
plank walls and wicker furniture. Kitty hadn't been to the Miami hotel
since her father had first opened it, but as she recalled, it had a sense
of luxury that set it apart.

In addition to the touches of her father's particular style, the three
hotels had two other unifying elements. One was an adjacent nightclub with a big band and a Spanish theme. The other was a suite high

above the busy streets that always sat waiting for him or his guests, just like the one Kitty entered on the top floor of the Vanguard at that very moment.

Loco sat patiently on the couch, wagging away, while Kitty rifled through some magazines on the glass coffee table. Hidden under the stack, she located a carefully placed book. She curled up beside the dog, turning to one of the many marked pages. "Let's see what inspiration we can find in here. I need a plan," Kitty murmured.

The doorbell startled Kitty out of reading. She slid the book back under the stack of magazines and picked up the glossy on the top. She opened it to an article about achieving the perfect blush effect. "Come in," she called.

Loco bounded off the couch to greet the girl who entered. Henrietta let out a happy gasp. "Ooh, someone looks so pretty," she cried, leaning down to pet the dog.

"Why, thank you," Kitty said. "Must be this new lipstick."

Hen giggled. "Not you, silly. Although you always do look pretty. Did little Miss Loco have a trip to the groomer's?"

"She did." Kitty wrinkled her nose. "She looks good, but they never dry her enough. Everything smells like wet dog."

"I still can't get over it," Hen said, straightening up. "A salon for a dog."

Kitty clicked her tongue, and Loco ran to rejoin her on the couch. Hen dropped onto the chaise longue. Though *dropped* wasn't the right word. Hen had all the definition and heft of a mosquito. She pretty much drifted everywhere she went.

"Whatcha reading?" Hen reached for the magazine.

"Nothing, actually. Couldn't keep my mind on it. I just had a 'meeting' with Papa, you know."

"About what?" Hen asked. "It wasn't bad news, was it?"

"It's nothing I can't fix."

"I believe that. So what did he say?"

Kitty stroked one of Loco's silky ears. "Papa seems to think it's high time I got married."

"But you don't even have a boyfriend. Who are you supposed to marry?"

"As luck would have it, Papa's already got someone picked out."

"Really?"

"Yes. Andre." Kitty stuck out her tongue. "Good thing Papa's in the hotel business. He'd be a lousy matchmaker."

Hen shook her head. "I'll say. So what did you tell him?"

"What could I say? He said either I marry Andre or work as a maid in the hotel."

"He's not serious, Kitty. He can't be. He'd never make you work."

Kitty pushed herself off the couch and inspected her makeup in the large mirror on the wall. "He wouldn't. That's what worries me. He must be attached to this Andre idea if he didn't give me a real alternative."

"Why not set you up with a trust fund?"

"He says he's made mistakes with me, that now's the time to put me on the straight and narrow. I think he wants me to settle down with someone stable. And Andre's stable, I'll give him that."

"So what are you going to do?"

"What I always do." Kitty flashed her reflection a smile. "I'm going to play Papa like a fiddle."

"You're so bad." Hen's eyes shone with admiration.

"Problem is, I'm not sure yet how to get around him this time. I need a plan, and until I have one, I'm going to have to play nice with Andre." Kitty started for her room, which was on the left of the French doors that led from the living room to the massive balcony. "Come on. Let's go freshen up the war paint. I think we need to go out tonight."

❋ TWO ❋

Hen lay down on the four-poster bed in Kitty's room, her tiny body dwarfed by a sea of lacy pink pillows. Kitty took a seat on the poufy cushion of the stool at her vanity table. While Kitty touched up her nail polish—always Arden Pink Perfection—she let Hen offer suggestions of ways to get out of her predicament. Kitty pretended to consider each of Hen's thoughts while she silently considered the other, equally serious dilemma she was facing. That problem was not one Hen could help Kitty with, since Hen refused to admit that her fiancé, Charles, qualified as a problem in the first place.

Charles Remington was the king of what Kitty's father derisively called "the tennis club set." He seemed perfect: handsome, a talented athlete, and a member of all the right clubs and societies at Harvard. He strode with purpose and cracked other men's knuckles with his handshake. On paper, the match was unimpeachable: a union of two families who dominated the New York social register and had done so for generations. In such elevated circles, this was just the way things were done. Hen and Charles were thrown together as children because their families' beach houses were side-by-side, and it didn't matter one bit that they had nothing in common except coastline property that their ancestors laid claim to when they arrived on the *Mayflower*. Once their parents had decided they should marry, the relationship was set in stone. Unfortunately, Charles was not a particularly faithful partner.

When they were newly engaged, Hen was quick to cover for Charles by embroidering the details, even as news of his conquests filtered down the grapevine. Hen always had some explanation to excuse his behavior—wasn't he so kind, paying for that girl's drink? She must have forgotten her handbag. Oh, that girl he shared a cab with must be the sister of a friend from college.

Then he'd done something Hen couldn't explain away. She'd come back from a summer stay at her family's beach house, shrunken from days of crying. Kitty had comforted her on the couch in the penthouse living room, handing her tissues and urging the whole story out of Hen.

After Hen revealed everything, Kitty had leapt up in a fury.

"You've got to ditch him, that's all there is to it." She paced the room. "Somewhere public. Make a scene. He'll be sorry he treated you like this when we're done."

"No." Hen's voice was a miserable croak.

Kitty had rejoined her on the couch, placing a hand on Hen's. "You can't stay with him after this."

"Mother said we're not to split up. So we won't. Mother said I'll forget about it. So I mean to forget. We'll forget." She'd locked eyes with Kitty, and Kitty had no doubt who *we* referred to.

Despite Charles's most outrageous offense, Hen's mother had made certain that Hen would never be the one to break it off. Liberating Hen from Charles would be Kitty's duty alone. She couldn't let her dearest friend spend a lifetime with a man like Charles. It would be cruel. He had to go. Kitty welcomed the task, even though it wouldn't be an easy one. After all, she owed her friend.

The truth was that Kitty had been trying her best to take care of Hen for the entire history of their friendship. Hen was the first girl

Kitty met when she enrolled at Alastair Preparatory Academy in the sixth grade. It had taken the better part of a year to convince Papa to let her transfer to Alastair from the dreary Catholic school she previously attended, but Kitty was already thinking of her future. She knew greater social possibilities lay elsewhere, and she'd found them in the person of Henrietta Bancroft.

Most teachers at Alastair assigned seating based on alphabetical order, but Miss Turner allowed the students in her care to choose their seats. Kitty had scanned her new homeroom, evaluating potential friends. Since all the girls wore matching plaid skirts, blue cardigans, and saddle shoes, she didn't have much to help her distinguish the wheat from the chaff. She rejected one girl for the oversized bow in her hair, and another for her snooty smirk. Then, at last, she spotted Hen: shirttail untucked, shoelace untied. Kitty had decided that the easiest way into her new social world was to find a partner who needed Kitty's help as much as Kitty needed hers. She could tell from Hen's hopeful, welcoming smile and glance at the empty desk beside her that Hen was on the lookout for a companion.

At first, Kitty imagined she would merely tolerate Hen as she advanced in the pecking order, but Hen had defied Kitty's expectations from the start. As soon as she learned Hen's family name, Kitty understood that her new friend's less-than-sophisticated toilette would never damage her reputation. If she wore a clown costume to school, the other girls would all be wearing red noses the next day. Her place at the top of the hierarchy was immutable thanks to her pedigree, which meant she wasn't much interested in the cold symbiotic partnership Kitty had hoped to establish. Instead, what Hen wanted was someone who was different from the baby debutantes she'd grown up with.

Hen wasn't much for confrontation, but once she had befriended Kitty she was fiercely loyal. When the other girls tried to snub Kitty that first week at school, Hen's quiet choice to sit with Kitty at lunch every day meant that the other students began to accept Kitty, at least outwardly. They had to, if they wanted to keep a Bancroft at their table.

Though years had passed, Kitty continued looking for ways to repay Hen for the initial—and life-changing—kindness no one else would show her in the classrooms of Alastair Prep. Getting rid of Charles would be an enormous undertaking, especially with Hen's formidable mother as a barrier, but preventing a lifetime of misery was not inappropriate in light of the debt Kitty owed.

Hen's voice broke into Kitty's thoughts. "I love this lipstick," she said, holding up a sultry red.

"Is that the color you want to wear tonight?" Kitty blew on her nails.

"No way. Too bright for me." Hen laughed.

"You think they're all too bright. Here." Kitty handed her a tube of a light rose color. "This will look great on you."

After attending to her own makeup, Kitty grabbed a full-skirted blue dress with a frothy underskirt out of her closet and insisted her friend borrow it before they left the suite. "I've got shoes you can borrow, too."

"But I'm not trying to impress anyone," Hen said, making her way to the bathroom to change anyway. "Charles already knows what I look like."

You and every other girl in a ten-mile radius, Kitty thought, gritting her teeth. "So Charles is joining us, then?" she asked Hen, raising her voice so she could be heard through the bathroom door.

"Yes." Layers of fabric muffled Hen's voice. "He's going to meet us downstairs."

Kitty clipped an earring on her lobe and inspected her makeup one final time. "I'm going to ring Papa, too. Better make sure Andre's at the club tonight. Don't want to waste our time there if we could be somewhere more exciting."

"But your father's clubs are exciting."

"You just think it's fun that the drinks are free." Kitty pulled the receiver to her ear. After two rings, Miss Jones answered. She asked Kitty to hold, and then her father spoke.

"Yes?"

"Papa, it's me. I was wondering if Andre is working this evening at the club. Thought it might be nice to go down and see him."

Kitty could almost hear her father's smile straining his face. "Well! That will be very nice. Yes, he'll be there tonight. And tell him he can leave Herman in charge for closing. In case you kids want to go out after."

"Thanks, Papa. I'll tell him." Kitty sighed and set the receiver back in the cradle. "Just peachy."

"What is?" Hen said, emerging from the bathroom.

Kitty stifled a giggle. "You've got the dress on backward, Hen. Let me help."

After the dress was righted, Kitty and Hen took the elevator down to the first floor. This time, instead of turning down the long, quiet hallway that led to the offices, Kitty headed toward the noise of the club, which drifted subtly through the lobby.

Charles stood at the double doors of the entrance. Kitty noted that his gaze lingered on her décolletage before he even glanced at Hen. Still, it was Hen he reached out for. At least he still had the good sense to pay some attention to his fiancée.

"Darling," he said, pulling her close and kissing her cheek. He turned. "Hello, Kitty. How are you?"

"Fabulous, as always."

He opened the door and she swept past them, nodding at the man standing behind the host's stand.

"Good evening, Miss Tessler. Always good to see you," the man said, opening a second door for them. The three walked inside, passing the long bar and heading to the circular booths nearest the stage. Booths ringed the outer edge of the room, each one covered in a screaming red leather that matched red paper lanterns hanging from the ceiling. Kitty had always thought of paper lanterns as more of a Chinese thing, but apparently to her father they gave the club a Spanish feel. About half of the tables filling the floor in the center of the room already had guests seated at them; by the end of the evening, there wouldn't even be room between the tables to stand. A small dance floor just in front of the stage gleamed with a fresh coat of polish.

"Kitty! Hello." Andre's voice thundered behind Kitty. She flinched, then caught herself.

"Why, hello yourself," she replied, turning to him. He was a bearded mountain, with a wide grin and friendly eyes. Not awful looking, Kitty had to admit, but not the kind of man she was looking for. He greeted the others, then focused his attention back on her.

"Your father told me you were dropping by. Said you wanted to have a drink?" He raised his thick brows.

"I thought . . . well, I know how busy you are." She patted her hair, hoping she was giving the impression of being properly awed.

He took a handkerchief from his breast pocket and wiped his forehead. "I'm getting the act set up for the show tonight. The guys just got into town, and they arrived a little late. But afterward . . . sure." He grinned at Hen and Charles. "Let's get you all a table up front. You're going to love these guys."

Andre guided Kitty, Hen, and Charles to a booth at the corner, closest to the edge of the stage. Kitty slid around from one end of the bench to the other, Hen following her lead. Charles sat beside Hen, lifting the menu and studying it, though he never ordered anything more adventurous than a rare steak with a baked potato. Andre leaned over to light Kitty's cigarette.

"I want you to meet someone," he said. "Back in a second."

Hen shot a quizzical look at Kitty, who shrugged. "Beats me," she said under her breath. "Probably some crusty old investor type."

A waiter in a red jacket approached the booth. "Miss Tessler, how nice to see you and your friends this evening."

"Hello, Malcolm." Kitty pouted, looking at him through lowered lids. "Will you be a darling and get me a sweet little drink? You know what I like. Oh, and make it a double. These jokers are already boring me to tears."

Hen elbowed Kitty and turned to Malcolm. "She's mean as a snake, isn't she? Just a sherry for me, please."

"Of course," Malcolm said. He took Charles's drink order and headed back through the growing crowd near the bar. Charles excused himself to go to the restroom, leaving the girls alone to gossip.

Kitty turned back to Hen. "Free drinks are not enough consolation for an evening with a Bolshevik."

"He's an attractive enough fellow, though," Hen said, gazing at Andre as he talked to some men on the other side of the room.

"If you like lumberjacks."

Hen shrugged. "Nothing wrong with a good lumberjack."

"You wouldn't touch a lumberjack on a dare," Kitty said, laughing.

"Maybe dare me and see," Hen said with a wicked smile. Her jaw slackened in an instant as something over Kitty's shoulder caught Hen's eye. "Oh, my word."

Kitty swiveled to follow Hen's gaze and saw Andre making his way back to the table. Then she saw what had knocked Hen's train of thought off the rails. Two men followed close behind him. One was a wiry fellow in a white jacket with an unfashionably long fringe of wavy black hair. The other was the most gorgeous man Kitty had ever seen who wasn't projected onto a movie screen. He had warm brown skin and a toothpaste-ad smile, which beamed at the girls as he walked toward them.

Andre stopped in front of the booth, smiling proudly. "Kitty, Hen— I'd like you to meet two of the members of the Miami club band. This is Max Zillman, the bandleader, and Sebastian Armenteros. He's our singer." He turned to the men. "Kitty is Mr. Tessler's daughter. And her friend is Henrietta Bancroft."

Sebastian leaned forward. "It's a pleasure to meet you, Miss Tessler. We've heard a lot about you from your father. You are as beautiful as he says."

Kitty offered Sebastian a hand, and a pleasant tingle ran up her arm when he gripped her fingers. "Please, it's Kitty. Nice to meet you," she said, her voice a little throatier than she might have liked.

Hen giggled beside her, and questions started rushing out. "You gentlemen are all the way from Miami? How do you like New York?

Is it very different?" She raised a hand, and Kitty noted a tremble in Hen's fingers.

"You'll have to excuse my friend," Kitty said, taking a drag off her cigarette. "She's not used to meeting such handsome boys."

Hen's mouth twitched. Kitty knew she was fighting the urge to stick out her tongue in retaliation for the comment.

"Well, she'll do just fine with me, then," Max said, reaching out for Hen's hand. "I've never been too good-looking for anyone."

"Oh, please." Kitty fluttered her lids, giving Max a demure smile. "No need to be so modest."

He glanced at her, unmoved, then looked back at Hen. "Nice to meet you, Henrietta."

"Call me Hen. Everyone does." Hen's cheeks were bright pink.

"Kitty? Hen? You two are just a couple of barnyard animals, aren't you?" Max said with another quick glance at Kitty. Hen laughed hard. Kitty's smile strained at the corners of her mouth. Max had his full attention on Hen, complimenting her dress. *The dress she borrowed from me*, Kitty thought. She focused on Sebastian.

"But you do like New York, don't you? It's the center of the world, after all," she said.

"Oh, yes, we are enjoying New York," Sebastian said, his words rolled smooth by his accent. "But you know, Miami has an advantage over your city."

"What's that?"

His eyes sparkled. "It's so very . . . hot."

Kitty was grateful Charles returned to the table at that moment. Sebastian's suggestive smile and the purr of his accent had her ready to pour her ice water straight on her head. On seeing Sebastian, Charles jutted out his chin.

"Who's this you've got with you, Andre?" he said, his own nasal tennis club accent a hint stronger than usual.

Another round of introductions distracted the four men, and Kitty leaned in to Hen. "Holy Toledo. Ricky Ricardo's got nothing on him, huh?"

Hen shushed her. "I thought Max was very nice."

"Hmph. Nice and dull." Kitty slumped back into the cushion and stubbed out her cigarette.

Hen smirked. "You're just mad that he didn't fall all over you."

"I am not. Besides, Sebastian seemed interested enough for both of them."

"Yes, he did. But you'd better behave. I don't think it counts as spending time with Andre if he's in the room while you're flirting with some other guy."

"Who cares?" Kitty sniffed. "Men love a little competition."

At last, the drinks arrived, and Max and Sebastian left to set up for the show. A crowd of about twenty other musicians had already taken the stage, pulling instruments from cases and taking their seats. Andre left to check that things were running smoothly in the kitchen and bar. Hen and Charles started up a conversation about one of Charles's Harvard classmates, someone Kitty didn't know, so she sulked and sipped the vodka and pineapple juice Malcolm had brought her. At least someone knew how to make her happy.

The houselights dimmed as the ones over the stage brightened, and Max took center stage. He spoke at a quick clip, like a radio presenter, and the words slid into each other. "Hello, and welcome all to the Alhambra Club, the hottest spot in the coolest city in the world." For a split second, Kitty was convinced he looked right at her. There was a strange flutter in her chest that she did her best to ignore.

"I'm Max Zillman and we are the Zillionaires," he continued. "Our home base is Miami, Florida, in the glorious Imperium Hotel and Ballroom, another fine Tessler Hotels property. It's my pleasure to present to you our lead singer, straight from Havana, Mr. Sebastian Armenteros."

Sebastian stepped beside him, his smile only made more brilliant by the glare of the lights. *"Bienvenidos, damas y caballeros."*

Hen tittered again, and Kitty was afraid she was going to have to dump cold water on Hen instead of herself. Though she had to admit that the beautiful language rolling off Sebastian's tongue was worthy of a little swooning.

"Whoa there, buddy." Max grasped Sebastian's shoulder. "They didn't come here to hear you talk." He faced the crowd. "How'd you like to hear a little music, folks?"

A cheer went up from the tables, and a drummer on stage tapped out a beat. Max lifted a trumpet to his lips and started to play. The sound was burning sunlight cutting through fog. The brassy notes were as bright and brilliant as the light bouncing off the golden surface of the trumpet's horn. They filled the room with a shine Kitty could hear. She sat, fixed, unmoving as Max played. The wavy fringe she had dismissed earlier as a fashion faux pas now shook and gleamed as he leaned back, as if dragging the sounds from deep within himself instead of blowing them through the instrument. Sebastian's low, silky voice caught her attention when he began to sing, but the distraction only lasted a moment. Max's trumpet blared once more, grabbing hold of her. She had the strangest feeling that if she held up her hand toward the sound, her fingers would be singed. Her stomach swooped.

The longer she sat there watching him, the more the shimmering sounds became a buzz of hornets in her mind. She had to admit Hen was right, though she'd never say it out loud. Kitty wasn't used to men ignoring her, especially not in favor of Hen. Hen's better qualities took time to get to know. Kitty's were all out on display; most men made that clear enough by tripping all over themselves to talk to her. How many times had Hen joked about being invisible when Kitty was around? This guy had reversed their roles, and Kitty had not liked the feeling.

Kitty jumped at Hen's hand on her arm. Hen lifted her brows but only said, "Wow, they're good, aren't they?"

Kitty shrugged.

"Are you coming to Mother's party tomorrow?" Hen continued, unfazed by Kitty's disinterest.

"Hmm? Oh, sure. What time?"

"She said seven."

"You staying with me tonight?" Kitty asked, swallowing the last of her vodka pineapple.

"Can't. Mother wants me home early in the morning to help with last-minute party things."

The band reached the end of the tune, and the people in the club applauded. Kitty looked up to see Andre weaving through the tables toward them.

"Maybe Bebe could make herself useful for once. But I know how your mother relies on you," Kitty added quickly, not wanting to press the perpetually sore topic of Hen's younger sister. "Anyway, it's too bad. We could've put on some records. Maybe listen to some music that came after the dinosaurs." She indicated the band with a nod.

"Oh, stop." Hen swatted Kitty's shoulder. "That song's only a couple of years old. *'Quizás, quizás, quizás . . .'*" Hen leaned in with a knowing look. "Or is it the guy playing the song that's bugging you?"

"You're the one who needs to stop. I don't care about that trumpet player," Kitty said, even as another wave of annoyance went through her at the thought of Max's slight.

Andre grinned at the two girls as he reached the table. "What's mean ol' Kitty saying now? Nothing bad about me, I hope."

"No, no," Hen rushed to assure him. "She was complaining about the song, though heaven knows why."

"Because she likes to complain, don'tcha, Kitty?" He held out a hand and Kitty scooted over to make room in the booth.

Charles leaned over Hen. "She sure does."

Kitty frowned. "Awful boys."

"Now, don't be that way. We're only teasing," Andre said.

"It's a compliment, Kitty. Means you've got high standards," Charles said, reaching past Hen to rub Kitty's shoulder for a beat too long. "Nothing wrong with that."

Kitty smiled, suppressing the desire to whack his hand. Instead, she leaned over to Andre, moving beyond Charles's reach. "Any song that's more than a year old doesn't belong in a nightclub, in my opinion. And who has a big band in a club these days?"

"Your pop is about the only one. The Latin stuff they play seems to help, though," Andre said. He turned to Charles. "I keep telling him, he needs to ditch the band and get some dancing girls. That's what everyone else has these days, dancing girls. But Mr. Tessler, he says there are plenty of girls on the dance floor here. Girls a guy actually has a chance with."

Charles nodded at the thickening crowd in the room. "You can't argue with success."

Andre looked at Kitty. "What about you? You want to dance?"

Kitty held up her glass, sloshing the remaining slivers of ice. "I want a drink."

"Anything you want." Andre stood and waved over a waiter.

Hen laid a hand on Charles's arm. "I'd like to dance."

"Sure thing, lovey." Charles stood and Hen scooted out of the booth. Kitty nearly gagged at the pet name. She'd suggested to Hen that perhaps another name would be more dignified, but Hen always replied that it was the pet name Charles's father used with Charles's mother. Hen thought that was endearing. Kitty thought it was Oedipal.

After securing Kitty another vodka pineapple, Andre made his way back to his duties. He'd offered to keep her company while the other two danced, but Kitty wanted time to think.

"I wouldn't dream of keeping you from your work," she said. "The whole place must be lost without you, even for a moment."

Andre's chest puffed out, and he strode through the club with renewed purpose. Kitty took a pack of matches from the bowl in the center of the table and lit another cigarette. The slow, aching sounds of "Sophisticated Lady" drifted from the stage, a song that really deserved a good cheek-to-cheek, but Charles and Hen danced like they were at a junior cotillion. Kitty noticed he kept one eye over Hen's shoulder on a curvy redhead's backside.

Kitty's gaze wandered to the stage, and she found Max looking intently at her, deep in thought. She jerked her focus back to her drink. On any other evening, with any other man, she would have stared right back. She should have at least felt gratified that she'd won his attention. But all she felt was a prickle of heat in her cheeks. She couldn't fathom what about him made her hide her eyes, nor could she understand why she couldn't bring herself to look up at him again. Though the song was over, the trill of a trumpet lingered in the back of her mind.

✤ THREE ✤

Kitty endured another couple of songs—and turned down a few dance requests, so Andre wouldn't feel slighted—before signaling to Hen that she was ready to go. Charles drove Hen home, and Kitty went upstairs to the empty suite. She awoke the next morning to a cold, wet nose sniffing under the blankets for her. Loco whined, and Kitty scratched the dog's ear.

"You know anyone else who woke me up before nine would be dead, don't you?" she murmured. "Come on, silly girl."

Kitty had gone to bed in her slip, so she only had to pull on a dress and shoes. She went out to the living room, Loco padding behind her. She heard a soft snore and turned to see her father fast asleep sitting up in his leather armchair. The radio played at a low volume beside him.

"Papa." She tapped his arm.

"Hmmm." He blinked awake. "Goodness, what time is it?"

She checked the clock. "About nine."

"I'd better get down to the office." He stood and stretched. "Did you have a nice time with Andre last night?"

"Oh, yes. But, you know, he was so busy . . ."

Her father rubbed his chin. "I should give him an evening off before he heads down to Miami. You kids can go to a nice restaurant or something."

"What a good idea." Kitty kissed his cheek, pleased to hear that Andre would be leaving town soon. She could easily avoid him when he was over a thousand miles away. "Ooh, I just remembered, I need a few things from the store. Do you have a few dollars to spare?"

"What things? You have everything." He folded his arms across his chest, but his tone was teasing.

"Stockings. Little necessities."

He smiled and pulled out his wallet. "Twenty dollars is probably too much, isn't it?"

She held out a hand. "I'll bring you the change."

"You never do," he said, shaking his head.

"Thanks, Papa." She slipped the bill into her purse on her way to the foyer. She called a good-bye over her shoulder, shrugged into her coat, and grabbed Loco's leash from its hook. The dog followed her out to the elevator, and they rode down to the ground floor. As they walked outside, Kitty was grateful she'd put on her heavy coat. Frost clung to the stair railing, and a blast of icy wind hit them as they stepped onto the sidewalk.

"All right, Miss Loco," Kitty said under her breath. "Let's do this quickly." But she knew her request was futile. Loco followed a strict routine of walking about five feet, sniffing a spot on the sidewalk thoroughly, and then smiling up at Kitty, as if she'd achieved some great triumph. Kitty would tug the leash, and they would move forward another five feet, where Loco would repeat her sniffing and smiling.

Loco did not disappoint. Kitty thought of all the evil things she would do if a human ever dared string her along this way. Not even her father could get that level of indulgence out of Kitty. For Loco, however, she had infinite patience. After about a half hour, the dog finally relieved herself, and Kitty took her back up to the suite.

The dog watched from under dancing eyebrows as Kitty put on

makeup. She patted Loco's head. "Don't miss me too much today. I'll come back to take you out again before the party."

Hen's mother's party wasn't starting until seven o'clock, so Kitty had plenty of time to visit one of her favorite places. With her father's twenty tucked in her purse, she walked back out onto the street, heading to Macy's with a new dress for Mrs. Bancroft's party on her mind. The air outside had already warmed up considerably only an hour after her walk with Loco, especially for late November. The frost had melted from the railing outside the hotel.

Kitty walked up a block and cut through Herald Square. The sidewalks had filled up, and she preferred dodging pigeons to bumping along with other pedestrians. She waited at the curb for a few bright yellow taxis to pass, then crossed 35th Street to dash under the awning to Macy's glass front doors. She could have found her way to the ladies' department blindfolded. The wooden escalator took her upstairs, where shoppers already crowded around the racks and glass tables filled with merchandise.

She paused at a display of three mannequins, each wearing a different full-skirted dress. One had a velvet halter top, embellished with a sparkling silver brooch, and a tiered cream skirt. Before Kitty could look around for a clerk to help find her size, a voice rose above the chatter of the other patrons.

"Miss Tessler!" A slender brunette practically skipped over. Kitty could almost hear the *ding* of the cash register in the girl's head.

"Hello, Barbara," Kitty said. "How are things?"

"Busy." Barbara swept a hand toward the other patrons. "But never too busy for you. What can I find for you today?"

Kitty pointed at the dress in the display. "Do you have that one in my size?"

"Of course." Barbara clucked her tongue. "That dress is going to look gorgeous on you. You have the best eye for things like that." She rushed off and returned a moment later with the dress, then escorted Kitty to the fitting room.

The dress fit her like a dream, and the wine-red top was a perfect contrast to her fair skin and platinum blond hair. The skirt especially set off her curves. Kitty admired herself in the three-way mirror at the end of the fitting room hallway, twirling a bit to get a look at the skirt's flare. Barbara squealed her approval. Satisfied, Kitty changed and went to pay. At the counter, she threw in a pair of gloves and some stockings. If her father asked her, she wanted to be able to say she'd put the twenty he gave her to its promised use, even though the dress meant there would be no change after all. But he was right; there never was anyway.

She went back out to the street, stopping at the corner. The weather had grown so warm that even her cardigan was too much. She took off her sweater and placed the bag by her feet. She had just knotted the cardigan around her shoulders when she heard a familiar voice behind her.

"If it isn't Kitty Tessler," the girl said.

Kitty whipped around to face her. "You know good and well it is, Marjorie."

Another girl joined Marjorie. Both had the same salon-pressed golden curls, though Marjorie was taller and far slimmer than her friend, Patricia. "We only wanted to say hello," Patricia said, her voice dripping with false sweetness.

"There, you've said it. This truly is the city where dreams come true." Kitty placed her hands on her hips.

Marjorie smirked. "Doing a little shopping this morning? How nice. And at Macy's. I'm sure that's a swell store if you're willing to settle for ready-to-wear. But that would be good enough for you, I suppose."

Kitty sighed. Marjorie and Patricia hadn't changed since the first day she'd met them at school. Their families were part of Hen's crowd, but Hen had never counted them as friends. Kitty certainly didn't either. They had never missed an opportunity to remind Kitty that her father's fortune did not make Kitty their social equal.

"Sorry, Marjorie. I know it must be hard to wait for weeks for your tailor to deliver up yet another fashion disappointment."

The smirk slid from Marjorie's face. "My fiancé seems to like what I wear just fine."

"Harold Daughtry wouldn't know high fashion from a burlap sack, so I don't know if I'd go around bragging about that," Kitty shot back.

Even Patricia had to fight hard to keep her defensive frown from turning into a smile at that remark. Harold was a blobby, freckled lawyer whose primary virtues were his bloodline and the fact that he had given Marjorie the golf ball–sized diamond she sported on her left hand.

"You've got no class, Kitty Tessler. You never have, and you never will." Color rose in Marjorie's cheeks.

"Oh, shut your trap. You just stopped to say hello? What a load of bunk. Have a nice day. I'm all out of rude things to say." Kitty breezed past them, heading back toward the Macy's entrance. When Marjorie and Patricia had cleared about half a block, Kitty signaled the security officer standing at the glass doors.

"Excuse me, sir? Do you see those two girls? The blondes?" she asked.

The officer peered down the street. "The one in the blue dress?"

"Yes, and the other in the green. I stopped to say hello—I know them from school, you see—and they told me they'd filled their purses with things from the store. They didn't pay or anything." Kitty pressed her hand to her chest and blinked rapidly. "I couldn't believe it, but I knew it would be wrong not to say something."

The officer nodded, his mouth a tight line. His eyes never left the girls. "Thank you, miss. You've done a good thing."

"Oh, no, thank *you*," Kitty said. He sprinted off toward Marjorie and Patricia, and Kitty smoothed her hair and started back toward the hotel, humming a bit to herself. She always enjoyed when she had the opportunity to give someone a little bit of just deserts.

⇥ FOUR ⇤

Kitty arrived at Hen's apartment right at seven o'clock, mindful of how much Mrs. Bancroft prized punctuality. Though there was always a hint of coldness in their encounters, Kitty hoped that with enough interaction she could secure Mrs. Bancroft's full approval. It would only help in Kitty's quest to someday join the ranks for which Mrs. Bancroft served as gatekeeper.

A white-gloved attendant took Kitty's fur wrap and showed her to the parlor, where the rest of the guests sipped cocktails and chatted. Huge, full-story windows looked out over the city lights, and the gloss on the wood floors gave the whole room a warm glow. Kitty strolled in with the sense that she always had at these parties—that she belonged here, in this type of gathering, with these people. Not being born to it simply meant she had to work to place herself here, but she deserved this charmed life. She knew it.

Mrs. Bancroft, a tall and willowy woman, met Kitty near the arched doorway. "Kitty, how are you this evening?"

"Just fine, and you?" Kitty took Mrs. Bancroft's outstretched hands and wondered for the millionth time how genetics had given Hen her mother's delicate limbs and none of Mrs. Bancroft's natural grace. Hen's mother's blessings were all physical, while Hen's were in her heart.

"Very well, thank you." Mrs. Bancroft gestured to the other side of the room. "Hen's over there by the settee. I'm sure she's been looking for you."

Kitty doubted Hen could have been looking for her long, given that the party had only officially been going on for three minutes. She kept that observation to herself and thanked Mrs. Bancroft. "I'll go say hello."

"Do. Oh, and try some of the punch," Mrs. Bancroft said, her eyes already on the next guest.

Hen stood near the windows with her back to Kitty. Kitty shook her head. Where Hen's mother was wearing a pearl-trimmed navy gown with a sweeping hem, Hen had chosen a dowdy pale blue number with long sleeves. She looked like she'd gotten lost on her way to church.

As Kitty crossed the room, she scanned the guests to see who she knew. Naturally, Hen's little sister Bebe was present, surrounded by a rapt audience of college-aged boys. All of their mother's traits that had skipped Hen had settled firmly on the younger Bancroft girl.

Before Kitty could make her way to Hen, she spotted Charles. He was heading over to greet Bebe, but Kitty threw herself in his path. "Hi, Charles. Have you already lost Hen? She's over there."

"Ah." Charles tore his gaze from Bebe. "Yes, thank you. I was just going to ask Bebe if she'd seen her."

Kitty linked her arm with his and pulled him toward the window. "Glad I could save you the trouble."

Hen spotted them and waved. Kitty's heart sank. Hen stood with a couple of men, most of whom she had set Kitty up with at one point or another. One of them let out a low whistle. As she let go of Charles's arm, Kitty struggled to remember the man's name—Barry? Larry? Harry? All she could remember from their date was that he was a banker. Kitty had known from one look at his oily black hair and outdated suit that the match was doomed.

"Look here, gents. It's the lovely Kitty Tessler," he said, sidling up next to her. The other men in the group drew closer, a circling school of sharks.

"It sure is," she said dryly.

"Did you get all dressed up like that for me?" he asked, letting his gaze linger on her bare shoulders.

"No," she said, one flat syllable. The boys howled, and Barry-Larry-Harry's face flamed up to his scalp.

Hen gave Kitty a warning look. "Do you want something to drink? Charles, will you get her something?"

"I was just going to, lovey," he said.

"Thank you," Kitty said.

"Be nice," Hen said, leaning in to Kitty's ear. "You could still have a chance with any of these guys. One bad date doesn't matter that much."

Kitty cringed. The last thing she wanted was another chance with a single one of them. She smiled at the group, and the man closest to her took it as an invitation to shoot her a slimy grin. As he started to advance, she blurted out, "Will you excuse me? I'm going to the powder room. Be right back."

She nearly sprinted away from the cloak of cologne. The bathroom was occupied, so Kitty ducked into an alcove. Why hadn't she been able to stick it out with any of those boys from the living room? Boring conversation, bad suits, no taste—she had to admit to herself that those were not truly disqualifying factors, not if tolerating them meant she got the prize she was after. Even an existing girlfriend was an obstacle she was willing to work around if necessary. The problem was that none of those men had the social leverage to pull the daughter of a self-made man and granddaughter of immigrants out of her nouveau riche no-man's-land. She'd need a Rockefeller or a Vanderbilt if she wanted to someday host these parties instead of attending them.

Kitty sighed, the weight of her father's ultimatum sitting heavier on her shoulders. She shook her head and started back down the hallway toward the party but heard Hen's voice coming from an open door down the hall. Kitty doubled back. Standing in a small, dark study were Hen, Bebe, and Mrs. Bancroft.

". . . happening again. And now I want you to do something about it, Mother. Please," Hen cried.

"Can I please be excused? He came up to me. I didn't do anything," Bebe broke in, throwing her hands up in frustration.

Kitty's hand flew to her mouth. *Oh no. Not again.* The sight of the three of them dragged her back to that horrible weekend in August, when Hen had come back from her beach house devastated. When the depths of Charles's sleaziness had been revealed. Still, Kitty felt Hen's mother had come out looking worse than Hen's fiancé.

The Bancroft family beach house was mere steps away from the Remingtons' summer retreat, and all summer the two families were particularly in each other's pockets. Charles and Hen had been together for years, so everyone expected them to finally formalize the arrangement between them. Sure enough, Charles had finally proposed, and Hen had eagerly accepted. Mrs. Bancroft invited every blueblood in Newport to celebrate the engagement. But at the party, Charles slipped off for so long that Hen had gotten worried. When she went in search of him, she found him in a compromising position with her own teenaged sister.

Hen had run to her mother, hysterical, expecting Mrs. Bancroft to throw Charles out and pack Bebe off to boarding school. Instead, she sent Hen to her room with a glass of water, an aspirin, and an admonishment to "not make a scene." Early the next morning, Hen found herself sequestered in the library. The only members of that second, less festive party were Hen, Mrs. Bancroft, Charles, and Bebe. Hen was assured in no uncertain terms that she didn't see what she thought she had, and she would forget what she'd seen as soon as possible. The engagement would not be broken off for such a silly "misunderstanding," as Mrs. Bancroft had termed it. She guaranteed Hen that she'd keep close watch on Bebe to be certain no other similar misunderstandings occurred. No whiff of scandal would ever leave that room. Bebe had apparently had the good sense to stay silent, her teary eyes on the Savonnerie carpet beneath her feet.

Kitty was no friend of Bebe's after hearing Hen's story, but she reserved her full wrath for Mrs. Bancroft and Charles. Even she could see that Bebe was just a spoiled kid captivated by the naughtiness of seducing her sister's fiancé; she'd never been the kind of girl who thought through the potential consequences of her actions. And she did seem to truly regret causing Hen such distress. But Mrs. Bancroft and Charles had both known exactly what they were doing, and now it seemed Charles wasn't even willing to keep his end of the bargain to steer clear of Bebe. That had to be the meaning of the impromptu conference she was witnessing.

"Shouldn't Bebe leave the party?" Hen asked.

"I don't want to have to leave the party just because of him," Bebe said.

"Keep your voices down," Mrs. Bancroft said, her voice hard and dangerous. Kitty watched her round on Hen, her eyes weary. "You know they can't avoid each other forever. We're all going to be family soon. We're going to have to be together. That includes Bebe."

"I promise, I didn't do anything to encourage him," Bebe piped up.

Hen rubbed her forehead. "I believe you. But, Mother—"

"That's enough," Mrs. Bancroft said. "Bebe is not leaving the party, and we're not canceling Christmas and every other family event because you can't get over something that happened one time. Stop being so dramatic."

Hen swallowed hard. "It's not just one time."

"It was, I swear—" Bebe began.

"I don't mean with you." Hen turned to her mother, eyes pleading. "There . . . there are other girls."

Her mother waved a hand. "He's a man. None of those other girls have his grandmother's ring on their finger, do they?"

"I just don't think I can bear it. Not for my whole life." Hen's chin wobbled.

Mrs. Bancroft grabbed Hen's arm. "He'll probably stop once you're married. But you will marry him. I will not have a daughter who is disgraced by a broken engagement, not when the Remingtons are involved, do you hear me?"

Hen stood silent. Kitty realized her fists were clenched so tightly that her nails were digging into her palm. She shook out her hands and prayed this would be the moment Hen would stand up to her mother. After a shaky breath, Hen spoke.

"Yes, Mother. I'm sorry."

Kitty didn't hear Mrs. Bancroft's response. Her heart raced as she strode away from the study. This was why she had no choice but to intervene. Nothing would ever improve between Hen and Charles. He couldn't even leave her sister alone with Hen standing a few feet away. Kitty found an empty room and leaned against the wall inside. Even though the breakup would be satisfying, what she really wanted was a way to make him feel some of the pain Hen had.

The thought leapt like a spark from the flame of her anger. Once Charles was single again, where would he turn his interest? Sure, he had a list of beauties on call. Bebe probably wasn't safe either, though Kitty doubted his parents would be interested in setting him up with another Bancroft after the older one dumped him. But if she managed everything just right, Kitty herself had a good chance of snagging him.

She didn't need love to marry, not like Hen. Kitty had always sought a marriage with other advantages. Charles was certainly no sappy romantic, and he'd have to be intrigued by such a mutually beneficial partnership. His flirting made it clear he found her attractive, and she'd been preparing since childhood for the role of society wife. Once he was attached to her, she could have a lifetime of making Charles suffer every indignity he'd earned by mistreating her best friend. No one was as good as Kitty at devising appropriate punishment. He deserved anything and everything Kitty and Hen could dream up. There would be no more crying in side rooms for Hen. Kitty had a clear vision of sitting with Hen at some grand restaurant, toasting with champagne bought with Charles's money while scheming about the next torture he would have to endure. And then Hen could go home to a man who was worthy of her.

But would Hen really go for a plan like that? Seeing her ex-fiancé with her best friend? Kitty had a lot to consider before the idea could become reality. In the meantime, she had to get out to the party to make sure Hen knew that at least one person supported her.

⊰ FIVE ⊱

Kitty spent most of the week after the party avoiding her father's questions about whether she was spending time with Andre. She also wrestled with her idea about securing an engagement to Charles when he and Hen parted. In the heat of anger, the thought had seemed brilliant. As she cooled off, the genius of it seemed to fizzle, too. For one thing, winning the affections of someone she hated would require deception on a whole other level than what she was used to. For another, Hen might be hurt by the suggestion, and Kitty wanted to avoid that more than anything. Still, the notion had its appeal, so she had a hard time dismissing it entirely.

On Friday night, she was relieved when Hen phoned to say that Charles had gone with his father to a lodge party, and Hen was on her own that weekend. Kitty had already decided to go down to the club that night to throw a little hope Andre's way and get her father off her back. Hen had eagerly agreed to join her. Now Kitty could enjoy the evening with Hen without Charles there to spoil it. Kitty noted with a laugh that Hen asked if Sebastian would be singing that night. Her friend really was a bit infatuated with the handsome Cuban.

Hen arrived late in the evening, unexpectedly detained when Mrs. Bancroft and a friend decided to share the car back from the dinner party they were attending. Kitty spotted the three of them exiting from her spot in the lobby, and her stomach fluttered. She might have hated what Mrs. Bancroft had done to Hen, but she still desperately wanted to impress the society maven. Kitty had schemed for years to get Mrs. Bancroft into one of her father's properties, so she could see how up-scale they really were, but none of the attempts had succeeded. Now Mrs. Bancroft was walking through the front doors. Kitty rushed over.

"How wonderful to see you, Mrs. Bancroft," Kitty said. "And you, Mrs. Fowler. Are you two joining us for some entertainment this evening? I'd love to give you a tour of the hotel."

Mrs. Bancroft smiled tightly. "We really haven't got the time, sorry to say. We're just popping in to powder our noses. The driver is waiting for us outside."

"Of course. Right this way." Kitty led them on the long route to the restrooms, determined to make the most of the unexpected good fortune. The two women went in, and Kitty and Hen waited outside the door.

"We don't have to wait for her," Hen said. "She can find her way back out. Come on, let's go get a table."

"You go ahead," Kitty said. "I don't mind waiting."

"Suit yourself."

"Tell Sebastian I said hello," Kitty teased. Hen lifted her nose and proceeded down the hall to the club without a word.

As Kitty waited, she realized she could entice Mrs. Bancroft to at least look at the ballrooms as a potential space for one of Hen's wedding celebrations. She opened the restroom door but paused when she heard her own name drift out. As the women touched up their makeup in the anteroom, Kitty could make out most of their conversation. She stood still, careful not to make a sound.

". . . it's so big of you to let Hen carry on with her," Mrs. Fowler said.

"She's not the ideal choice, as you know," Mrs. Bancroft said. "But she is such a little glamour puss. I keep hoping her fashion sense will rub off on Hen. I'm just thankful her father doesn't seem to have any Red leanings."

The other woman laughed. "Not with the money he's making. Tessler's a capitalist, not like those Rosenbergs. No chance of his daughter filling Hen's head with all that Commie nonsense."

"True," Hen's mother said. "And at least she's not a Jew. A lot of those Russians are, you know."

"So many of them. You couldn't have that."

"Besides, once Hen's married she won't have time for school friends anymore. We can finally shake her off." She clicked her tongue. "All his money from nightclubs. And this . . . place."

The contemptuous tone burned in Kitty's ears. She didn't want to listen anymore. Closing the door as softly as she could, she hurried back out to the lobby. It wasn't the first time she'd heard disparaging remarks about her family's origins. At least they hadn't stooped to calling her "Russki"—or worse—like the kids at Alastair Prep. What really hurt was listening to those women scorn everything that her father had made while they stood in his creation. And she had hoped Hen's mother would see that even if Kitty's family tree didn't recommend her, her years of loyal and loving friendship to Hen should. Apparently, all Hen's mother saw when she looked at Kitty was a mannequin. A possibly Communist mannequin.

Kitty paused in the hallway near the entrance to the club. She realized that her idea to snare Charles would have the additional bonus of throwing a little misery Mrs. Bancroft's way. Kitty smiled to think how galling Hen's mother would find it to attend the wedding of a Remington and the granddaughter of Russian immigrants. She could make sure Mrs. Bancroft got a seat in the front pew. Hell, she'd even provide the monogrammed hankies for Hen's mother to weep into. Given what she'd forced Hen to do, she deserved all that and more.

When Kitty finally entered the club, she found Hen watching the door with concern.

"I was about to come look for you," Hen said as they sat in the booth.

"Sorry about that. I got sidetracked."

Hen waved at the bar area. "Andre's here. He already stopped by to say hello."

"Goody." Kitty pasted on a smile as Andre joined them. She turned and caught a glimpse of Max onstage, and the flare of irritation she was already battling swelled. "They sure are enjoying an extended stay, aren't they?" she said.

Andre laughed. "They've only been here for a few days, Kitty. Did you think your father would bus them all the way up here for a one-night show?"

"Why are they here at all?" Kitty asked.

"Drumming up business for the Miami hotel. We want to remind people that there are still some places in this world where the sun shines."

"I think I like the regular band better," Kitty said with a huff.

"Don't be silly, Kitty." Hen nudged her. "These guys are really good."

"I'm with you, Hen," Andre said. "C'mon, you gotta like them a little. Look how many people are on the floor! That never happens. The house band always plays that slow music. At least Max knows a couple of peppy tunes."

As if on cue, the band struck up an instrumental version of "Embraceable You." Kitty raised an eyebrow triumphantly.

Andre threw up his hands and stood. "I'll get you girls some drinks."

After he left, Hen wagged a finger at Kitty, her eyes gleeful. "Bad girl. You're not playing nice."

"Do you want me to end up with Andre?" Kitty shrugged. "You and my father might be the only ones. Andre doesn't seem to care at all."

Hen's eyes were strangely sad as she watched him at the bar. "Poor Andre. You never know, he really might like you. He's so nice."

"Poor Andre like hell. He's not even working that hard for me. A little odd if he's as interested as Papa seems to believe, don't you think?"

"That's how men are," Hen said. "You don't see Charles running to get me drinks, do you? Andre probably thinks you're a sure thing, since he works for your father and all."

"If he thinks a girl like me is a sure thing for a guy like him, I've got news for him."

"Who cares what he thinks anyway?" Hen poked Kitty's arm. "Let me set you up with someone. If you have a steady guy, maybe your father will ease up a little."

"If you suggest Barry or whatever his name is, I'll stab you with this fork." Kitty tapped the silverware on the table with a pink fingernail.

"His name is Harry, and I wasn't thinking of him. Let's see . . . there's Alfie's cousin. He's a lawyer. . . ." Hen counted off wealthy cousins and friends of friends, but the list of names once again turned Kitty's thoughts to Charles. None of them would suit her ambitions as well as he would, yet another point in favor of taking him for herself. The men Hen suggested were wealthy, sure. Their family names graced a campus building here, a bank there. But Kitty's new money required that she have the best of those old names if she wanted to legitimize her standing. A name that was printed on street signs and engraved over the entrances to museums. A legacy that went back to the founding fathers. A name that even the boys Hen had in mind spoke in hushed tones. No one else could give her the advantage that a Remington would. The Harrys of the world were dukes and earls. Charles was a prince, even if his behavior was more that of the frog.

Her resolve began to solidify. She could punish Mrs. Bancroft, destroy Charles, and take her rightful place in the world with one action. The only sticking point was still Hen's acceptance of the notion. That would likely be an issue of timing. Once Kitty helped Hen find a more honorable partner, she could reveal her intention to make Charles miserable and secure Hen's blessing. After all, she had never failed to convince Hen of what was best before.

Kitty pulled her attention back to Hen, listening politely to the list of bachelors, then steering the conversation to the much more pleasant

topic of winter fashions. Andre occasionally dropped in to offer another round of drinks or to join them for a few moments. He took
full advantage of those brief interludes to brag about how much work
Kitty's father entrusted him with. To her, it sounded like Andre was
an overworked servant. But she brightened at the reminder that Andre
was off to Miami when the band left New York.

"That's right, Papa mentioned you're going down there." She sensed
she hadn't flirted with Andre properly that evening, so she flashed him
a smile. "You're going to come back so tanned. I think it will look swell
on you. Don't you think, Hen?"

Hen blushed, nodding hard, and Andre grinned.

"I'll probably be inside working too much. But wouldn't you like to
get a little sun? Maybe sit by the pool? You ought to come down with
me. Your father said it's been years since you saw the place. Hen, you'd
have to come, too. I'd make sure you both had a good visit."

Kitty almost blanched at the thought.

"You are just too sweet, Andre. A Miami vacation would be the
tops. But I couldn't have you worrying about entertaining me while
you're working so hard. Some other time."

"It wouldn't be a distraction," Andre said quickly.

"Mmm-hmm. Some other time," Kitty said.

She was spared from further discussion by Max's voice in the microphone. "Thanks to all you gents and lovely ladies for a wonderful
evening. Once again, we are Max Zillman and the Zillionaires. Lead
singer, Sebastian Armenteros."

Andre started up from the table. "It's already sign-off. Better make
sure everyone's set for closing."

Max wrapped up his good nights to the house, and the band began
packing up. Reluctant clubgoers took the last watery swigs from their
glasses and pulled out wallets to pay.

"What do you want to do now?" Kitty asked.

"We could go upstairs and listen to records. I don't feel like going
to bed yet," Hen said.

Kitty drummed her fingers on the table. She glanced up at the stage and saw Sebastian chatting with the bass player. The light hit the angles of his face, making him look for all the world like a statue of a Greek god. After the bruising Hen's mother had given Kitty's ego, Kitty could stand a little soothing admiration from a good-looking singer. She got up from the table so fast she nearly upset the drinks.

"I want to find out what he's doing after," she called over her shoulder. A bewildered Hen leapt to her feet and followed.

Kitty approached the stage with a sway in her hips, but it wasn't Sebastian who spoke first. It was Max.

"Now I see why your pop is so successful," he said. "You single-handedly keeping this place afloat?"

She narrowed her eyes and looked past him at Sebastian. "No."

"No? But you sure do hang here a lot." He leaned on the microphone stand.

"Mmm."

"What can we help you with?"

"I'm waiting for Sebastian, that's all."

Max leaned back, calling over his shoulder. "Hey, Sebastian. You've got an admirer."

Kitty's face burned, but she straightened her back. Sebastian walked over with a puzzled smile.

"Hello, good to see you," he said.

"I was just . . . I thought I'd ask . . . what are you doing after?" She had to stop herself from stomping her feet like she used to when she was a little girl and she didn't get her way. Of all people, that stupid trumpeter shouldn't make her tongue-tied. She must have looked cool enough to Sebastian, though. He brightened at her question.

"Nothing interesting, I'm sad to say. We'll probably go back to the boardinghouse."

"The boardinghouse?" Kitty said. "You aren't staying in the hotel?"

Max laughed and stepped toward them. "Your dad doesn't make money by giving things away." He gestured to Kitty. "Well, maybe giving drinks away to his daughter. But not hotel rooms to his employees."

Kitty's jaw clenched. She kept her eyes on Sebastian, ignoring Max's dig. "It's too early to go to bed. Why don't you come upstairs?"

Hen walked up in time to hear Kitty's offer and grabbed her elbow. "Kitty, may I speak to you?"

Kitty jerked her arm free. "Not right now." She hadn't meant to snap, but between Max's demeanor and Hen's interruption, her frustration was boiling over.

Sebastian glanced from Kitty to Max. "Ah, better not. We're practicing early tomorrow morning."

Hen pulled Kitty out of his earshot. "Thank goodness he said no. What are you thinking, inviting a bunch of musicians upstairs? You know your father isn't home."

"I can invite up whoever I want. Don't you think real musicians would be more fun than some old records?"

"I thought you said you didn't like their music!" Hen threw her arms in the air, exasperated.

Kitty looked up at the stage. Sebastian and Max were as deep in conversation as the two girls were. "I don't. But I sure like the way Sebastian looks."

"I do, too. But, Kitty . . ." Hen leaned in, her voice hushed with embarrassment. "I mean . . . he's as good as colored, isn't he?"

Kitty paused a moment, caught off guard. "He's Cuban. Since when do you care?"

"I don't . . . not really. But Charles and his parents are very sensitive to that sort of thing. If it got back to them that we were alone with him . . ." She shook her head. "And Max. I think he might be a Jew."

"Sharp eye," Kitty said dryly. "I didn't invite Max anyway, did I? Look, how are Charles's parents ever going to hear who was in my apartment?"

Hen crossed her arms. "Sebastian said no. There's nothing to worry about."

Sebastian stepped forward. "Excuse me, Kitty?"

She smiled brightly, first at Hen, then at Sebastian. "Yes?"

"On second thought . . . Max and I are not tired. We would like to come up with you, if that's all right."

"Sure. We'll have a real party." Kitty hid her dismay that Max seemed to think the invitation extended to him. She needed smooth and charming right now, not flinty and sarcastic.

Hen glowered. "Won't Andre want to come up? We should wait for him."

Kitty waved a hand. "He's so busy."

"Won't you at least ask?"

Kitty thought for a moment. "Fine." She wound her way through the tables, passing the final few patrons as they prepared to leave. Andre stood at the bar, looking over a closing inventory sheet. Kitty glanced back over her shoulder to be sure Hen was watching.

"Sorry to bother you." Kitty laid a hand on Andre's arm, and he abandoned the sheet. "I know you have so much to do."

"Never too busy for you." He dabbed at his temples with his hand-kerchief.

"You are a doll. Anyway, Hen and I are pooped. We're heading up-stairs. I hope that's all right."

He nodded. "Of course. I hope you had a good evening."

"Oh, the best," Kitty said. "A couple of the fellas over there are going to walk us up. They want to see the view. But I thought I ought to check with you." She lowered her chin. "Don't want you getting the wrong idea about me."

Andre's smile took over his face. "No, no. I wouldn't. And, hey, give those boys a drink, will you? If you're not too tired for a few minutes of entertaining."

"Well . . ." She tilted her head. "Okay. But only as a favor to you."

"Maybe I should come up later," he said, looking past her.

"I would love that, I really would. What time will you be done here?"

"Hour and a half, maybe two."

Kitty sucked in a breath through her teeth. "Ooh, that's so late."

"It is," he said, his tone apologetic. "Tell you what, give those boys a drink, then kick 'em right out so you and Hen can go to bed."

She squeezed his arm. "Thanks, Andre."

Hen's cloudy expression persisted as Kitty crossed the floor to her. "What did he say?"

"He insisted we take the boys up for a drink."

"Did he really say that?"

"Yes." Kitty waved at Andre, who waved back and gave her a thumbs-up.

Hen sighed. "Fine. You win."

Kitty pinched Hen's arm. "Come on, let's have some fun."

❖ SIX ❖

When they arrived at the suite upstairs, Kitty poured drinks for the other three. Max and Hen sat on the couch, and he barely thanked her for his cocktail. She guessed other girls might find his dark eyes and full lips appealing. Maybe he thought his looks were substitute enough for good manners, but Kitty disagreed. Or perhaps musicians didn't feel the need for the same etiquette as polite society. She shrugged him off and smiled as Sebastian joined her at the bar cart on the other side of the living room, clearly only interested in conversation with Kitty.

He gazed out the long window at the buildings that surrounded the hotel. "The buildings in this city are all very tall. Not like Miami."

"Oh, no?" She handed him a drink.

"I feel like I'll hurt my neck looking up on the street. But all those buildings block the sun. Miami is much brighter."

Kitty swallowed a sigh. Not riveting conversation, but his accent was pretty. Now here was a guy who could get by only on appearance. "I guess it would be," she offered.

Sebastian glanced across the room to where Max and Hen sat. He must have decided they were too far away to hear him, because he leaned in to Kitty and spoke under his breath. "I'm sorry Max came up with us. I know you didn't invite him."

"It's fine, really." She shook her head, hoping she looked as if it was, indeed, fine.

"He thought I'd sneak up here anyway. Said it was easier to come with me." Sebastian's smile could have melted butter. Kitty's face warmed.

"Is that the sort of thing you'd do?"

He stared into his glass, failing miserably at looking guilty. "Well . . . I might have been a little bad once or twice. With girls like you. He thought he needed to keep an eye on me."

"I see." Kitty's stomach quivered. *Girls like you.* Her conversation with Hen about Charles's parents' objections came back to her. Kitty and Hen were evidently not the first white girls to find Sebastian charming. She knew segregation was more of a formal institution in the South than in New York, so he'd likely found himself in real hot water before. Hen broke into Kitty's thoughts, calling her over, and Kitty crossed the room back to where Max and Hen sat.

At least Hen had relaxed somewhat. Kitty couldn't say whether Hen's change in attitude was more the result of the heavy cocktail Kitty had poured for her or the realization that this little private rebellion had almost no chance of making it back to Charles's parents. Either way, Hen's tinkling laugh had gotten louder, and her initial worries about their companions didn't seem to concern her anymore.

Kitty's attention was diverted when Loco ran in. At the sight of the dog, Sebastian lit up. He settled on the braided rug, delighted when Loco climbed onto his lap.

"What is her name? She is a beautiful dog," he said. Loco licked his hand, her whole body wiggling, and he laughed.

"Her name's Loco," Kitty said.

He startled. "You named your dog Crazy?"

She shook her head. "No! She's named after Betty Grable's character in *How to Marry a Millionaire.*"

"But she's a girl, isn't she?"

"So's Betty Grable."

Sebastian smiled. "Loc-a. If she's a girl, the name should be Loc-a."

"Why is that?"

"Everything in Spanish is either boy or girl. Girl is *a*. It's a softer sound, more feminine. Better for girls."

"Loca." Kitty cocked her head. "I'll never get used to calling her something different now. Guess she's stuck with a boy name."

"She's still beautiful, though."

"Yes, she is." Kitty clicked her tongue and Loco settled on the chaise longue beside her.

"*How to Marry a Millionaire?*" Max leaned in. "You know that wasn't meant to be an instructional film, right?"

Kitty wondered if that was supposed to be funny, but the lame attempt at humor must have landed with Hen. "It's Kitty's current favorite. She's already dragged me to see it about twenty times."

Kitty lifted her chin. "Don't exaggerate. And you liked it too."

"Not as much as you." Hen turned to Max. "When her father gave her Loco, he'd already named her Peanut. After Kitty saw the movie the first time, she insisted on changing the name. The dog hadn't been Peanut long anyway, so she didn't seem to care. She just comes no matter what Kitty calls her."

"I take it Kitty gets what she wants," Max said.

Hen flipped a hand. "Oh, always. That's her specialty."

"I don't get what I want all the time; no one does." Kitty took a cigarette from her case, and Sebastian took a match from the table to give her a light.

"I don't know," Hen said. Her drink sloshed as she gestured. "You always find a way out of the things you don't want to do. Like with your Andre problem. I bet you've already got a plan for him, don't you?"

Max and Sebastian looked from Hen to Kitty, but Kitty cut off their questions. "I'd rather not talk about that while I have people over."

Hen's eyes widened. "Oh. Oh, right. Sure."

Kitty didn't want Max, and especially not Sebastian, knowing about her father's mandate. Now, at least, she had a suitor picked out, which would help her avoid pairing up with Andre. But to get Charles, she had to force the breakup. She'd been trying to puzzle that out for too long with too little success. The others turned their conversation toward music, while Kitty sat back on the chaise longue and let her mind wander. She did her best thinking when she wasn't trying to think.

She almost laughed when she noticed that Hen kept staring at Sebastian. Hen would gaze at him until her eyes lost focus, then catch herself and snap her head back up. Kitty could hardly blame Hen for that. His smooth skin, strong jaw, and dark brown eyes made it hard to look away. Still, for all Hen's fretting about what Charles's parents would think of Sebastian's skin color, it sure didn't seem to bother Hen herself much.

Kitty opened her mouth to tease Hen and froze. Her solution was sitting right in front of her; Hen had practically gift-wrapped the answer for her. She had to get Hen away from Charles and throw her at someone else. For all Charles's escapades, he'd never want anyone to think his girl had run around on *him*. From the way Sebastian's mere presence was now making it hard for Hen to keep up with her side of the conversation with Max, it wouldn't be too difficult to engineer a romantic situation . . . or at least the appearance of one. After all, Hen would never cheat. It only needed to seem like she could.

Kitty snapped out of her daze when she noticed Hen was no longer staring at Sebastian but at her. "You look like the wheels are turning," Hen said, a note of apprehension in her voice.

"No, no." Kitty yawned theatrically. "Goodness, it is late, though."

"Maybe we'd better go," Max said.

Sebastian raised an eyebrow at Kitty. "Maybe you just need another drink?"

"I like his plan better," Kitty said with a nod in Sebastian's direction. She stood and stretched. "So how much longer are you boys in town?"

"Only another week," Sebastian said.

Kitty spun around, leaving her half-poured drink on the bar. "No. But you just got here."

"It's a two-week engagement. We've got to get back, save the Miami club from the amateurs they've got down there right now," Max said.

"It's a pity, that's all." Kitty turned back to finish mixing her cocktail. "We've barely gotten to know you." *And I need Sebastian to make my plan work*, she thought.

"Andre is coming to Miami, isn't he?" Sebastian asked. "When was the last time you visited?"

Kitty sat back down beside a now-sleeping Loco. "Papa took me once when he first opened the Imperium. I was only nine or ten. I barely remember it."

"That's a real shame," Sebastian said. "You ought to come down. You would have a wonderful time, don't you think, Max?"

"Oh, yeah. Sure." Max sipped his drink, eyes locked on Kitty.

"Then you must come," Sebastian said. "You too, Hen."

Hen's eyes lit up, and Kitty nearly choked on her drink. She could have kissed Sebastian. Maybe she would, one of these days. He'd made a perfect plan even better. She and Hen could accompany Andre to Miami. Everything fit so beautifully. Her father would be pleased with her "interest" in Andre, Hen would be over a thousand miles away from Charles and her mother, and Sebastian would be close at hand to provide an enticement into trouble.

"Now that you put it that way . . ." Kitty couldn't suppress her smile. "I'd say it's too good to pass up. Hen? What do you think?"

Hen's head bobbed up and down. "Oh, yes."

Oh, yes. Kitty could absolutely make Miami work.

Max shot a look at Sebastian. "Hey, you know, we should go. Practice is early. I don't want you sleeping through it."

"Are you sure?" Kitty directed the question at Sebastian.

"Yeah, we are." Max stood and picked up his glass from the coffee table. "Should we put these in the sink?"

Kitty waved him off. "Leave them. The maid will get them in the morning."

Max tilted his head and looked at her for a long moment. He exhaled hard and set his glass back down. "Come on, Sebastian. Bye, girls."

"Good-bye, Kitty. Hen." Sebastian patted Loco on the head. *"Buenas noches, Loquita."*

"Let me walk you to the door." Kitty started to follow them, but Max spoke without turning around.

"We know where it is, thanks."

She wasn't sure if it was her imagination, but it seemed like he shut the door a little harder than he needed to. Hen's wrinkled brow confirmed it.

"You think he's all right?" Hen asked.

Kitty sank back onto the chaise. "Oh, who cares?"

Hen giggled and crossed the room to rifle through Kitty's record collection. Kitty scratched Loco's ear and pondered Max. At first, he'd seemed merely indifferent to her, but now he seemed to actively dislike her. He also seemed determined to stick close to Sebastian, which wouldn't make her plan for Hen any easier. If she was going to make sure Hen and Sebastian had time alone, something that at least looked scandalous, it would mean separating him from his self-appointed chaperone. She sighed. In Kitty's experience, there was only one sure-fire way to distract a man from his mission. She would have to be her own bait and seduce a guy who had just slammed a door on her for no good reason.

Well, she thought, *no one could ever accuse me of shying away from a challenge.*

❋ SEVEN ❋

To set the trip to Miami in motion, Kitty needed her father's approval. Though he gave her more than enough spending money, the cost of a plane ticket far exceeded the leftovers in her purse from shopping and trips to the movies. The band would take their bus back to Miami, but Andre bragged that he would fly down ahead of them. She didn't want to imagine what a multiday bus ride with a bunch of musicians would look like. She had to fly too.

For her father to agree, he'd have to think he'd had the idea first. Kitty called down to his office on Tuesday afternoon, knowing Mondays and Tuesdays were slow days. In fact, for a while they'd had a standing Tuesday night dinner date, although the little tradition had fallen by the wayside some time ago.

Her father answered the phone in an unusually gruff voice. "Kitty? What is it? Do you need money?"

She thought for a moment about delaying the conversation, but Andre was leaving next week. There was no other time. "Can't I call my own father without some ulterior motive?"

"You? I doubt it."

"You're a grouch today." She kept her tone light and playful.

He sighed. "Got some bad news about a property I wanted to buy in Atlanta."

"Poor Papa. What do you say we go out to dinner? You need a little distraction."

"Dinner, eh?" He snorted. "You think that's going to get Atlanta off my mind?"

"I know a charming dinner companion can."

This time he laughed. "You're on. Where do you want to go?"

"I think you can guess," she said.

"Keens. Nothing but the best."

Kitty twirled the phone cord around her finger. "Why bother with anything else? I'll call and get reservations. How does eight o'clock sound?"

"See you there."

Step one complete. Nothing would butter up her father more than a good steak and a glass of Bordeaux. Of course, she'd already called the restaurant as soon as she had the idea to ask her father. Posing as his secretary, she'd had no trouble securing a table for Tessler, party of two, even with short notice.

She took Loco out for a quick walk before getting ready for dinner. The unseasonable warmth of the week before had faded back into a start-of-winter chill, and Kitty was grateful to climb into the warm bath when she returned to the suite. After washing up, she pulled on a fluffy pink robe and went to her vanity to comb her hair and reapply makeup. The final touch was a navy blue sweater set and white wool skirt. She pulled on her gloves and shoes, checking that they matched her purse, then left the apartment.

The elevator doors opened on the lobby to reveal her father waiting for her. He held out his elbow, and she linked her arm in his.

"You look pretty as a picture," he said as they walked out onto the sidewalk. The glow of neon signs above the buildings gave everything a colorful sheen. Between the signs, the headlights of taxis, and the streetlights, there was no need of the moon, which hid behind clouds.

"Thank you. You're not so bad yourself." Kitty took a deep breath. The smoke-tinged air was brisk, slightly damp. It could mean snow. She pulled her coat tight.

With his free hand, her father adjusted his hat. "Kind of you to say, but I'm coming off a hard day."

"Yes, what happened in Atlanta?" she asked. They paused at the crosswalk.

"It's complicated. I don't expect you to worry about it, though."

"I'm not worried. I'm curious."

Her father led her around the corner. The door to the steakhouse was just ahead, under a brown cloth awning. "You really want to know?"

"Sure. It'll make great dinner conversation." She knew her father would, at best, end up glossing over the details of his missed opportunity. He always said he was sure the business would bore her, but she suspected he thought she wouldn't understand. He was probably right. But playing interested would soften him up.

Her father held the door for her, then stepped ahead of her at the maître d's station. "Tessler, party of two."

"Of course, sir. Do you have a table preference?"

"A booth, please. In the corner."

The maître d' led them through the dark rooms to a booth on a back wall. When Kitty was younger, she liked to crane her neck up throughout the meal and try to count all the ceramic pipes on the ceiling. Her father would list names of all the important men who'd taken part in the restaurant's unique tradition by purchasing a pipe for a postdinner smoke there. The pipes were hung from the ceiling when not in use. By the end of the night, her neck would ache from staring up, and she never got an accurate count. She smiled at the memory as she slid into the booth.

"What's got you so cheerful?" her father asked.

"I'm always cheerful." Kitty glanced over the menu.

"Well, I'm happy to be here with you. It's been a long time since we had a chance to go to dinner together, hasn't it? I thought you might not want to be seen on the town with your old man anymore."

"There's no one I'd rather be out with, Papa." A twinge in Kitty's heart surprised her. She enjoyed spending the evening with her father. Why had it been so long since she'd made the time?

"So, what are you softening me up for this time?" The corners of his mouth twitched.

"To pick up the check."

He laughed. The waiter came over to get their drink orders. He started to list the specials, but Kitty and her father always got the same meals: lamb chops for her, a steak medium-rare for him. After the waiter left, her father asked again about Kitty's motives.

"You know me too well." She sighed. "I wanted to talk to you about Andre."

Her father crossed his arms over his chest. "I won't change my mind, Katarina."

"No, that's the thing . . ." She picked at the edge of her napkin, her gaze drifting to the wall beside them. She had to keep her performance subtle to set the trap. He wouldn't buy that Kitty had fallen madly in love with Andre overnight. After a sufficient pause, she said, "You were right. He is a nice guy." She hesitated, and her father took the bait.

"What? What's the matter?"

"You've got him going to Miami so soon. We're just getting to know each other better."

Her father smiled. "Is that all? Oh, you girls are all the same. He'll be back in a month."

"A whole month? Doesn't that seem a little long? What if he meets a girl in Miami, what will you say then?"

"I don't think he'll meet anyone." But worry clouded her father's eyes.

Kitty sat back, still fiddling with the napkin. "You're right. I know you're right. And he'll be back . . . let's see, next week is the first of December . . . January? New Year's?"

"The first week of January." Her father shifted a bit in his seat.

"Oh." Kitty drooped. "I was hoping he might be back for the New Year's parties. I'll need a date. I'm sure Hen can find me someone, though. Going alone would be too embarrassing. Andre would understand, don't you think?"

The waiter delivered their cocktails, giving her father a moment to think. Kitty played with her swizzle stick and tried to look appropriately forlorn.

"Sure. He'd understand. Can't go alone." Her father stared at the ice in his drink, his face lined with effort.

"Oh, good. If you think so, then I know it will be okay. And a month really isn't that long." Kitty perked up.

Her father regarded her critically. "I have a thought."

"Oh?" Kitty prepared her look of surprise.

"How would you like to go to Miami?"

Kitty's mouth rounded into an O. "Miami?"

"Sure. You haven't gone out of town in ages. A beach trip would be a treat for you."

"I don't know, Papa. A whole month? I don't want to be away for that long. And Andre will be working all the time. What will I do by myself?"

"You occupy yourself pretty well here."

She felt a flicker of frustration at having to offer this piece of the puzzle, but she was so close to her goal. "I've got Hen here."

Her father threw up a hand in triumph. "She ought to go with you. You girls can have our suite. I'll find another room for Andre. There's no way Hen's going to say no to a Miami vacation, is there?"

Kitty brightened. "I suppose I could ask her what she thinks."

Her father reached a hand across the table, and she gripped it. "There, doesn't your papa take good care of you? You didn't think Andre was right for you, but I knew."

Kitty's stomach knotted as a serious concern she hadn't thought of before occurred to her. "Wait. That means we'd be apart at Christmas."

Her father pressed his lips together for a moment. "Maybe I could make it down there. We'll see. But you should go. Have a good time." He grinned. "Get away from the snow."

She couldn't return his happy expression. Small family though they were, they had a few traditions, and opening presents on Christmas morning was the one Kitty treasured most. When she'd been too young to go shopping on her own, her nanny had taken her out to the stores. She'd always get him a tie and tie clip, because he trusted only Kitty to help him accessorize.

Kitty was grateful for the arrival of the waiter with their dinners. She swallowed down the lump in her throat. She shook off the last of her sentiment and refocused her energy on the rewards the trip would bring. After all, one Christmas in the grand scheme of things was nothing. "Ooh, that reminds me. I'll need a ticket, won't I? Isn't Andre flying down?"

"Of course. My daughter's not riding on the bus with the band." Her father took a bite of his steak. "Perfection, as always. How's the lamb?"

"Divine." Kitty took a bite and followed it with a gulp of her drink, to wash away the last lingering doubts about the timing of her Miami trip.

⇥⇤

Kitty's father assured her that his travel agent would arrange everything, so all she had to do was confirm that Hen would be able to go. She called Hen the morning after dinner with her father.

"You're really and truly going to Miami?" Hen squealed across the phone line. "Wait . . . does this mean you've changed your mind about Andre?"

"Don't be silly." Kitty sprawled on her bed, Loco snoozing in the curve of her hip. "If Daddy's paying for a Miami trip, why would I miss it? Andre will be working all the time. I'll get to have some fun. But you have to come."

"I don't think I could. We've got Mother's holiday party, and Charles won't want to go to the New Year's Ball alone."

"He'll survive. You've gone to a million events with him. Come with me."

"I'll have to ask Mother."

Kitty sat up. *Damn that woman.* "You don't need to do that. Just tell her you're going. You're an adult, for God's sake."

"Kitty. You know Mother. She's not going to let me jaunt off for a month without some say in it."

"Well, ask her then." Kitty flopped back down, and Loco grunted in protest at the shifting. "I want to get everything settled. Besides, don't you want to go?"

"Oh, yes. It sounds like a dream. And I wouldn't mind putting the winter coats away for a while."

Mrs. Bancroft's words in the hotel the other evening sounded in Kitty's head. *I keep hoping her fashion sense will rub off on Hen.* "Look, if you want to go, tell her it's a shopping trip, okay? Tell her I'm helping you buy a summer wardrobe. Or a wedding trousseau. Miami is one of the most fashionable places in the country."

"So is New York," Hen said.

"Yes, but you've seen everything here. The Miami winter lines inspire everyone else's summer lines," Kitty said, all patience. Hen must be throwing away those *Vogue* magazines Kitty passed along.

"If you say so. I'll talk to Mother today."

"Good. Why don't you come over tonight? Hopefully your mother will say yes, and we can plan."

"Charles wants to go out to dinner. Mind if he comes?"

"Sure. Don't forget: shopping trip." Kitty's mind raced as she hung up the phone. If Hen got permission, Kitty could use the evening to get her scheme under way.

As she was trudging down the sidewalk behind Loco that afternoon, Kitty realized she could get more than one chess piece in motion at the club that night. She needed to draw Max's attention, however reluctant he might be to like her. A night at the club would be the perfect time to play the vixen for his benefit. Then, once he was on the hook, she could keep him from interfering with Hen and Sebastian. Little did Hen know the sacrifices Kitty made for her.

Kitty selected her favorite dress, the sapphire satin with a low-cut back and full, swishing skirt. Accented with flashing diamond studs, her silver heels, and just a dab of Femme de Rochas perfume, she went down to the club like a knight in armor.

Even Charles and Hen, who were as used to seeing Kitty as their own reflections in the mirror, did double takes when she walked into the lobby.

"Seen a ghost?" she asked, kissing Hen on the cheek.

"You look gorgeous," Hen said. "Who's all that for?"

"Me," Kitty said with a sidelong smile. "So, what did your mother say about Miami?"

"Miami?" Charles looked from Hen to Kitty.

Hen shuffled her feet. "Oh, yes, well. Kitty's going to Miami, and she's invited me along. I didn't get a chance to talk to Mother yet, though. She was out all day."

Charles smiled. "Sounds like a fine idea to me."

I just bet it does, Kitty thought. No telling what he'd get up to with Hen away for a month.

"Really? You don't mind?" Hen asked him.

"Sure. So long as you girls behave yourselves." He wrapped an arm around Hen's shoulder.

"What kind of trouble could we get up to?" Kitty asked, all sweetness. "Let's go in."

The three entered the club and the maître d' led them to a front booth. Charles and Hen ordered meals, but Kitty demurred, saying she'd already eaten. The truth was if she wanted to look sharp, she couldn't wolf down a cheeseburger in front of everyone. Instead, she contented herself with a cocktail.

Thanks to some supply order mix-up in the kitchen, Andre only had time to come over to say a quick hello, but he made a point to say he hadn't wanted to miss them. He seemed unusually glad to see them. Kitty began to worry that maybe work had been responsible for his distractedness with her, and maybe he really did have a crush on her. If so, that was something she'd have to address. She couldn't let him think he had a real chance, and the trip might only give him hope.

After they ate, Charles and Hen moved to the dance floor. Kitty had to wait through two songs before getting her own invitation. She accepted, glad for an opportunity to get in front of Max. She might have preferred a more suave partner, though. The man standing in front of the booth, who introduced himself as Ed, had a gut, a plaid jacket, and a bald spot. But Kitty was not one to waste an opportunity, especially not as the band struck up the opening notes to "Kiss of Fire."

Sadly, Ed did not know how to tango. Not that Kitty was an expert in that type of dance, but she might have opted for less of the shuffling Ed was inclined to. She angled herself so that she was in the halo of light at the edge of the stage and threw as much style as she could into her own steps. She knew she'd made an impression even before she glanced up, when she heard Sebastian's smooth voice stumble on the word *burning*. When she looked up, her suspicions were confirmed. Sebastian had his eyes locked on her, a slight grin on his face.

Max, however, didn't seem to notice Kitty's hard work. He glanced at her once, then closed his eyes as he worked the stops on the trumpet. She worked Ed's less-than-confident lead to her advantage and maneuvered closer to where Max stood. When he opened his eyes again, however, he looked past her into the darkness of the club. The song ended with a flourish. Kitty thanked Ed glumly and declined the offer of a second dance. She had to let her back dry after being pawed by his sweaty palms. She walked back over toward the booth. At the corner of the stage, she paused and turned slowly. Max was watching her, his gaze moving up her exposed back. A tingle followed the line of his eyes up her spine. At last, when their eyes met, she flashed him the hint of a smile, and he looked away.

A giddy, bubbly feeling flooded her head. The familiar feeling of a win. But she couldn't let it distract her from the second part of what she hoped to accomplish that evening. Her chance came when the band took a short break and Hen returned to the booth with Charles for fresh drinks. While they waited for the waiter to return, Kitty excused herself to ask Sebastian something about Miami.

Sebastian's eyes lit up as she approached the stage. "Hello, Kitty. You look especially pretty tonight."

She tilted her head. "As pretty as Loco?"

He laughed. "Prettier. You like the songs tonight?"

"Always." She glanced over her shoulder, then leaned in to Sebastian. "So, listen. My father is sending me to Miami with Andre after all."

He lifted his brows. "That's great. But you won't spend all your time with Andre, will you? Can I steal you away to go dancing?" His eyes sparkled. "I'll make sure you have fun."

"I don't doubt that," Kitty said. "I've invited Hen to come along, but I think she's a little reluctant. Would you mind talking it up to her? Tell her how exciting it is, how much she'd like it, that sort of thing. She'll listen to you."

"Of course. Yes. I will be happy to."

"But don't tell her I told you to. She'll think I'm meddling."

Sebastian agreed. Kitty went back to the table and stood beside Hen. "Will you come with me to the powder room?"

"Sure," Hen said. She slid out of the booth and followed Kitty across the dance floor. She offered Hen the lipstick and freshened her own. As they made their way back to Charles, Sebastian called Hen over.

"What do you think he wants?" Hen whispered.

Kitty shrugged. "Better go see. I'll keep Charles company."

Hen nodded and walked over to the stage. Kitty slid back into the booth just as the waiter brought their drinks. Charles didn't acknowledge the waiter. He watched Hen with a furrowed brow.

"What's that about?" he asked. Hen had her face just inches from Sebastian's, and she was giggling with her hand on her lips.

"It's nothing," Kitty said. "He had a question about her family. Guess they're a big deal everywhere. He sure knew the name Bancroft."

Charles nodded and some of the tension left his face. "Right. Naturally."

"So you think our little trip is a good idea?" she asked.

"I think it's high time Hen got out of the city, somewhere other than Newport," he said, though his tone was wary. "She doesn't travel enough."

"I agree," Kitty said. "And don't you worry a bit, I'll keep her out of trouble."

Charles chuckled, now relaxed. "I'm not worried about Hen."

"No, why would you be?" Kitty leaned toward him and pointed. "Isn't she the silliest thing, though? Look at how she is with him. Hen's no flirt, but that's about the closest I've seen from her."

At this, Charles's face tightened more than before. He took a sip of his martini and said nothing. Kitty settled back, careful to hide her smile.

⧽ EIGHT ⧼

Charles and Hen left the club shortly after Hen's chat with Sebastian, with Hen far more eager to broach the subject of the trip with her mother. Kitty waited for the band to finish, then invited Sebastian to come up to the suite again. She wanted to get an idea of what was waiting for her in Miami. Max overheard and piped up.

"Rehearsal is later in the morning," he said. "Mind if I come, too?"

Kitty raised an eyebrow. This time his self-invitation had nothing to do with playing chaperone; that much was obvious. Men were so easy. All it took was one dress and the right look, and they couldn't help themselves. "The more the merrier," she said.

Andre's massive frame drooped as Kitty approached him at the bar. "Tough night, huh?"

He rubbed his eyes. "It was."

"I've got some good news for you."

"Oh, yeah?"

"Yeah. Papa's sending me with you to Miami."

Andre brightened. "Well, that is good news. And Hen's coming, too, of course?"

"Sure. Couldn't go without Hen."

"You two will love it, I promise you that."

"I'm sure we will. I was hoping to talk to Sebastian and Max about what Miami's like. Get their take on things. I know you'll do a great job showing us around, but I don't remember anything about it. They're coming up to the suite. Want to join?"

He sighed. "I'd love to, but this night has me beat. Don't worry, I'll help fill you in on the plane trip. You are flying with me, right?"

"Papa's getting it all settled."

"Great." He cast an eye at the stack of papers in front of him. She patted his arm.

"Get some rest, will you?"

"Will do." He turned back to his work, and she headed upstairs to get the bar set for her guests. Max and Sebastian rang the doorbell to the suite just as she was setting out the ice bucket.

"We had to help pack the equipment," Sebastian explained. He did a poor job of concealing his drifting gaze as he looked around the living room.

"Looking for someone?" Kitty asked.

Sebastian laughed. Kitty clicked her tongue and Loco came skittering out of Kitty's bedroom. The dog launched herself at Sebastian, who lifted her in his arms. Sebastian's appeal to girls seemed to extend beyond his own species.

"Looks like you've got yourself a boyfriend, Loco." Kitty patted the dog's head and went to the bar. "Can I get you boys a drink?"

She poured cocktails for them as Max sat on the couch. Sebastian sat on the rug, a contented Loco on his lap. He cooed at the dog in Spanish.

"You don't have to sit on the floor, you know," Kitty said, handing him a glass. "She's allowed on the furniture."

"I don't care," Sebastian said. Kitty did a double take.

"Mind." Max took the second cocktail Kitty offered. "You don't *mind*."

"I don't mind," Sebastian repeated. "Sorry, some expressions stay in my head better than others."

"I wouldn't want to try to learn English." Kitty took her own drink and sat on the chaise. "I had a hard enough time with grammar in school."

"You weren't a scholar, eh?" Max studied the spread of fashion magazines on the coffee table pointedly.

Kitty kicked off her shoes. "I didn't say that."

"There's no shame in it. I'm sure there's a lot of fine journalism in . . . what is this?" He picked up a glossy and held it between his finger and thumb. "*Mademoiselle?* Ooh là là."

"Max . . ." Sebastian said, his tone a warning. Max ignored it and kept his focus on Kitty.

She cocked her head. "In that one, I only look at the pictures."

"That's about what I expected." Max returned the magazine to the pile.

"What does that mean?"

"I don't mean any offense by it." He sat back against the cushions of the couch. "You don't strike me as a bookworm, that's all."

"I'm sure that Max can find another topic," Sebastian said.

"Don't be silly. I'm intrigued that he's such a quick study. He's only talked to me a couple of times, but he knows everything about me. Come on, Amazing Dunninger." She swept a hand from her head to her shoes. "What do you observe?"

Max rubbed the back of his neck. "Look, your efforts aren't wasted, that's for sure. I was just curious about how a girl like you fills her day."

"I don't read every article in *Mademoiselle*, that's true. Doesn't mean I'm not a reader."

"Oh yeah? So what's the last book you read?"

She lifted her chin, in her element now. "That's hardly fair."

The corner of his mouth twitched. " 'Cause you don't read."

"Because I *re*read. The last book I read is one I've read a million times. I like the classics." She sat up. "Though you seem to favor dime-store detective novels, if your investigative skills are any clue."

At this, Max sat up straighter. "The classics? Is that right?"

"You better believe it."

Their back-and-forth had a brief pause as Sebastian stood. He held up his hands. "Sorry to interrupt. If he's going to do this, I need a drink." At the bar cart, he turned to Kitty with a sympathetic smile. "He always does this. Would you like to know what does the trick? How to make him be polite?"

Kitty delivered her answer with her eyes locked on Max's. "Now why in the world would I want him to be polite? Don't worry, Sebastian. I can handle him."

A smile crept up Max's face. "So, I think you were about to list your favorite classic novels?"

"I guess you don't think Dickens is classic?"

Max snorted. "I don't see Dickens appealing to a girl like you. All those smelly orphans . . ."

She stood and crossed to the coffee table, fishing the dog-eared book from under the pile of magazines. "How about *Great Expectations*?" She tossed it into his lap.

He turned the book over in his hands, then flipped through the pages. "This isn't your pop's book? I could see him reading it."

"I like Estella. You should read it. It proves it's entirely possible for a girl to have both style and brains."

"And to string guys along, if I recall."

"She's smart. She knows what she wants and how to get it."

Max set the book back on the coffee table. "So you've read *Great Expectations*. That's one. Anything else?"

She sat back. "I like *The Merchant of Venice*."

"Oh, I bet you do."

"I like Portia." Kitty reached for her cigarette case. "There's a woman with guts. The Wife of Bath is pretty good too. Knows how to dress, and she didn't even need fashion magazines."

Max watched Kitty for a moment without responding. Sebastian, whose head had been going back and forth like a metronome, had abandoned the conversation and sat playing with Loco in the corner. Kitty blew smoke toward the ceiling. She felt certain Max was working on another volley, so she was surprised when he pulled a small brown journal out of his pocket.

"Fair's fair. Here's what I'm reading right now." He offered the journal to her. "I got the poem from a book from the library and copied it out so I could keep it with me."

She read the title and the first few lines. "'Little Gidding'?" she asked. "What's that?"

"It's a town. And a church."

"And a poem, apparently." She set the journal on the coffee table, beside the copy of *Great Expectations*. "Is it any good?"

"It's very good. I've read it a lot. It's a hard one."

Kitty shrugged. "Why not read two or three easier ones? Take you about the same amount of time. Much less work that way."

For the first time in the conversation, Max dropped her gaze. "I'm being serious with you right now."

"If you get to crack jokes about Estella, I can joke too."

"It's clear I misjudged you. I'm sorry. Really."

His straightforward tone caught Kitty off guard. "Thank you."

He nodded and put the journal back in his pocket. "Anyway, you wanted to know about Miami, right? That was the reason for this friendly visit. Sebastian, tell her about the beach, would you?"

Sebastian looked up from his game of tug-of-war with Loco. "I get to talk now?"

"Tell Kitty about Miami and don't be sore." Max pointed at the bar. "Mind if I refill?"

"Not at all." Kitty lounged on the chaise once more, toying with her earring as Sebastian described the restaurants and clubs that awaited her in Miami. She half listened, replaying the conversation with Max. Handling someone's dismissal of her with a well-timed barb was a reflex by now—Kitty had been doing that most of her life. She was far less equipped to handle sincerity.

". . . and you'll have to take Loco out to the beach," Sebastian continued, unaware of her distraction. Kitty gasped.

"Loco! She won't be able to fly with me. I guess I'll have to leave her here." Her heart sank. Between missing Christmas morning with her father and the prospect of a month without Loco, Kitty was ready to reconsider the trip.

"She can ride on the bus with us," Sebastian said without hesitation. He turned to Max. "That will be all right, don't you think?"

Max glanced from Sebastian to Kitty. "Sure. Of course. Can't leave her here."

"I'll take very good care of her, I promise," Sebastian said.

"I'm sure you would. But how would she get back?"

"Some musicians from the band here are coming with us, aren't they?" Sebastian asked Max. "They will probably return when Andre does. And we will make sure she goes with someone who you can trust. If I don't find someone, I will bring her back myself."

"Well, that settles it," Kitty said. "Loco, I guess you're coming to Miami."

They said their good-byes shortly after, leaving Kitty alone with the puzzle of Max's behavior. He seemed to be testing her, probing for something, but she wasn't sure what. Sparring with a worthy opponent had been a refreshing challenge, even if he had thrown her for a loop with his sudden change in attitude. *What an odd bird*, she thought. At least conversation in Miami wouldn't be dull.

NINE

Hen called the next morning to say that she'd secured her mother's permission to go to Miami, a huge relief to Kitty. Following Kitty's instructions, Hen had pitched the trip as a shopping excursion, and Mrs. Bancroft had agreed without hesitation. The only question Hen's mother had asked was if the airline would charge for extra luggage, since she wanted Hen to take an empty suitcase to fill with new clothes. Kitty assured them both that an extra bag would be no trouble, since they could each carry up to forty pounds of luggage, and they could always ship back anything they couldn't pack.

Though Kitty had initially planned to go shopping herself to prepare, she decided to heed her own sage advice and purchase her vacation wardrobe in Miami. She'd take a few items, of course, but the stores in New York would only have winter clothes. Most of Kitty's summer wear would be hopelessly out-of-date by Miami standards. Buying outfits in Miami was the smartest course of action. She packed a light suitcase and carried an empty one of her own.

Sebastian stopped by the night before her flight to pick up Loco. Kitty handed over a hefty satchel with Loco's food, favorite toys, and blanket. She also gave him ten dollars and the direct phone number for the suite at the Imperium, with strict instructions to call if anything happened. She was nearly at the point of tears, but Sebastian reassured her that he would care for Loco like she was his own. His clear excitement at having the dog to accompany him on the long ride eased Kitty's nerves. At last, she relinquished the leash, and Loco was off to Florida with the band.

The next morning, Kitty put on the only weather-appropriate dress she'd found when she'd done a last-minute sweep of Macy's, a short-sleeved fuchsia number with a flared skirt and shiny black buttons up the front. She pinned a black, pearl-studded half hat into her curls and clipped large rhinestone studs on her earlobes. The finishing touch was a turquoise pair of Claire McCardell sunglasses, which she tucked in her handbag. Kitty would add those on the tarmac, where her father planned to take a photo of her boarding with Andre and Hen.

"Are you excited to fly?" her father asked as his driver steered them through the streets toward Idlewild Airport. "Remember, it's bumpy. That's normal, so don't let it make you worry."

"I won't, Papa." She rolled the strap of her handbag between her fingers. "When are you coming down?"

"I haven't quite worked it out yet. Don't worry about me. Just have a good time, all right?"

Kitty nodded and kept her eyes on the beams of the bridge as they flew by the car window. The truth was, she was a bit nervous about flying, mainly about the possibility of needing the airsickness bag. She didn't exactly want Andre to have an enduring memory of her throwing up into a bag, even if she wasn't serious about him.

At the airport, they handed her luggage off to the porter. Hen and Andre were waiting at the gate, and they all went out to the tarmac together when it was time to board. They joined a line of people who had the same idea, and they waited as each group posed on the stairs to have their photo taken. Finally, it was their turn, and the three travelers squinted into the sun as Kitty's father snapped the picture.

"Oh, wait," Kitty called. She pulled her sunglasses out of her bag. "Take another one, Papa."

Someone below them on the stairs groaned, but Kitty ignored them. No excuse for not getting the best picture possible. She waved at her father one last time, then boarded the plane with Hen and Andre.

A smiling stewardess met them at the door. They offered their tickets, and the stewardess led them to four seats near the front of the plane. The seats were arranged in sets of two, facing each other, with a table between them. Hen and Kitty sat next to each other, with Andre on the other side of the table.

"Isn't this lovely? Like a train," Hen said.

"The deluxe cabin is the only way to go," Andre said. "I suggested it to Mr. Tessler. Thought this way it would be easier for us to keep each other company."

Kitty would have preferred to sit with Hen alone, but she had to admit the seating was divine. She was especially pleased when the stewardess came around a few minutes later to take orders for cocktails and to hand out the menu. The lunch in the deluxe cabin featured marinated mushrooms and steak. If this was air travel, Kitty could see herself flying more often.

The plane shuddered to life. The whine of the engines startled Kitty, and she glanced to see if more experienced travelers looked nervous. The stewardesses chatted happily near the front, and Andre studied his menu. No fear there. Kitty turned to Hen and saw her own worry mirrored in Hen's wide eyes. The recognition made both girls laugh, and Kitty patted Hen's hand.

"Mother said takeoff is the scariest part," Hen said as the plane rolled down the runway.

Kitty jerked her head back to look at Hen. "When has your mother ever been on a plane?"

"She went on some luxury flight with Father when I was a baby. Said it was awful, that she'd never do it aga—oh." Hen pressed her lips together. "Well, that was a long time ago. I'm sure this will be different."

"It'll be fine," Andre said. "I've done this plenty."

His calm reassured Kitty for the briefest of moments, until the plane began to rise. A sudden pressure settled on her whole body, pushing her into her seat. Outside the window, the skyline tilted. Though Kitty expected her nerves to get worse, instead she felt liberated at the thought that she was free from the earth. The plane leveled, and she looked out the window. Manhattan truly looked like an island from that height, instead of the energetic world it was at street level.

The city's buildings shrank to the size of toys, then disappeared into the distance. The stewardess brought postcards with a photo of the plane on them, and the girls busied themselves scribbling notes to their families. Andre slipped his postcard into his pocket.

"Don't you want to drop one in the mail?" Kitty asked.

"Who would I send it to? Your pop?"

Kitty pressed her lips together as she realized she knew very little about Andre's family. "Your friends in the city wouldn't want to see the plane?"

"Nah, they'd think I was bragging." He smiled.

"I'm just surprised a guy like you doesn't have a girl," Hen said.

Andre laughed. "Not at the moment, no."

"What about brothers or sisters? Wouldn't they like to get a card from you?"

"Don't have any. No family in the city to speak of. My pop died when I was a kid, and my mom never remarried. She died a couple of years ago." His tone stayed light and amiable. "It's just me."

"I'm so sorry," Hen said.

"Hey." Andre leaned forward. "Nothing to be sorry about. I'm happy—got my job, it keeps me busy. Got friends who have me over for holidays. Plus there's Mr. Tessler." He nodded at Kitty. "He's a good man. I'm fortunate to work for him."

Kitty sensed Andre wanted her to respond. "He's glad to have you. Says so all the time." As soon as the words came out of her mouth, she realized they were true. What she hadn't known was how much Andre looked up to her father. That was clear from the way Andre brightened at the idea that her father talked about him.

"Yeah?" Andre shook his head. "Good man, good man."

A jolt of turbulence interrupted them, and Kitty gripped the handles of her seat. She decided a lighter meal was the best idea, in case her stomach revolted against the rocky treatment. When the stewardess came to take their orders, she asked for the cold salad plate. Hen followed suit, but Andre opted for the steak. He was an experienced flyer, so Kitty reasoned he must be more used to the ups and downs. He seemed completely untroubled, pulling out a deck of cards as the plane took another dip.

"Either of you play gin rummy?" he asked. Kitty declined, taking out a magazine, but Hen agreed excitedly. It was all Kitty could do not to roll her eyes. Of course Hen would waste a glamorous plane trip on an old ladies' game just to avoid hurting someone's feelings.

The trip went by surprisingly fast. A couple of rounds of cards, a delicious meal, and a few magazines later, Kitty glanced out the window to see cerulean water. A thin band of buildings curved around a larger landmass to the west.

Andre spotted her looking. "That's it," he said.

"South Beach?"

"South Beach." He grinned. "You girls are in for a treat."

Hen leaned over Kitty to gaze at the view. As Kitty watched her friend admiring the sight of Miami for the first time, she reminded herself that the plane's descent meant the beginning of her plan. If all went the way she hoped, everything would be different by the time they flew back home.

❖ TEN ❖

MIAMI

DECEMBER 1953

Before Kitty could even step outside the plane's open door, a burst of hot, sticky air made her gasp. The short sleeves that she thought would make her dress so perfect for the Miami temperatures were little help, and she could feel every fiber of her stockings clinging to her legs. Each step she took down the stairs brought her closer to the pulse of heat from the tarmac. Her father had been right; she sure wouldn't have to worry about snow.

Andre, Kitty, and Hen went to baggage claim, where porters began laying out suitcases in a long line. They pointed out theirs, and Andre slipped a porter a few bills to follow them out to the taxi line.

"We don't have a car here?" Kitty asked, fluffing her curls away from the beads of perspiration now dotting her temple. Next to her, Hen fanned herself and exhaled hard.

"It's in the shop," Andre explained. "Don't worry. We should have it in the next few days. South Beach is like New York, though. You can walk to a lot." He chuckled. "Just not the airport."

Kitty forced a smile and climbed into the back of the cab with Hen. Andre directed the cabbie to Collins Avenue, and they pulled onto the street.

All she remembered from her previous visit were the bright whites and vivid colors of the buildings. Despite the memory, the tropical rainbow still took Kitty by surprise with its vibrancy as they passed the hotels, resorts, and restaurants that led to South Beach. The sooty grays and browns of New York, along with the tall buildings, darkened every street and corner. Miami's yellows were lemon, its pinks were candy, and everything was edged with chrome. She felt more awake, as if she'd come out of a long, refreshing sleep. Miami was alive, and it wanted Kitty here.

They pulled into the circular driveway in front of the gleaming white Imperium Hotel. The cabbie opened the back door, and Kitty sucked in a breath of warm salt air. Unlike the stale air on the tarmac, the light breeze at the hotel carried a promise of cool ocean water.

A gangly bellboy with light brown skin raced out and began unpacking the trunk before the three travelers could even step out of the cab. When he spotted Andre, the bellboy set down the suitcase he was carrying and stuck out his hand.

"Mr. Polzer, good to see you. They told us you were coming today," he said.

"How are you, George?" Andre shook the boy's hand.

"Always a beautiful day at the Imperium, sir." George's words had a practiced air. "And which one of your lovely companions is Mr. Tessler's daughter?"

Andre waved Kitty forward. "This is Miss Tessler, and her friend is Miss Bancroft. They're in the presidential suite."

"Yes, sir."

Andre pointed out the girls' luggage, and George piled it onto a cart. He disappeared into a side door, and Hen and Kitty followed Andre through the wide glass doors of the main entrance. Since the Vanguard was Kitty's home, she never really thought of it as a hotel. She saw strangers in the elevator, of course, but thought of the daily commotion as a normal part of life. Standing in the lobby of the Imperium, she could see her father's work for what it was. The spacious room brought back a recollection of her first visit as a young girl, with the sea air drifting through the lobby and the wicker furniture.

Now Kitty could appreciate the subtleties of how her father had incorporated his taste into the unique Miami ambiance. The wood plank walls she remembered as white actually had a hint of pale blue, a constant reminder of the turquoise water that awaited just on the other side of the lobby. Cool white marble floors provided an oasis from the humidity they'd just escaped. And the shining metal accents on the check-in desk occasionally caught rays of sunlight from the long windows that looked out over the sands and pool. Kitty made a mental note to tell her father how much she liked it when she called to let him know they'd arrived safely.

The man at the check-in desk greeted Andre warmly. He gave the girls keys to the presidential suite and practically begged them to let him know if they required anything. As the three walked to the elevator, Kitty turned to Andre.

"When is the band arriving?" she asked.

"It usually takes them three days, with stops. I'd say Friday morning."

"Do you think they'll call before then?"

Hen laid a hand on Kitty's arm. "I'm sure Loco's fine. Sebastian said he'd treat her like his own."

"I'm not worried," Kitty said quickly. "Just want to make sure I'm ready to pick her up. I don't want him to have to watch her once they're here."

"I'll let you know as soon as I get word," Andre assured her. "You two would probably like to freshen up, right? Let's meet for dinner at seven. I have some work to do, but I'll meet you in the lobby."

Kitty and Hen agreed, and they stepped onto the elevator as Andre headed back toward the hall leading to the right of the entrance, which Kitty assumed led to the offices. He threw a look and a final wave over his shoulder before the doors closed. *Now he can't even walk away without looking back?* Kitty thought. *Yep, all the classic signs.* Andre had fallen prey to her usual effect on men. She'd have to put some work into convincing him to give up on her by the end of the trip. At the moment, though, she needed to concentrate on Hen. Kitty calculated that the few days it would take for the band to arrive would give her time to set her scheme into motion. Once Sebastian arrived, she could begin working to throw Hen in his path.

The elevator doors opened onto a hallway with wide double doors at the end. A golden plaque announced that the girls had arrived at the presidential suite. Inside, the suite was decorated with the same light colors and glittering accents as the lobby. The windows on the far side of the room looked out over the ocean, and the tips of palm fronds waved just outside.

"I suppose our bags are in our rooms," Kitty said. "Let's change out of these traveling clothes and explore, what do you say?"

"Sure. I'm going to get a bath first. I'm sweating like a hog," Hen said, shaking her jacket in an attempt to air out.

Kitty fluffed her hair and batted her lashes. "Ladies don't sweat, they glow."

"Then I'm glowing like a hog."

Kitty laughed and headed to the door on the left side of the living room, more out of habit than anything. She opened the door to find she'd guessed wrong; Hen's bags were waiting instead. Kitty hadn't thought that she'd get her father's room, but since he wasn't there, it was the most logical. "You're in here," she told Hen.

She changed into a pair of high-waisted shorts from the previous summer, glad she'd saved them. Once Hen was bathed and changed, the girls decided to head out to the pool. Unfortunately, all Hen had to wear were long-sleeved dresses and blouses. Kitty helped Hen roll and pin the sleeves on her shirt, wishing she had a second pair of shorts to offer her. *We've got to go out shopping as soon as possible*, she thought.

The patio was already crowded with people when they walked out. Children splashed in the kidney-shaped pool, teen girls lounged on blue-striped chairs, and couples drank from glasses with tiny paper umbrellas at the outdoor bar. A young man passed Kitty and Hen, taking a moment to gaze appreciatively at Kitty's exposed legs. She smiled and lifted her sunglasses.

"Hello there." She nudged Hen. "I think Miami suits me."

Hen had her eye on a tanned, shirtless man preparing to dive into the deep end of the pool. "I think it suits anyone with a pulse and eyes," she said.

The girls stretched out on deck chairs and traded assessments of the handsome guys on offer at the pool. Kitty considered that even if she couldn't work Sebastian into her plan with Hen, there were many other boys of all types. Temptation lay all around, and Charles was miles away. As Kitty soaked up the warm sunshine, she thought she might even have time for a little romance herself before all was said and done. She didn't care a thing about love, but romance? Romance she liked.

❊ ELEVEN ❊

Kitty made short work of getting Hen to a store for more heat-appropriate clothing. On the recommendation of the front desk clerk, they took a cab to Burdine's Department Store the morning after they arrived. At the sight of the store's bubblegum-pink walls and bright blue ceiling streaked with fake clouds, Kitty wished she'd been more specific about their fashion needs. But she quickly realized the dresses and rompers on sale were nowhere near as tacky as the décor.

Though the items they purchased at Burdine's were charming and summery, they were hardly the kind of haute couture Hen's mother would expect from the trip. The next morning, Kitty called around to make appointments at several designers, including Alix of Miami. The large showrooms with live models and champagne for Kitty and Hen were more along the lines of what Kitty had expected. Hen bought some evening wear, and Kitty pointed her to a few pieces for her trousseau that would satisfy Mrs. Bancroft. At another designer, Kitty treated herself to a strapless two-piece bathing suit, yet another pair of shorts, and several daring tops.

As they waited for the band's return, they shopped in the mornings and spent the afternoons at the pool. They met Andre for dinner in the hotel restaurant both evenings, mostly as a convenience to him. He had a hard time pulling away from work long enough to take them out but promised to show them more of the town on his first day off. The girls discussed going to some of the clubs Andre told them about, but decided to wait until they had a man to go with them. Kitty was not going to show up at a club without at least one date between the two of them; it would reek of desperation. For the first time, she was sorry they didn't have Charles. If nothing else, he was a reliable escort.

Andre's excitement as he met them for dinner each night gave her cause for concern. A hug for each of them when they walked in the first night turned into a kiss on each girl's cheek the next. She knew it wasn't a sign of the budding friendship among the three of them. It must have been an effort to get a little physical contact with Kitty. Though she wanted to convince her father that their relationship was progressing, she couldn't have Andre do something foolish like propose to her. At the rate they were going, a couple of weeks might be enough to convince him he should. She'd have to continue to flirt, but make sure he'd want nothing to do with her in the end. And, as with her father, Andre would have to believe that his decision was entirely his idea. The tricky part was how to achieve that, which kept Kitty's mind whirring.

Andre had told Kitty and Hen that the band should arrive around eleven o'clock on Friday morning so the girls had gone down to wait a few minutes before. At last, the band pulled up in a weather-beaten bus to the hotel's entrance. The members staggered off, more bags under their eyes than in their hands, and headed to the back parking lot to pick up their cars. Sebastian and Max were among the last off, with Sebastian cradling Loco in his arms. Kitty rushed out the door as soon as she saw them.

"My sweetheart," she cried, reaching for the dog.

Sebastian grinned. He was the only one who walked off the bus looking fresh enough to star in a commercial. "Now I'm your sweetheart, eh?"

"Don't tease me," Kitty said. Sebastian handed the wriggling dog to her. "Thank you for taking such good care of her."

Max leaned in. "How do you like Miami so far?"

"It's swell," Hen said. "But we haven't seen much. We've gone shopping and had dinner here. Oh, and we love the pool."

"That's not Miami." Max shook his head. "Sebastian, we've got to take them out. Can you call Marcela?"

Marcela? Kitty thought. Andre hadn't mentioned any club owned by a woman, and he knew all the owners. "What's the name of Marcela's place?" she asked.

"No name," Sebastian said. "It's a friend of ours. She has a little house party most nights."

"I think Andre's planning to take us out tonight. We'd really hoped to go to the Park Avenue Restaurant," Kitty said quickly. Wherever these musicians were going, and whoever Marcela was, Kitty doubted the outing would be to her usual standards.

"Andre's working tonight," Hen said. She either didn't notice or was ignoring the daggers Kitty was staring at her.

"I'm sure you two don't want to go out tonight, after such a long trip," Kitty said.

"It will be our only chance to have the whole evening and see our friends for a few days," Sebastian said. "We start playing at the club again tomorrow."

"We'll sleep all afternoon anyway," Max added. "But don't let us force you if you've got better things to do."

Kitty considered for a moment. She didn't want to go to some other-side-of-the-tracks dive, but she did need for Hen to spend time with Sebastian early and often if her ruse was going to be convincing. "Where does she live?" she asked at last.

"She has a little place just over the Causeway in Riverside—that's where Sebastian and I live," Max said. "Like Sebastian said, it's really more of a house party than a club, but it's the real Latin scene."

"The best live music in Miami," Sebastian added. "Except for when we play, of course."

Again, Kitty hesitated. "I can't say I know what to wear to a house party."

Max shot her a knowing look. "I'm surprised to hear there's any occasion you can't dress for."

"No need for anything special," Sebastian said. "Very casual."

"It sounds like fun to me," Hen said. "Come on, Kitty. What do you say?"

"Sounds swell," Kitty said, fighting mental images of a dilapidated shack. One night wouldn't kill her. "What time should we be ready?"

"We'll pick you up at nine," Max said.

"Meet you out front," Hen said, shooting Kitty a pointed look. Once Max and Sebastian were out of earshot, she crossed her arms on her chest. "What was all that about?"

"I was going to ask you the same thing. Why are you so eager all of a sudden?"

"You know I'm excited about the Park Avenue, but we can go there with Andre," Hen said. "Don't you think it's nice of the boys to invite us to meet their friends? You could have been a little more gracious about it."

"You're the gracious one, not me. Besides, wouldn't you rather go somewhere a little more . . . to our taste?" Kitty asked.

"I'm curious about the rest of Miami."

"You're curious about Sebastian."

Hen blushed, but a giggle escaped. "So what? He's handsome, is that so bad?"

"No, though I'm starting to think you're drawn to a scandalous type of man. Lumberjacks? Now 'good as colored' musicians? What would Charles's parents think?" Kitty teased.

"That doesn't matter as much here, does it? They're for sure never going to see me going to Marcela's," Hen said.

The girls headed up to their suite to plan their outfits for the evening. Once back upstairs, Kitty set Loco down, so the dog could begin her thorough inspection of the rooms. Hen looked at her reflection in the hall mirror and fluffed her hair.

"I wasn't going to wash my hair today, but I suppose I will if we're going out," Hen said. She pursed her lips. "Though maybe I should catch just a tiny nap first. Who knows how long this thing might last tonight? I want to be fresh."

"I think I'll go out to the pool," Kitty said. "Just for an hour or two."

"Wake me up when you get back in, will you?" Hen asked. She patted Loco on the head, then went off to her room and closed the door.

Kitty changed into her new bathing suit, taking a moment to admire it in the bathroom mirror. She collected her *Vogue* and sunglasses and was just about to walk out the door when the phone rang. Hoping it would be her father, she picked up.

It was a man on the other end of the line, but not her father. "Kitty? Is that you?"

"Charles? How are you?" She kept her voice low, worried Hen might hear.

"All's swell here, though probably colder than where you are."

She rolled her eyes. *No, we're building snowmen in Miami.* "I'm sure that's true."

"You girls enjoying yourselves?"

Inspiration lit up her mind. "Never a dull moment. Do you miss us?"

"Of course. But I'm staying occupied."

"I'm sure you are." *Probably with every hussy in Manhattan,* she thought.

"Is Hen around?"

Kitty paused for dramatic effect. "I know she wouldn't want to miss a call from you, but she's sleeping, and I hate to wake her. I just got up myself. We had a bit of a late night," she lied.

"She's still asleep? But it's . . . hmm. Will you ask her to call me later? Though I am going to the club this evening. Maybe before she goes to bed?"

"That depends on how long you plan to stay up. Our sweet Hen has really taken to the Miami nightlife."

Now it was Charles's turn to laugh. "You don't say."

"You'd be mighty surprised if you saw her. But, goodness, I don't want to get her in trouble. We'll just say she's having a very nice time and leave it at that."

"Trouble? What exactly is she getting up to?" He sounded more hesitant.

"Me and my mouth," Kitty said. "Don't you worry about a thing. I'm keeping an eye on her. It's all in good fun, nothing at all to worry about."

"I see." His voice was full of false cheer. "Well, have a good time tonight. And will you please ask her to call me tomorrow?"

"I will, but don't go waiting by the phone too early," Kitty said brightly. She hung up the phone with a smile. Charles was suspicious now, all right. She'd give the ideas she'd planted a few days to marinate, and then it would be time to escalate.

⇥⇤

When Kitty and Hen walked out the front door of the Imperium, they found Max and Sebastian waiting for them on the sidewalk of the roundabout. Max looked at his watch.

"Right on time," he said. "I would've thought you'd make us wait."

"And I didn't think a couple of musicians would be so punctual," Kitty said.

"Look at us. Full of surprises." Max glanced at Hen, then back to Kitty. "You two look great."

"Thanks," Hen said. "Kitty must have put on a thousand different—"

"Oh, they're not interested in the process," Kitty said. "Just the result. Is this your car?"

"It's my car," Sebastian said, his whole face glowing. He opened the door so Kitty could climb in.

The car was a beauty. It had to be ten years old, maybe more, but the ruby paint shined like it was still fresh and wet. Whatever trivial sum Sebastian made singing at the club must have been poured directly into the purchase and upkeep of the Ford convertible he now stood beside proudly.

"I think Hen should have the honor of sitting up front. I'll ride in the back." Kitty didn't say that she knew her much-shorter hair could stand the breeze in the back better than Hen's. Neither of them had brought a scarf, and Kitty had spent too long pinning Hen's curls for her work to come flying apart when Sebastian hit the gas.

Max opened the back door, and Kitty slid in onto the gray cloth seat. He ran around the back and climbed in beside her. Once Hen and Sebastian were in, they were off. Max and Sebastian related tales from the bus trip, and Hen was especially amused by the story of a clarinetist who nearly got left in a small Tennessee town when he took too long in the restroom. Kitty half listened, reacting at the appropriate moments, but her attention was mostly on the view. The farther they got away from the hotel, the more the buildings started to change. She watched, a quiver in her stomach, as the neat square restaurants and shops of South Beach became less orderly. The stucco gave way to wood.

Kitty broke into the conversation. "You say this is near where you live?"

Max turned to her. "Sebastian and I share a place on this side of the bridge. Why?"

"Making sure we know our way," Kitty said, hoping she covered the waver in her voice. She hadn't seen many people who looked like Max since they'd gone over the Causeway.

"Don't worry," Sebastian said. "We go to Marcela's at least once a week. We would not forget the way."

Max looked at Kitty but said nothing more. She angled her face away so that he couldn't read her expression. On the street, she saw knots of people, some standing and talking, some walking. There was more variety of skin tone within each group than she'd ever seen in the entirety of her street in Manhattan.

By the time they pulled up to a row of tightly packed two-story buildings, Kitty's insides burned. The boisterous music coming from their destination wafted out into the street. This plan was already taking more mental fortitude than any she'd ever hatched. But when she saw Hen's face light up as Sebastian helped her out of the car, Kitty regained her courage. Max helped her out of the car, studying her carefully.

"You all right? You look pale," he said.

"I'm ready for a drink," she said with a smile.

"Sure you are. Hope you like rum."

"No vodka?"

"Not at Marcela's." Max tilted his head toward the door. "C'mon."

TWELVE

Kitty took a step toward the screen door in front of them, but Max caught her arm. He and Sebastian walked around to the side of the building, guiding the girls around a few broken bottles, then entered through an open door on the side. The row house's lower floor had been converted into a single large room, and brightly painted columns remained where walls had once stood. In the far corner, a dinged-up refrigerator sat behind a woman at a card table filled with liquor bottles and glasses. The music Kitty had heard drifting into the street now blared from a trio of musicians in the opposite corner, near the window. About a dozen people crowded near them, dancing. No one took advantage of the handful of mismatched chairs against the wall.

Over the music, a voice rang out. "My boys, you are back at last," the woman at the table called. She rushed over to Max and Sebastian as fast as her tight skirt would allow.

Max hugged her. "Good to see you, Marcela."

The woman and Sebastian began speaking Spanish, though she did pause to plant a bright red kiss on Max's cheek. The tips of his ears turned pink, and he rubbed his face with his handkerchief.

"You two sure are favorites," Kitty said.

Her voice caught Marcela's attention, and the woman's hazel eyes widened. "You brought girlfriends!" She rushed forward and took Kitty's hands. "They never bring girls to me, never. Let me get you a drink. You like rum?"

"Ah . . . sure." Kitty forced a smile. A glance at Hen revealed that she was equally overwhelmed. "How much do I owe you?"

"For you, free." Marcela dropped ice from the refrigerator into two glasses, then filled them halfway with brown liquid.

"We drink for free now?" Sebastian asked.

"Not you. The girls. For you, ten cents." Marcela held the drinks out to Kitty and Hen, paying no attention to the boys' groans of protest.

Kitty liked the sugary smell of the rum. She took a gulp to help settle her nerves and wished she'd worn something else. Hen was the only other woman in the room wearing a full swing skirt. Some had curve-hugging skirts like Marcela's, and a few wore similarly snug capris. All of them had bare shoulders, and most had long hair piled high. At least Kitty's layer of eye-catching lipstick fit the scene. She edged to the window where Hen had claimed a chair, hoping to feel a wisp of the cool night air. Though they had just come in, the warmth of the packed bodies had already caused sweat to break out on Kitty's skin. She sucked an ice cube out of her glass and let it melt on her tongue.

Max paid for his drink and crossed to where Kitty stood. "Are you sure you're okay?"

Kitty didn't answer. She was fixed on Sebastian, who was asking Hen to dance. "I hope she doesn't stumble too much. Dancing was never Hen's greatest talent."

"She'll be fine with him. He's good enough for both of them." Max tapped a finger against his glass. "What about you? Do you want to dance?"

"With Sebastian? Absolutely."

"With me. I know you're good. I saw you showing off that night in New York."

She thought about how Max had looked at her as she left the dance floor that night, and the back of her neck tingled. Just as quickly, she recalled their odd interaction in her apartment. Still, she couldn't say no; it was her job to distract him. She placed her drink on a nearby chair and held out a hand. They went closer to the musicians but still kept a little distance from the other dancers. She marveled that only three musicians could make music so loud. The sound pulsed under her skin.

Max laid a hand on her waist and pulled her close. He smelled like Burma-Shave and pomade. She could feel his hip bone against hers, and this time the heat in her face had nothing to do with the crowded room. He pressed his cheek against hers and whispered in her ear, "Just move with me."

Then he moved—one long, languid stride followed by a few staccato steps. His hand felt unexpectedly strong through the fabric of her dress. He guided her so effortlessly, she felt as if she'd known the dance her whole life. She pulled back.

"Where did this come from?" she asked.

"Years of practice. I've been coming to this place for a long time." There was a wicked look in his eye. "Why? Do you like it?"

"I'm surprised you wanted to dance with me," she said. "Last time we talked you didn't seem so interested."

He reeled her out, holding her at arm's length for a beat before pulling her close again. "But now it turns out you've got brains under all that style. That changes things."

She touched her cheek to his once more, speaking softly in his ear. "You like me better because I've read a couple of books, huh?"

"Does that bother you? I'm betting you like it when a guy's interested because of your looks." His hand slid from her waist to her back.

"A cute girl doesn't do it for you?" She tightened her grip on his shoulder.

"A pretty birdbrain doesn't do it for me."

"And what are you going to do if I am a birdbrain? Then you'll only be interested because of my looks. I'm betting that would bug a guy like you."

"Then I'll have to get to know you better. Find out which you are."

The song came to a dramatic end with a final pounding flourish from the bongo player. Kitty held Max's gaze for a moment before going to retrieve her drink. *So he is interested*, she thought. *Good.* One more box checked off on her list. A little more interest, and she might be able to separate him entirely from his wayward friend.

An idea came to her so suddenly that she was shocked she hadn't thought of it before. One of those intimate moments with Max might be of more use to her than simply throwing Hen in Sebastian's path. Max would be the perfect person to get her off the hook with Andre. She could talk Max up, ask when he would be coming back to New York, little tidbits like that. Then, when Andre started to suspect her interest, she could arrange a little romantic interlude with Max near the end of their time in Miami for Andre to stumble upon. He'd know he never had a chance, and he'd probably think the whole trip was Kitty's way of seeing Max again. Only a dope would want to go after a girl who'd used him that way.

At last, all the major elements had come together. Max would get Andre off the table and solve the problem of her father's demands. If Andre wasn't interested, Kitty's father could hardly insist that she marry him then. He'd have no choice but to change his ultimatum, maybe to something more palatable, especially if she had an alternative husband lined up. And she would. Sebastian would help her separate Hen and Charles and, once Hen approved, Charles would be hers for the taking. All she had to do was arrange the proper timing, and soon everyone would have exactly what they deserved. Kitty would have her new social sphere, Hen the right match, and Charles all the payback he could handle.

Flush with excitement, Kitty eagerly agreed when Sebastian asked her to dance. She expected him to be the superior dancer of the two men but was surprised to find that he and Max were evenly matched in terms of skill. Every so often, she threw a glance over Sebastian's shoulder to be sure Max still had his eyes on her. Even though he'd asked Hen to dance, Kitty was pleased to find that he was, indeed, watching her every chance he got.

"Are you having fun?" Sebastian asked when they took a break.

"I am," Kitty said, taking another sip of her drink. She liked rum, as it turned out. "It's different from how I pictured Miami."

"There is more than one Miami," he said.

"Which one is this?"

He grinned. "This is *cubano*. So much like Cuba. Although Marisol there—" He pointed to a tall, dark-skinned girl with a green print dress. "She is *dominicana*. Alonso is from the Dominican, too. But the sounds, the flavors, the people creating a party out of nothing . . . it's so much like my home. Well . . . some parts of the island." A cloud flickered over his expression so quickly, Kitty thought she'd imagined it.

"Cuba's easy to get to from Miami, right? Maybe Hen and I should go while we're here."

He shook his head. "You may not want to go there right now. There was some . . . trouble this summer. Some people are unhappy." He paused. "It might not be over."

Before Kitty could respond, Sebastian stood. "I'd better ask Marcela to dance," he said. "She doesn't like to sit for long. Excuse me."

She nodded, still puzzled. The only things she'd ever heard about Cuba involved movie stars and tropical drinks. She couldn't picture movie stars sweltering in a converted living room, though. There was a more glamorous side to Cuba; Kitty had seen it in magazines. Sebastian must have grown up in the wrong part, she concluded. Perhaps that was why he was in Miami now.

Hen sat down in the chair next to Kitty, panting slightly. "Who would've thought Max could dance like that? Wowee."

"He's made an impression on you, has he?" Kitty swirled the few slivers of ice that remained in her glass.

"Nothing close to the impression you've made on him." Hen leaned in. "Don't look now, but I think you've still got his eye."

Kitty flicked her gaze over to the makeshift bar and found Max watching her. "He thinks he's hot stuff."

"After dancing with him, I'm inclined to agree," Hen said.

"I thought Sebastian was your guy."

"You know very well that Charles is my guy." Hen's expression darkened. She sat up and brightened once more as Max approached with a fresh drink in each hand.

"Thought you two might be thirsty," he said. The girls accepted their drinks, thanking him. As he sat on Kitty's other side, Hen raised her eyebrows at Kitty. Kitty resisted the urge to swat Hen. Even though she had been trying to hook Max, she didn't want Hen teasing her about her success. Or worse, believing that Kitty actually liked him. Fortunately, Sebastian returned from his dance with Marcela a few minutes later. He asked Kitty to dance, but she declined, and Hen took her place.

"Are you waiting for me to ask you again?" Max said.

"I'm enjoying my drink and the music, thank you." Kitty dabbed at an errant drop of condensation that had landed on her skirt. "So where does Marcela find all these people? Surely she doesn't hire a trio for every house party."

"She's what you might call a talent finder," Max said. "Marcela loves music, and she has back-of-the-house connections at pretty much every club and venue on the other side of the Causeway. She's been helping people find jobs so long, now people send musicians to her."

"Is that how you and Sebastian met her?"

"Actually, she introduced us. I met her through a friend at a show down at the Lyric, and she had me an audition at the Imperium within a week. Practically everyone here either plays at the resorts or will soon enough." He pointed across the room to a balding man. "Marcos there plays the trombone at the Park Avenue. The girl beside him is Daniela. She sings, but she hasn't found a gig yet. I think Marcela has big plans for her. Bigger than the clubs."

Kitty studied Daniela's cream-colored skin and wide brown eyes. "She's certainly pretty enough to be a star."

Max stood. "Come on, I'll introduce you."

Though she began to feel more at ease, especially after meeting some of Max's friends, Kitty couldn't shake the sensation that she was more of a curiosity than a guest. She didn't fit in, despite the warm welcome, and she felt it acutely. When they finally climbed back into Sebastian's car to return to the hotel, she felt a relief that was also, in a way, uncomfortable. She stepped into the lobby of the Imperium, resolved not to think about it any further. After all, she'd never see that place or those people again.

THIRTEEN

The jangle of the telephone woke Kitty far earlier than she had expected. She cleared her throat in an attempt to make it sound like she'd been awake for hours. Even more unexpected than the call was hearing Max's voice on the other end.

"Did I wake you?" he asked, his voice as sunny as the view from Kitty's window.

"Of course not." She rubbed her eyes with one hand.

"That's too bad. If you can't sleep late when you're on vacation, when can you?" he said. "I mean, obviously *you* can sleep late any time you want, I suppose."

She gritted her teeth. So he was still intent on teasing her. "Is there something I can do for you, Max?"

"I was thinking about how you girls said you hadn't seen the real Miami yet."

"I believe you were the one who said that. Besides, you said the party last night was the real Miami. Problem solved."

"Here's the thing," he said. He sounded just the tiniest bit unsure. Maybe even nervous. "I'm playing tonight, so I can't ask you to dinner. I thought I'd take you out to lunch."

"Hen and me?"

"No, just you." He paused. "And just me. Unless you think Hen would mind."

Kitty's mind snapped out of its dazed, half-asleep state. Max was asking her on a real date, of all things. This part of her plan was falling into place faster than she could have hoped. "Lunch sounds swell. What time will you pick me up?"

"Sebastian is going to give me a ride to the hotel, but I thought we could walk. It's only about a mile down the road."

She dreaded what the sticky sea air would do to her hair, but she agreed. "Where are we going exactly?"

"To get a real taste of the South. Don't worry, you'll love it. But maybe don't dress fancy, okay?"

Kitty agreed with as much strength as she could dig up. What a delightful lunch date—she'd dress in rags and then walk a mile in the heat to some dump. After she hung up, she chose a pair of red shorts, flat sandals, and a sleeveless gingham blouse that tied at the bottom. There was no reason to look like a peasant, no matter where they were going.

Once she was properly primped, she went out to the living room, where Hen sat in her pajamas, reading a magazine. When Hen saw Kitty, she did a double take.

"I didn't think you'd be up and dressed so early," Hen said.

Kitty called Loco over and hooked the dog's leash on. She might as well get it over with quickly. "I'm going out to lunch."

Hen slapped the magazine closed. "With who?"

"Max." Kitty walked Loco to the door of the suite, but Hen leapt into her path.

"Just you and Max?"

"So it would seem."

Hen studied Kitty with a tight-lipped expression somewhere between smug and pleased. "Was this arranged last night, or was that the call this morning?"

Kitty sighed. "Does it matter?"

Hen pushed her shoulder. "Don't get worked up. I'm not think-ing it's true love forever between you and a trumpet player. It's lunch. You're entitled to enjoy yourself. Someone should." Hen caught herself. "But won't your father be angry if he thinks you're not serious about Andre?"

"That's why Andre doesn't need to hear about this." *Not yet*, Kitty thought.

Hen twisted an invisible key at the corner of her mouth. "Not a word from me."

"Thank you."

"And I think Max is pretty dreamy, personally. I didn't at first, but—" Hen fanned herself. "That dancing."

"Yes, I know." Kitty couldn't help but smile. "'Wowee.'"

Hen giggled. Her curiosity satisfied, she stepped out of the way so Kitty could take Loco out.

Sebastian and Max pulled up to the roundabout in front of the hotel a little while later. Kitty waited in the lobby to give her hair its last few minutes of undisturbed beauty. When she spotted Sebastian's car, she walked outside into the white sunlight. Max got out of the car, and Sebastian sped off with a wave.

"Where's he off to?" she asked.

"He works in the kitchen at a hotel a couple blocks over," Max said.

"Two jobs?"

"Plus he picks up day shifts at the pool."

"All that money for his car, huh?"

"I think he sends a lot home." Max gestured down the street. "Ready? It's this way."

They took a left down Collins Avenue and fell into an easy pace. "Any chance you can let me in on our secret lunch location now?" Kitty asked.

"You like chicken?" he asked.

"Who doesn't?"

"Then you're going to like this place," he said. "I'm glad you agreed to come out. Like I said last night, I wanted to get to know you."

"What do you want to know?"

"You grew up in New York, right? And I know you like to read. What else do you like?"

She had prepared for conversation, but she wasn't sure how much of the truth she wanted to share with Max. Very few of the men she went out with bothered to ask her much about herself. After all, she didn't have a high-powered career or a golf handicap. They usually waxed long about themselves, allowing her to play the coquette when they paused to draw breath. That suited Kitty fine. She could try that angle with Max, but she sensed it wouldn't work.

"The usual, I guess," she said. "Fashion. Nightclubs, dancing. Having a good time."

He was quiet a moment. "That's what I assumed at first, to be honest. Another silly rich girl. But I don't think that's true."

"You have a strange way of complimenting someone." She glanced at him. "Are you telling me I don't like those things?"

"What you read, the way you talk. I'm saying there's more on your mind than fashion. I want to know what it is."

"Sorry to disappoint, but that's me." *Time to deflect*, she thought. "What about you? A musician's life must be more interesting than mine."

"Oh, no. You're not getting out of it that easy. It's just you and your pop, huh?"

Kitty let out something between a sigh and a laugh. Why did this guy want her life story? "What are you hoping to unearth? I don't have that much going."

"You're the daughter of one of the most ambitious, hardworking men I ever met. That's not nothing. You've got to have a little of that in you."

"Just because my father is ambitious doesn't mean I am."

Max paused again. She was learning not to like that. "It's something in your eyes," he said. "Some kind of fire."

"Amazing what a little mascara can do. Anyway—" Kitty stopped short. A larger-than-life sign on a nearby building declared PICKIN' CHICKEN. "Oh, good grief. Tell me that's not lunch."

"What's the matter? I thought you liked chicken." Max's voice was full of false innocence.

Kitty turned to him, ready to give him an earful of her opinion on eating with her hands. Then she saw the mischievous flash in his eyes. Something in her couldn't ignore the challenge. She straightened her back. "I love chicken. Let's go."

The inside of the Pickin' Chicken was no less offensive than the pink neon sign outside. Families with squealing children filled turquoise vinyl booths, and the thick smell of grease wafted from the kitchen. Kitty glanced around out of habit, then chided herself. *No one is going to catch you in this place. No one important is here.* She took her seat with as much dignity as she could and accepted the chicken-shaped menu from the hostess. Even the place mat was a jumble of hand-drawn chickens, all in full squawk, as if the proprietors feared their patrons would forget the theme without constant reminders. Kitty flipped the place mat over, glad for the reprieve of the blank side.

Fried chicken was, indeed, the only real option on the menu. Kitty and Max both ordered the luncheon special and Cokes.

"Look," Max said, "I know this isn't your type of place. But maybe you'll like it. The fried chicken is tops. The best is dipping it in honey—they bring some on the side."

Kitty looked out the window at the busy street. "Honey. Gotcha." She jumped as Max reached across the table to touch one of the curls at her temple.

"I bet you rushed right out the minute you saw *Roman Holiday* and asked them to cut your hair just like Hepburn's, didn't you?" he said.

At last, an opportunity to be flirtatious. "Who wouldn't want to look like a princess?"

"Did you go to school? College, I mean?"

Damn. He wouldn't be distracted. "Nope," she replied.

"Where'd you get all those books?"

"The usual places. I know where to find books, Max. You sure have a lot of questions."

"I want to know more about you. Do you travel much?"

Kitty stifled the urge to point out that he'd asked another frigging question. Instead, she replied with a query of her own. "Why should I?" She smiled. "Everything I need is in New York."

He sat back against the booth. "You're living in a small world if all you need is New York."

"It's true. New York has it all."

"It can't be true."

"How come?"

He grinned at her. "Because you're not in New York right now. Must be something you need here."

Kitty fiddled with the corner of her place mat. The urge to speak honestly bubbled up. Maybe it was his demeanor, or his suggestive smile. He could see that there was more to her. Hadn't he said that? She thought of Harry, who had droned on about portfolios or something all evening before trying to grope her in the cab afterward. Max wanted her to talk about herself. She knew better than to do that, but the words came anyway.

"New York may be a small world, but I'm going to be at the top of it one day."

He pointed at her. "There it is. A genuine answer. That's what I wanted."

Kitty was spared from responding to that by the arrival of their food. Max, who seemed to be placated, did not press further on the topic. He turned the conversation to his other favorite restaurants in South Beach, and she mentioned a few spots he might like in New York. The feeling that she'd said more than she ought to weighed on Kitty, but she brushed it away. She hadn't said anything of substance. After a couple of weeks, she'd never see him again. As long as she didn't tell him too much, she didn't need to worry.

The messy chicken was followed by bowls of warm water and

lemon, so Kitty was able to clean her hands before they left the restaurant. She slid her sunglasses back on as they walked out into the parking lot.

"I have to admit, that was delicious," she said.

"Thought you'd enjoy it," he said. "Maybe we can go again before you leave."

"Maybe." She glanced at him out of the corner of her eye. It was only a half invitation, and she still couldn't get a read on how he actually felt about her. One moment he would tease, the next he would probe, and in another he would pull back. She had to make sure the hook was in deep before she tried to reel him in, or she might find herself without a necessary element of her plan. Fortunately, Kitty knew the best way to loosen a guy up. To get into his head. To entice him to romance.

Just add booze, she thought.

FOURTEEN

That night at dinner, Hen and Andre chatted while Kitty quietly plotted. She could get Max drunk enough to loosen his tongue if she invited him up to the penthouse one night when the band wasn't playing, but she ideally needed him to be alone when she invited him. A group gathering would offer him too many places to hide. Getting rid of Hen would be easy enough, since Hen thought she was wise to a budding romance between Max and Kitty.

As for extending the invitation, an opportunity produced itself more easily than she'd anticipated. On one of the band's breaks, Max came over to their table.

"Hey, Andre. Is there anything going on at the club tomorrow afternoon?" he asked, after greeting the girls.

"Nope. It's all yours," Andre replied.

"Swell. Thanks." Max started back for the stage, turning one last time to wink at Kitty. Her face burned, but Andre had been absorbed in the last bites of his steak and had missed the wink.

"What does he need the club for?" Kitty asked.

"He likes to play new songs here alone," Andre said. "Something about testing the song in the acoustics of the space."

"So he doesn't bring the band?"

"He really doesn't like any employees here while he's testing—wants the club empty, if he can get it. Sunday afternoon is usually perfect."

Kitty nodded. *That* is *perfect*, she thought. She could stop by tomorrow afternoon and catch him on his own. She'd fill Hen in before he came up and encourage her to go for a walk on the beach with Sebastian if he happened to tag along with Max. Two birds, one stone.

"Did you girls go shopping again today?" Andre continued. "You're going to break the hinges on those suitcases if you're not careful."

"No shopping today," Kitty said. "We've nearly run out of places to go, and Hen still has half an empty suitcase."

"I've got good news, then." He pulled out a brochure and set it on the table by Kitty's plate. "Some company is hosting a big fashion show here at the Imperium. It's not for a few weeks, but I thought you might be interested. I can get you invitations."

Kitty inspected the brochure. "Thanks, Andre. That would be swell."

"And I have an idea for tomorrow, if you don't have plans," he said. "First, I have to say I'm sorry that I've been so busy."

"Oh, we understand," Kitty said quickly. "This place doesn't run itself."

"They'll have to manage without me for a couple hours. I've taken the whole afternoon off. I mean to make good on my promise to show you Miami." He beamed. "We're going to Parrot Jungle. The birds do tricks, and you can even hold them and get your picture made. You'll love it."

Kitty couldn't think of anything she'd rather do less than go stare at birds, especially if the trip kept her from getting Max on his own. She flicked her eyes at Hen, who was already glowing.

"My grandmother used to keep parrots. I loved holding them. They're so beautiful. I can't wait," Hen said. Her lips tightened when she saw Kitty's expression. "I don't know if that's Kitty's cup of tea, though."

Even if Kitty was no bird enthusiast, the attraction did sound like something Hen would enjoy. She couldn't very well deprive Hen of some fun, then turn around and ask her to sit alone in the hotel room while she went downstairs to talk to Max. She'd have to make declining sound altruistic. Hen might be hesitant about being squired around by Andre without Kitty, even if Andre was as harmless as a monk.

"Why don't the two of you go?" Kitty said, putting on her best concerned face. "Hen's right, I don't much care for birds, but it's so sweet of you to offer. I hate to be the reason you two don't get to do what you'd like. I'm happy sitting by the pool."

Thankfully, Hen didn't look uncomfortable at all with the suggestion. "Are you sure? Wait. What am I asking? Of course you're sure." She poked Kitty. "Every time you see a bird on the street, you jump."

Kitty poked her back. "I'll lend you my umbrella. With all those birds flying over you, you might want to protect your head."

The next day, after Hen had left to meet Andre, Kitty took the elevator to the lobby. She breezed through and headed down the short hallway to the right of the reception desk, hoping the busy desk clerk wouldn't pay too much attention to her. Before she went to see Max, she had two stops to make.

At the end of the hallway were three doors, each with a brass nameplate. The one at the far end was labeled NICOLAS TESSLER. Satisfied, she headed back toward the lobby. She took a left out of the main entrance and cut through a break in a line of hedges to circle around to the side of the building where the offices' windows would be. She found herself at a small concrete patio, with an awning and a few chairs. As she suspected, the manager's office had a window that looked out over the patio. Otherwise, the area was secluded, sheltered by a ring of short, scrubby trees on one side and the hedges on the other.

"Perfect," she said, walking back through the hedges to reenter the hotel. What better place to stage a romantic interlude for Andre to stumble on than right by the office that he must use when he was in town? He'd have a view perfectly framed by the window. All Kitty had to do was get Max out there at the appropriate time, and she'd have her opportunity. Of course, first she had to make sure he would be feeling romantic. She passed back through the lobby to go down the long hallway toward the club to find Max and issue her invitation.

Through the circular window in the door to the club, she could see Max sitting at the piano on the stage. She pushed on the door, which let out a loud squeak but didn't open. Still, the noise was enough to get Max's attention. He looked up, and Kitty waved through the window. The dim light kept her from seeing his expression as he made his way to let her in. The lock clicked, and he swung the door open. His tense face gave her pause. Her prepared speech went right out of her head.

"I'm sorry to interrupt," she said.

"No, it's fine." He rubbed his forehead and his brow smoothed. "I was in my own world. Plus I didn't expect to see you."

"I gathered that." She peeked around him. "Were you playing piano?"

He stepped aside and waved her in. "One of my many talents. Come on in, I'll show you."

"Are you sure?"

"Yep." He led the way to the stage, where he sat on the edge of the piano bench. He patted the space beside him, and Kitty sat.

"Andre said you like to test out songs," she said, uncomfortably aware of how close his arm was.

"Yeah, I play the new pieces I'm thinking of adding so I can see how they sound in the space. If they don't work—not big enough, or something—I don't bother the band with them."

"But it must sound different with the full band and people in the club."

He placed his fingers on the keys and plunked out a few soft notes. "I can hear all of that in my mind once I've tested a few parts. Years of experience."

"So, trumpet and piano. Any other instruments?"

"And the congas." He gestured to a pair of standing drums near the back of the stage.

"My, my. You really are a man of many talents."

"You don't know the half of it, sister." He played a final chord with a flourish and turned to her. "Do you play?"

Kitty laughed. "My father would have loved that. He paid enough for lessons when I was younger for me to have made it to Carnegie Hall by now." She placed a tentative finger on middle C. "Sadly, I didn't practice as much as I should have. I think Papa gave up on me shortly after he heard me butcher Beethoven. He finally moved the piano out of the living room at that point. I think it's the one in our club at the Vanguard, actually."

"It's a fine instrument." He nodded. "Your pop does know music. He's one of the few club owners I know who actually care about the set list. First thing he asked me when I met him." Max stood. "Let's switch places. I'll teach you something. You can make him proud."

Kitty scooted to the left side of the bench, and Max sat on her right. "This is your part." He tapped out a *dum-dah-dum-dum-dum* a couple of times, then reached over her for her left hand. A little jolt went up her arm. She pulled her hand away.

"Oh, I'm afraid it's hopeless," she said airily.

He was far more focused on the idea of her playing than her reaction. "It's never hopeless." He played the five-note sequence again then held out a hand for hers. She lifted her hand, and he arranged his hand under hers, so that hers was resting on top. He moved their hands together to the keys and began playing the sequence. She could feel the muscles moving under his skin but tried to focus on the notes.

"I think I've got it," she said. He took his hand away, and she tapped the keys. The rhythm was slightly off, but at last she was concentrating on the sound enough to recognize the tune. Her guess was confirmed when Max began to play with his right hand.

"'Habanera,' right?" she asked.

"Just don't ask me to sing it in French," he said.

She stood and pretended to clear her throat ceremoniously. He smiled and took over both parts of the piano melody.

"*Si tu ne m'aimes pas, si tu ne m'aimes pas, je t'aime. Mais si je t'aime, si je t'aime; Prends garde à toi!*" she sang. He finished the tune with a flourish, then clapped as she bowed and sat back down beside him. "Papa loves opera," she explained. "I've been hearing that one since before I could walk."

"Turns out you have some talents of your own," Max said.

"Not an operatic voice," she said. "But close enough to the notes, I guess."

"Do you know what it means?"

Kitty glanced at the floor. She knew exactly what it meant—*if I love you, take guard yourself.* "Oh . . . no. I took Latin in school," she lied.

He looked at her for a moment, then seemed to catch himself. His fingers returned to the keys. "So what did you need to talk to me about?"

"Wh-what?"

"I'm guessing that's why you came down here. Unless you were looking for a music lesson."

"Oh. Right. That's right." *Damn it.* He'd knocked her off guard again when she was the one who needed the upper hand. And how could she invite him upstairs now? He'd assume she was interested in him . . . which was, of course, the impression she was hoping to give him. So why was she so flustered? Why couldn't she make her mind work around him?

"I wanted to invite you upstairs for a cocktail. The band doesn't play on Mondays, right?" she finally managed.

"Tomorrow night?" he asked.

"Yes." She tried to recover her coquettish demeanor. "I thought a drink would be a nice way to thank you for lunch. Don't go getting any ideas. Hen will be there. Why don't you bring Sebastian, too?"

He leaned in, grinning. "But Sebastian didn't buy you lunch."

She stood with a huff. "Forget I said anything. You're impossible."

He stood, too, stepping in close. "Nothing's impossible."

"Maybe not for you. For silly rich girls—"

"Maybe for them, sure. But they aren't you." He took another step toward her, but just before they touched, he moved past her and headed for the drums. "I've got plans tomorrow night. How about Tuesday? Want to say eight?" When she hesitated, he raised his eyebrows. "Wouldn't be polite to take back an invitation."

"Tuesday at eight," she agreed.

Kitty fumed all the way back upstairs. She had done it again, had spoken about herself without him saying anything at all. Having him interested was good, having him *think* she was interested was fine, but . . . the way her head was swimming? Not fine. Not good. True, she hadn't given away much. Her father's interest in opera was hardly a well-guarded secret. But something about the tone of her encounter with Max was different. Too intimate. He was getting to her, and she suspected he knew it.

She calmed herself as she settled on the couch in the suite's living room. Getting him talking about himself would be the objective of the drunken evening she was planning for him, and she had arranged that. She hadn't really lost any ground, she reminded herself. Still, what irritated her most was that she couldn't stop wondering who he had plans with on Monday.

❖ FIFTEEN ❖

Hen came back from her trip to Parrot Jungle chattering away. She shoved a photo of herself, her arms covered with birds, into Kitty's hand. Kitty pretended to admire it before dropping it onto the coffee table. The sight of all those birds on her friend's arms gave her the willies.

"They were gorgeous, you wouldn't believe it. There was a little yellow one that fell in love with Andre. Ate right out of his hand and sat on his shoulder nearly the whole time we were there." Hen sat beside Kitty on the couch.

"Honestly, I don't understand the fascination," Kitty said. "Parrots are just pigeons with a better color palette. At least none of them hit you with a . . . souvenir."

Hen rolled her eyes. "Well, we sure had fun. Andre is a great guide. You might need to spend more time with him. He could be more interesting to you than you think."

"I doubt that very much, but I'm glad you enjoyed yourself. And promise me that if you have the urge to do something like that again while we're here, you'll drag Andre instead of me."

"Promise." Hen stood and stretched. "Andre has some work to catch up on tonight, so you and I are on our own for dinner. Where would you like to go?"

Kitty nearly said *Pickin' Chicken*, then wanted to bite her tongue off. She cursed Max for taking her there; she'd been craving that chicken and honey every minute since. She offered a classier option, and Hen agreed, then went to her room to change.

Andre was able to meet the girls for dinner in the hotel the next night, and he joined them downstairs with more enthusiasm than usual. "Great news, ladies," he said, pulling out their chairs.

"Marlon Brando is coming to visit?" Kitty asked.

Andre jerked his head back. "What, did you hear something?"

"You said it was great news. That qualifies as great to me."

"Don't be silly," Hen said to Kitty. She looked up at Andre. "What's your news?"

"I'm taking the evening off tomorrow night, and I'd like to take you girls out." He sat down, clearly thrilled with himself. "I want you two to meet some friends of mine, real good folks. Got a beautiful place in Coral Gables. We always get a bridge game going when I come into town. I thought it would be nice to socialize a bit. And this time they won't have to find me a partner."

Kitty swallowed a groan. After Andre's big talk about hosting them in Miami, his offers consisted of being climbed on by birds and visiting some bridge-playing couple's kitchen. She should have known. Kitty noticed that, once again, Hen didn't share her reaction. Her friend was already nodding.

"That sounds swell, doesn't it?" Hen asked. "We'd love to go, thank you."

The waiter came over to take their drink orders, giving Kitty a moment to deliberate. She hadn't told Hen about inviting Max over yet, since she wanted Hen to think it was a more spontaneous plan. Sending Hen off with Andre again did remove one obstacle. Still, it meant she wouldn't have anyone to distract Sebastian if Max did extend the invitation to him. After all, she'd said he was invited, too. *Maybe having his friend around will get him talking quicker*, she reasoned, without much hope.

There was still the small matter of the fact that she'd already sent Hen and Andre off alone together yesterday. Much more of this, and they'd definitely start to get suspicious. She might have worried that Hen would forget about Sebastian, but that handsome distraction seemed to be falling through anyway. How could Hen flirt with a guy who was always working somewhere else? No matter—Kitty could adjust that piece of the plan. Any guy would do, even a fictional one, and Charles was already suspicious. Plus Hen had already said she'd go play bridge; Kitty couldn't rescind her acceptance for her. Kitty would have to find a good enough reason to stay behind a second time, and the next time Andre invited them somewhere, she'd have to go, no matter what. As increasingly boring as Andre's offers were, she wondered if that next outing might be to the cemetery.

"Gee. That does sound like fun," she said at last. "But, you know, Papa is calling me tomorrow evening. We keep missing each other, and I would hate to miss him again. Why don't you two go?"

"We couldn't leave you again," Andre said.

"But you can't have a five-person bridge game anyway," Kitty said.

"Sure you can—" Hen began, and then thought better of it. She turned to Andre. "I'd like to go. And Kitty has barely gotten to talk to her father."

"I don't mind. At all," Kitty said, thanking heaven Hen knew her as well as she did.

"If you're sure." Andre glanced between the two girls, hesitating. Kitty worried for a flash that he might think she was trying to get rid of him. Fortunately, Andre confirmed once more that Kitty didn't mind staying behind at the hotel, then dropped the issue.

A few men in dark suits began setting up on the stage, grabbing Kitty's attention. For a split second, she thought one of them was Max, and her heart began to pound, but she recognized that it was the band that played on the nights the Zillionaires had off. She swallowed hard and turned back to Hen and Andre, who were already deep in a lively discussion about bridge. Kitty graciously put on an interested face. No sense in sulking when they'd let her off the hook.

The next day, Kitty and Hen went out on the beach. A staff member from the hotel followed them down lugging two huge umbrellas with *Imperium* on each in blue letters. He set them up in the sand and assured the girls someone would come along in the evening to pick up the umbrellas, so they could leave them when they were done. The girls spent the day wading into the water, then drying off in the sun, with a quick trip for ice cream from a stand near the shore. Kitty tried to let her giggles with Hen divert her from thoughts of her impending evening with Max. After all, she could handle him.

They went back to the suite so Hen could shower and dress for her evening. Kitty showered but put on a dressing gown so Hen wouldn't suspect her plans. Hen came out of her room in one of her new rompers, her hair pinned in a pretty little twist. Kitty raised an eyebrow.

"Seems like all my years of work are finally having an impact," she said. "You look positively adorable."

"And you want all the credit, huh?" Hen put her hand on her hip.

"I think I get some, at least. Here, let me get you that lipstick that looks so good on you." She stood to go to her room.

"Are you sure it's all right if I go? I know you said it was, and I definitely know you don't want to play bridge. But you invited me on this trip, not Andre. I don't want you to be bored."

"Please don't worry," Kitty said over her shoulder. "It's only one night, and I'm looking forward to talking to Papa." She dug through her makeup case, found the lipstick, and returned to drop it in Hen's hand. "If bridge is what you call fun, well . . . enjoy."

"We will, thank you very much."

Hen applied a layer of lipstick and left. Since Andre's friends were cooking, Kitty was on her own for dinner. She changed into an emerald-green dress, put on makeup, and ordered room service. A glance at the bar in the room prompted her to call down to the club next. She spoke to Sonny, one of the bartenders Andre had introduced them to, and he promised to send up a couple of bottles of a regional treat.

The food and liquor had just been delivered when the phone rang. She looked longingly at the steaming shrimp on the plate, but picked up the phone. What if it really was Papa?

"Hello?" she said.

"Kitty?" Charles said.

"Yes, how are you?"

"A little worried, but I'm glad I caught you."

"Worried? Why?"

"Hen never called. Did you give her the message?"

"Of course I did. I thought she called this morning." In reality, Kitty hadn't said a word to Hen. The fact that Hen neglected to call was an unexpected bonus.

"Doesn't matter," he said. "At least I caught you on a night in. May I speak to Hen?"

"I'm sure she meant to call . . . we're staying so busy, you see." Kitty lolled on the couch, more comfortable than her tone suggested.

"Isn't she there?" Now he sounded really agitated.

"She . . . she's out."

"Who on earth would she be out with if not you?"

"Oh, I'm going later. I'm going to catch up with them. I was just waiting on a call from my father, that's why I stayed behind—"

"Kitty." Charles's voice grew stern. "Who is she out with?"

"Oh, you *know* them, it's no one to worry about. It's only Andre . . . and some—some friends."

There was a long pause on the other end of the line. "I see."

"Now, Charles. I'll have Hen call you tomorrow first thing. Then you'll hear her voice, and everything will be fine," Kitty said.

"Yes. Good night," he said.

Kitty hung up, delighting in making Charles just a bit unhappier. After all the times he'd run around on Hen, he deserved to be the one

sitting at home worrying. And now that Charles believed Hen was gal-
livanting around Miami, the innocent bridge game would sound like a
ridiculous cover-up.

An hour or so later, a knock announced Max's arrival. Loco raced
to the entryway, tail wagging. Kitty followed after to open the door.

Max stepped in, rubbing the back of his neck. "Thanks for inviting
me up."

"Glad you could come." She moved aside so he could enter.

"Sebastian did say I had to be sure to pet Loco for him." He bent
down to scratch the dog's ears.

"Oh, he's not coming?" she asked.

"Like I said, he didn't buy you lunch. No drink for him." Max kept
his eyes on the dog, so he missed Kitty's quick, triumphant smile.

"Where's Hen?" He straightened up and smoothed his shirt.

"Andre invited us to play bridge with some friends of his, and she
took him up on it."

"Let me guess. Kitty Tessler doesn't play bridge."

"No. She does not." Kitty led the way to the living room. "I hope
you're ready for a drink. I'm experimenting with rum tonight. The boys
at the bar downstairs sent me a bottle. They said this is the Miami
way to drink it, with lime juice and sugar. But you would know." She
held out the cocktail she'd poured for him, which she'd made sure was
heavier on the rum than hers was. Not enough to notice, but enough
to make a difference. They sat on the couch, and he tasted his drink.

"Good," he said. "Very Miami."

Kitty had prepared her questions, so that they wouldn't have to sit
in awkward silence. "So how is it? Being back on stage here, I mean?"

"Like being home. Something about it does feel different. Not that
I don't like New York."

"You sound wonderful in either place, truly." Though Kitty's tone
was practiced flattery, she wasn't lying. She'd judged from his reaction at lunch that a touch of sincerity on her part might get his words
flowing. "I had never thought of the trumpet as a particularly moving

instrument. You know," she added, "you think of violin, piano—those are the emotional instruments. And you do play piano too, after all. I don't think I'm explaining myself very well. But you play beautifully. You surprised me."

He laughed. "I know what you mean. And thank you."

"What made you choose the trumpet to play on stage?"

"Instead of a prettier instrument?" He held up a hand to stop her protest. "You're right, people don't normally think of trumpet music as soothing." He paused, then took another drink of rum. "I didn't want soothing, I guess. I wanted something that could be loud. Energetic. Angry. And something that could be spontaneous. The piano can do that, but not in the same way. A piano moans. A trumpet screams."

Kitty realized she was leaning in, fascinated. She relaxed her shoulders and sat back against the cushions. "How old were you when you started playing?"

"Ten. Which is pretty late. A lot of the guys in the band were playing since they could hold their instruments."

"Did you want to play before then?"

He scratched his temple. "You're the one full of questions tonight."

"You said you want to know more about me. Why shouldn't I want to know about you?" She looked up at him through lowered lids with a soft smile that was all pretense, finally feeling she was back in her element.

"Yeah, but I don't know more about you. Except now I know that you want to be at the top of . . . something. And you sing in French, but you don't speak it." He polished off his rum and set down his glass. "Can we drop the flirty routine and just talk to each other?"

She pressed her lips together. "I don't know what you mean."

"Sure you do."

She waited for him to say more. After a brief stalemate, Kitty stood and held out a hand. "I might as well freshen your drink."

"Thanks." He handed over the glass.

"I was telling the truth. I do think you're good."

"I believed you. I believed you meant that." He sighed. "I liked you when we met, and I couldn't figure out why. It bugged me, honestly, until you started talking about books. Once I realized what's going on under all that makeup and goo-goo eyes, I felt a little better about it. And then every time we talk, I get a little better view."

Kitty returned his glass, now full. "I'm so glad you were able to come to terms with the idea of me, I really am."

"Be honest. You like this better, don't you? When we're being genuine with each other?"

For the first time in her life, Kitty was at a loss for words. Not because she didn't have a quick answer prepared. She had a cutting negative response she would have preferred to use, along with a positive response that might get the conversation back under her control. The problem wasn't what to say, but what was *right* to say. Unfortunately, she couldn't read Max that way. She didn't know how to get him to bend. She aimed for neutrality.

"Don't they say honesty is the best policy?" she said at last.

"I bet you don't say that."

"Why would you think so?"

"Because you just took a full ten seconds to figure out how to answer me."

"You count too fast."

He took a swig of his drink. "Cute."

She lit a cigarette. "Here's a thought. How about you be honest with me for a little while, and I'll tell you how I like it."

"What do you want to know?"

"Whatever you want to tell me."

He slid closer to her on the couch. A tickle ran under her skin as he looked at her, a sly smile spreading on his face. "I want to tell you how good it felt to dance with you. I want to tell you how crazy you make me. I want to tell you that I haven't stopped thinking about you since I first heard you talk, really talk. Just being you, when you're not trying to be anyone else." He leaned in until only a few inches separated them. "How's that for honest?"

She lifted her drink between them. "It's a good start."

He sank back with a groan. "You think you're so smart."

"Helps that I *am* smart."

"Yeah, you are smart. But I don't know what kind of smart yet. And that is what's got me worried."

"What does it matter what kind, so long as I am?"

He shook his head. "And you saying that makes me worry you're the wrong kind of smart."

His answer struck her. What did he mean, the wrong kind of smart? She felt cornered, like she had all those years ago at Alastair Prep or when she'd overheard Hen's mother talking about her. All those times they'd reminded her how inferior she was. She couldn't help the words that came out next. "Aren't all of us the wrong kind of something? One way or another?"

He nodded, his eyes on the drink in his hand. "And you saying that makes me think you're the right kind of smart."

They both sat silent. Kitty cast about for some reply that would redirect the conversation. "You know, you're not really telling me about yourself."

"I asked you what you wanted to know. Go on, ask me something."

"What's your favorite food?" she asked.

"Come on, you're more creative than that."

"Too personal? You sure are giving up easily."

"Roast beef. My mom's roast beef, to be exact." He held a hand out to her. "It wouldn't be fair for you not to play along. What's yours?"

"Lobster."

"I was going to guess fried chicken from the way you were chowing down at lunch."

"Very funny."

"Now I've got a question for you."

She took a sip of her drink to stall but concluded that if she didn't like what he asked, she could give a non-answer. "All right."

"Where do you go to have fun? Besides Bloomingdale's, I mean. Where's your good time?"

"It's Macy's, if you must know. And my good time is the club, of course. You've seen how often I go."

He thought for a moment. "I don't know if I believe that."

"You should. I said it. Why wouldn't you think so?"

"Because you're always somewhere else when you're at the club. You're staring out, thinking. Where do you wish you were?"

"I don't know where you get these ideas, I really don't. And didn't your beef-roasting mother tell you it's rude to stare?" she said wryly.

"I thought that's what this whole thing was about," he said, gesturing at her dress and makeup. "Getting people to stare. Anyway, I've got one more question for you."

"I can't say I'm shocked."

"What does that mean, 'the top'? I'm being serious now. You said you want to be at the top—that was the first sincere thing you said to me. What did you mean?"

"You heard me when I said it. The top of society."

"But, look, you're already rich, right? Don't make that face, that's a fact. So what else do you want?"

"I want to be in that place where no one can question you. Where no one can hurt you. That's real. I've seen it. I know those people. Oh, sure, people can say anything they want behind their back, but it bounces right off. That's power."

"So you've been hurt."

Kitty stood and walked to the window. Frankly, she wanted to hurl herself out of it. He'd gotten her to do exactly what she didn't want, and he'd done it by turning her own silly interrogation against her. The worst part was, she recognized she didn't have to hide from him. The goal was to entice him, and it was clear the real Kitty was what interested him. Why play a game when she could have him much more easily by being herself? She only needed him to get rid of Andre, and for that, she only needed him to be comfortable kissing her.

She knew why. She couldn't be open with him because it might mean really liking him. She risked losing something, and risks were not what this plan was about. Security and a lifetime of happiness awaited her if she could pull off her scheme. To say nothing of Hen. If Kitty chickened out, Hen was stuck with a sister-humping bastard for as long as they both shall live. Kitty wasn't going to let that happen, not for a few days with some broke musician. But, she reminded herself, romance was okay. As long as she could still see herself ditching Max at the end, she would be fine.

Max placed a hand on her shoulder, and she jumped. She hadn't even noticed him get up.

"I think I'd better go," he said. He set his empty glass on the bar cart. "Early rehearsal tomorrow. Thanks for the drinks. Sorry if I said something I shouldn't have."

Kitty grasped for something flirty, something clever that would prove she was fine. Nothing came. "You didn't. Thank you for coming."

He nodded and walked toward the door of the suite. She twisted a lock of hair, certain she didn't want this to be the way they ended the evening.

"Hey," she called as he opened the door.

"Hey." He turned back to her.

"Maybe soon you can tell me about that poem. Another night? What was it? 'Little' . . . something?" she said.

The corner of his mouth ticked up. "'Little Gidding.'"

She took a step toward him. "Yes, that one."

"I'd love to. Good night."

He closed the door, and Kitty stood still for a moment, trying to slow her heartbeat. She grabbed a bottle of rum, one of the limes, and a glass. Loco followed Kitty into her room, where Kitty dimmed the lights. She had no idea how she was going to get back on her feet after this episode, but she knew it started with a stiff drink. Or two.

SIXTEEN

Kitty's head buzzed when she woke up the next morning. She sat up in bed for a moment, concentrating, until the events of the previous evening caught up with her. Hen must have come in quietly, because Kitty hadn't heard a thing. Then again, the way Kitty had laid waste to the rum, Hen probably could have come in with a marching band and Kitty still would have slept through it.

She downed a glass of water and threw on a dress to take Loco out. When she came back in, Hen was sitting on the couch talking on the phone.

"I'm sorry that I didn't call until now, but really, Charles," Hen said. "I don't understand why you're upset about a simple card game with a married couple." She paused. "Of course that's what I was doing. The musicians?" Hen blushed, no doubt thinking about the evening at Marcela's. "That's ridiculous. They weren't there. No, I'm not saying you're ridiculous."

Kitty sat on the ottoman near the window, unsure if Hen would want support or to be left alone. Hen's casual tone gave Kitty hope. One false accusation wouldn't be enough to make Hen give Charles a piece of her mind, but the fact that Hen didn't sound apologetic might mean she was finally reaching her breaking point with Charles. Hen turned to Kitty with pursed lips and a raised eyebrow that made Kitty stifle a laugh.

"If you're going to be this way, I don't think I can talk to you. You're not ridiculous, but you are being awfully silly. I'll call you later," Hen said. Kitty could hear the voice on the other end of the line grow quieter. "Okay. I love you, too."

Perhaps the distance from Charles had made Hen somewhat bolder, but the loving good-bye wasn't what Kitty had hoped to hear. She was also less than enthusiastic to see Hen's sardonic cocked eyebrow wilt when she hung up the phone.

"I don't know what's gotten into him," Hen said. "He's gotten some crazy notion in his head that we're running around all night with the band. You didn't talk to him, did you?"

"I did, but I told him you would call," Kitty said, close enough to the truth for her own comfort.

"And now I wish I hadn't." Hen stood, fluffing her hair. "I'm sure he just misses me, that's all. Men are so funny."

"I'm sure that's it," Kitty said, not wanting any lack of encouragement on her part to make Hen question what Kitty had really said on the phone to Charles. "Why don't we go to the salon today? *Gonna wash that man right outta my hair . . .*" She sashayed toward Hen.

Hen inspected the ends of her hair. "You said the magic words. I'm overdue."

Kitty piled Hen's curls on top of her head and turned her toward the mirror. "Maybe it's time you got a short cut, like me."

Hen swatted her. "You know Mother would skin me if I came home with anything above my chin."

"Permanent wave, maybe?" Kitty teased. "Nice bright color rinse?"

"Not a chance," Hen called over her shoulder, heading to get dressed. "I could do with a set and style, though."

Kitty phoned the concierge for the name of the best salon, but the concierge said he would arrange for an appointment and a car, so Kitty wouldn't have to spend her whole morning calling around town. She agreed to be downstairs with Hen at eleven o'clock to head to the appointment.

In the car, Hen maintained her livelier demeanor, but by the time she sat under the dryer, her expression had noticeably dimmed. The buzz of the fans made it impossible for Kitty to strike up any conversation, so she had to wait until they were in side-by-side chairs in front of the mirror getting the finishing touches on their styles.

"Guess you didn't wash him all the way out, huh?" Kitty asked.

"It's not that easy," Hen said with a sigh.

"You said it yourself. Men are just funny. I wish you wouldn't let it ruin your good time." Kitty glanced at the hairdresser out of the corner of her eye, but the woman was wholly engrossed in her work. "You are having a good time, aren't you?"

"Oh, yes. It's been such fun." Hen stared at her reflection for a beat. "I just don't know why he'd get so upset over a card game."

"He's not," Kitty said with authority. "And you have every right to have fun, even if it's not with him."

"You're right," Hen said, but her brow was still creased with worry. Kitty resolved to distract Hen any time she suspected her friend was ruminating about Charles.

That evening, freshly coiffed, the girls met Andre for dinner in the club. They had debated going out on their own, but Hen pointed out that Andre had said how much he enjoyed their company on those nights when he couldn't get away. Kitty was secretly glad for the excuse to go to the club. She wanted to see Max and make sure no awkwardness lingered around his visit. Her concern, she finally managed to reassure herself, was due to his vital role in preventing a decisive overture on Andre's part. She would never care otherwise what a guy like that thought of her.

Andre's wide eyes when he saw them confirmed the success of their trip to the salon. He greeted them with the now-standard kiss on the cheek, then stood back to admire them.

"You two get prettier every time I see you," he said.

"Must be that ocean air," Kitty said.

"Thank you, Andre," Hen said as he pulled out her chair.

Kitty looked around the room. "Is the band here yet?"

"Not yet. Why?"

"Well, I was thinking, it's a shame we haven't really thanked the band yet. Max and Sebastian were so kind to bring Loco down on the bus with them." Kitty turned to Hen. "What would you say to inviting the band up after they play? It can't have been easy to ride all that way with a dog. I thought it would make a nice thank-you."

Of course, Kitty hadn't been thinking anything of the sort. But the sudden idea seemed like a nice way of testing the waters with Max without chancing anyone discovering their time alone. She could at least trust that Hen's polite nature would prevent her from objecting to the invitation, but Hen's tight lips said she knew Kitty too well to credit the idea to altruism. Andre, on the other hand, didn't know Kitty quite well enough.

"That's a fantastic idea," he cried. "A real party, the boys will love that. I'll get the bar to send up drinks. The guys in the kitchen should be able to throw some snacks together, too." He also turned to Hen. "That is, if you're sure you don't mind them coming up to where you're staying. They're good boys, really. They won't get into anything they shouldn't."

"If you can vouch for them, then why not?" Hen said. "Such a generous offer, Kitty."

Kitty flashed her a confident smile. "Thank you, doll."

As soon as Andre left the table to make the arrangements, Hen scowled. "What's all this really about?"

Kitty pouted, trying to look innocent. "Why? Don't you think it's a nice idea? Sounds like something you'd come up with yourself."

"You want to know what I think?" Hen leaned in and lowered her voice. "I think you like the attention from Max. It's one thing to have a little fun, but it's not nice to lead him on when you can't be with a guy like that."

"Oh, please." Kitty reached for her cigarette case. "Because we had one low-rent lunch you think I'm leading him on? I'd hope it would take a little more than that."

Hen said nothing more, but her eyes were locked on Kitty when the band finally did start filing in. Kitty waved at Sebastian, who nodded back.

"Now, just so you know," she said, leaning in to Hen. "That was an innocent wave."

Hen cut her gaze toward Andre, who was chatting with the waiter. "Your father thinks you're here to get to know Andre better," she whispered. "That's not happening so far. I've spent more time with him than you have. You're going to end up cleaning toilets and mopping floors if you don't straighten up."

"How do you know inviting them up isn't so I can spend some time with Andre, hmmm?" Kitty said, keeping her own voice low.

"Because you wouldn't have to invite the whole band. You could just invite him."

"And then it would be the three of us, like it is practically every night at dinner." She laid a hand on Hen's. "Don't worry. There's no way I'll end up mopping floors. I've got it all figured out, I promise."

Max stepped up to the microphone. He introduced the band and, to her surprise, sat down at the piano.

"I hope it's all right with you good people," he said. "We're going to start it off a little different tonight." He played a few notes. "A little slower. But don't worry—we'll heat this place up in no time."

Applause rounded the room as he began to play. Kitty knew the tune sounded familiar, but a few bars weren't enough to clue her in. It was only when Sebastian began singing that she recognized the song. Her stomach flipped. Max joined in on the last line: "The best thing for you would be me."

Kitty was grateful for the low lighting, certain her expression would contradict everything she'd just denied to Hen. Maybe Max and Kitty had ended the previous night on better terms than she'd realized.

After the dinner plates had been cleared, Andre went to the kitchen to get the snack order arranged for the party. The girls debated going up to change clothes but decided to stay and have another drink. The waiter brought their drinks over, then pointed out two men standing near the bar.

"Those gentlemen have already paid for your order, with their compliments," he said.

"Well, that's silly," Kitty said. "Didn't you tell them our drinks are already on the hotel's account?"

"I tried to, but they insisted." He shrugged. "Enjoy."

"Some people," Kitty said to Hen as the waiter walked away. "Didn't they see Andre sitting with us not ten minutes ago? Pretty presumptuous if you ask me."

"You're not interested in dancing?" Hen asked. "This is the first I've heard that you don't like it when a man buys you a drink."

Kitty bristled. "Depends on the guy, doesn't it? Anyone who's dumb enough to buy a drink that was free in the first place doesn't deserve a dance."

The men, as she'd expected, made their way toward the booth. They had the same stiff waves in their hair, testifying that they'd overapplied Brylcreem in the hopes of looking smooth. The blond one spoke first. He looked barely old enough to walk in the door of the club.

"Hi, ladies. We were hoping we could tempt you to dance," he said, running a hand through his hair. Kitty waited patiently as he attempted to find a surreptitious way to wipe the styling cream on his trousers.

"Thank you for the drink," Hen said, "but we're not dancing tonight."

The dark-haired guy's brow wrinkled. His bloodshot eyes indicated he might have been hitting the bar harder than his friend. "But we bought you drinks. Now, is that any way to treat a guy?"

"She said 'thank you,'" Kitty said. She flashed him a bright smile, but her tone was an ice pick. "She's engaged, and I'm with someone. No dance."

"Aw, come on," the dark-haired one said. "You're not gonna get in trouble for one little dance." He reached out to grab Hen's arm, but Kitty stood between them to block him.

"Hey, what are you doing?" he asked.

"Listen," she said. "Think of it this way. You see a nice car parked on the street. You might admire it, right? Compliment the driver."

The dark-haired guy frowned deeply. "What are you getting at?"

Kitty took another step toward him. "You don't get to hop in and drive off." She took a long drink from the glass and handed it to him. "No matter how much you like the car. Get lost, fellas."

She sat back at the booth, leaving both men dumbstruck. At last, they turned to go, the dark-haired boy still clutching Kitty's half-finished drink.

Hen clucked her tongue. "You're still the best at that."

Kitty flexed her bicep playfully. "It's been a while since I had the exercise. Honestly, some guys get a few drinks in them and think they own the world."

"Come on, strongman. We'd better get upstairs and make sure we don't have any unmentionables lying around."

Upstairs, Kitty retrieved Loco and took her downstairs for a quick walk. The night was clear and just cool enough to take the edge off the humidity. Across the street from the hotel, the late-night crew of a store was hanging garland and tinsel. The warm days had nearly made Kitty forget that Christmas was on its way. With a pang of guilt, she thought of her father. He always relied on her to decorate their suite, and it would likely remain undecorated in her absence. Perhaps she could call the housekeeper to ask her to put up a tree or hang the wreath. He ought to have a little taste of the holiday to surprise him. She had to admit to herself that she hadn't called him as often as she'd meant to. Her good intentions always seemed to get derailed by her affairs in Miami. She made a mental note to call him the next morning and remind him to arrange his trip down for the holiday. He'd certainly want to be with her at Christmas.

When she returned to the suite, she put Loco in her room and freshened up her makeup. Andre arrived a little while later, joined by two waiters who laid out food on the banquette.

"Just a few things," he said. "They were busy in the kitchen, and I didn't want to burden them."

"It looks great," Kitty said. There were some cold cuts, small sandwiches, and sliced vegetables. She imagined most of it came from room service odds and ends, but the cooks had arranged it all to look nice. Andre deposited a few bottles on the bar cart as the waiters left the suite.

"Oh, you've already got rum," he said.

"When did you get that?" Hen asked.

Kitty waved a hand. "The other night, when you were out. Thought I'd try my hand at those rum cocktails they like so much down here."

"Looks like you tried several hands," Andre said, holding up the half-empty bottle.

"The first few came out wrong," Kitty lied. "Undrinkable. Had to toss them."

"I guess I'll let Andre make mine," Hen said. "Would you mind?"

About half the musicians came up shortly after Andre arrived, with the other half sending their apologies and heading home to their families. The ones who came had sweat-sticky hair and droopy lids, but they all smiled and thanked Kitty for the offer of a drink and food on her.

"I'm just so glad you all agreed to let Loco ride down on the bus with you," she said. "I would have been sad to leave her for so long."

"Say, where is Loco?" asked Billy, the trombonist.

"She's gone to bed," Kitty said. "Too much excitement for her." She was touched that he looked disappointed.

Max caught Kitty's eye. She instinctively glanced to Hen, who was trying to get the record player working. Andre stood and offered to help her. The other musicians were distracted by the food, including Sebastian. Kitty pointed discreetly to the entryway, and Max followed her over.

"What did you think of the playlist?" he asked.

"It's risky to start with a slow song, don't you think?"

"I think I'm willing to take a risk," he said.

She held out a hand, and he laced his strong, callused fingers with hers. Hen called Kitty from the living room, and they broke apart. Max let out a nervous laugh. She went first back into the living room, flushed and light-headed.

"Sorry, I was showing Max where to hang up his jacket," she said, watching from the corner of her eye to be sure he heard her. He obliged, opening the closet door, and she crossed the room to Hen. "What's up?"

"We can't figure this thing out," Hen said. "It's not like the one you have at home."

Kitty got the record player going, and soon the music joined the conversation that filled the suite. She almost didn't hear the phone ring over the noise. When she realized it was ringing, she sprinted to her room to catch it, assuming only her father would call so late. She was delighted to find it was Charles instead. *He may be a rat*, she thought, *but he's got impeccable timing*.

"Oh, I'm so sorry," she said, after they exchanged greetings. "Hen's busy at the moment." She shifted to be closer to the door, cracking it a little and angling the phone toward the racket from the living room.

"Busy doing what? I was afraid I'd wake you."

"We're having people over."

"What people?"

"Andre and one or two of the musicians from the club."

"Again?"

"Charles," she said, in her sweetest tone, "these people work for me. It's not what you'd call a social visit. I'm throwing them a little thank-you party for all their efforts. It pays to keep the talent happy in this business."

"Well, I'm sure she'll want to speak to me. Call her in, please."

Kitty peeked out into the living room. Hen had dissolved into giggles at something Sebastian had said. She was leaning on Andre's arm for support. Recalling their conversation at the salon, Kitty wasn't about to take Hen away from a good time to have an upsetting conversation with Charles. "You know, it looks like she already went to bed after all."

"How is she sleeping through that noise? Wake her up."

"That's really not necessary, is it?"

"I'll say what's necessary and what isn't." His nasal New England accent was in full effect. "Wake her up, Kitty."

She was tempted to ask, *Or what?* She held her tongue.

"This is getting absurd," Charles continued. "And to think I called to apologize."

"There's nothing to be angry about," Kitty said. "I've been with her the whole time."

"Except now." His voice got louder. "Who's to say what she's doing right now?"

"Good grief, Charles. She's sleeping. That's exactly what she's doing."

Hen chose that moment to let out a peal of laughter. The record was between songs, and the conversation had died out for a second. Kitty was sure Charles had heard it. Her guess was confirmed when she heard the click on the other end, followed by the dial tone.

She leaned against the wall. Of all the horrible things she knew Charles to be, Kitty hadn't ever known him to be such a hothead. The sooner Hen got rid of him, the better. And Kitty knew a golden opportunity when she saw one. That laugh had justified Charles's suspicions. Once Kitty confirmed them, he and Hen would surely be finished. Kitty could intercept his calls and discourage Hen from calling him until she was truly ready to call it quits. Keeping them from being in contact would have the added bonus of allowing Hen to enjoy her trip without having to defend herself to Charles.

Kitty slipped back into the party, pleased to see Hen dancing. She had barely finished her dance with Max when Sebastian asked her for the next song. Finally, Andre cut in. The two made quite a pair, as neither of them danced in rhythm with the song, nor with each other. At last, breathless, Hen sat on the couch beside Kitty.

"Looks like you're beating them off with a stick," Kitty said.

"Oh, they're just being friendly," Hen said. She downed the rest of the drink she was holding, and Kitty noticed Hen's eyes were swimmy.

"How many of those have you had?" Kitty asked.

"One fewer than one too many." Hen sat up straight, nose in the air, in an attempt to look prim.

"Make sure you stay on the right side of that equation."

"Listen," Hen said, her face settling into seriousness. "I'm sorry I gave you a hard time earlier about your father and about you not spending time with Andre. I know you'll figure it out."

Her voice was a notch too loud. Andre was standing on the other side of the record player, well out of earshot thanks to the music. Kitty turned to her right. Sure enough, Max was beside the banquette. His stiff posture indicated that he'd heard.

"Thanks," Kitty said, standing. "I'm going to grab a sandwich. Want anything?"

"Nope."

Kitty stood by Max, pretending to examine the sandwich offerings. He spoke as quietly as he could.

"That's the second time that Hen's mentioned something between you and Andre," he said. "Want to clue me in? Are you two an item or something?"

"No. Papa thinks Andre and I would make a good match. I disagree." She glanced over her shoulder. "I'm guessing Andre does, too. I've got to figure out a way to tell Papa that, but that's the reason he sent me to Miami. I wasn't going to miss the chance to . . ." She met Max's eyes, then focused on the food again. "Well, I didn't want to miss the trip. So I let him think whatever he wants. But that's why I'd rather we didn't tell anyone about our time together."

He faced her. "You want to hide me."

"That's not it at all. I just mean for now. Otherwise, Papa will make me come right home." She let her hand brush his as she reached for a napkin. "I'm not ready for that yet. Are you?"

Max thought for a moment. He sighed. "Sure. Have it your way."

"Come on. I have to do it like this. For now." She extended a hand. "Want to dance?"

He set his plate down. "Sure."

She slipped off her shoes and they moved into the open space in the middle of the carpet. At first, she worried they'd draw attention. But then, Hen had been dancing the whole time, and no one had cared. To her relief, Hen and Sebastian soon jumped up to dance again. Between Andre, Max, Hen, and Charles, Kitty had plenty to preoccupy her. For that moment, however, she focused on the feel of Max's arms around her waist.

SEVENTEEN

The next morning, Kitty awoke far earlier than she'd expected to the sound of church bells. No, not church bells. An alarm? Not urgent enough for an alarm sound.

The phone! She leapt out of bed. Even with her cloudy head, she still remembered the need to keep Hen from talking to Charles. When she picked up the receiver, however, it wasn't Charles on the other end of the line.

"Papa," she said, with a hard exhale.

"Hello, princess. How are you?"

"I'm so glad to talk to you. I was planning to call you, actually. I feel like we haven't spoken in months."

Her father laughed. "I think it's only been a few days since our last call."

"A few long days," she said. "So how's New York?"

"Cold. I'm jealous of all that warm sunshine Andre tells me you have down there."

Kitty frowned. Was Andre talking to her father more often than she was? "That's why you should come down. At least for Christmas. It's only two weeks away now."

"Less than that. I'll see what I can do."

The firmness in his tone kept her from pushing further. Surely he would make the effort to see her on Christmas, even if it was just for a night or two. Perhaps he planned to surprise her, and that was why he hadn't confirmed anything.

His voice broke into her thoughts. "And how's our girl?"

"I don't think Loco likes the sand too much. She's strictly a side-walk sort of gal. New Yorker through and through."

"Sounds about right." He paused. "So I have an idea for you."

"Oh, yeah?"

"I'm sending Andre on a little excursion. A scouting trip, I guess you could call it. Got it all arranged this morning."

Kitty blinked at the clock on the nightstand. Andre was already working this morning? It had nearly been sunrise when he'd left the suite. He really was a pack mule. "Oh?"

"The more I thought about it, the more I thought it might make a nice little getaway for him. Especially since it sounds like it's been hard for you to spend time with him like you'd hoped." Her father's voice took on a slight edge.

"Did he say that? We've had dinner together practically every night."

"And Hen was the one he took to a bridge game."

"You didn't think I was actually going to play bridge, did you?"

"Katarina. I need to know you're taking this seriously."

Kitty sighed. "I didn't know that meant taking bridge seriously."

"You aren't down there to lounge by the pool." His voice took a sharp tone she had rarely heard from him. "I expect you to do better, or you know what's waiting for you."

She answered with what she hoped was a suitably meek assent. "So where is he going?"

"Havana."

She nearly dropped the phone. When she'd sworn to go the next place Andre offered to take her, she had no idea it would be anywhere as exciting as Havana. "Why is he going there?"

"He's going down there to talk to some nightclub owners. After the Atlanta deal fell through, I had a man there approach me about—" He stopped short. "All that wouldn't interest you. The long and short of it is, I'm thinking of investing in a casino. Andre is so close right now, I thought I'd send him on over to see what they're doing in Havana."

"I'd love to go, Papa, thank you." She paused. "Hen too, right?"

"Of course. And please tell her it's my treat. I'll get the hotel and flight set up. Oh, and I'll send your passport down express."

They talked out a few more details, and her father closed with another stern reminder that Kitty should spend as much time as possible with Andre. She hung up the phone, head still spinning. For the opportunity to see the glamour of Havana, she might have agreed to hold his hand the entire time. She rushed into Hen's room and jumped onto the bed. Hen moaned in protest.

"Wake up, silly," Kitty said, popping Hen on the arm with a pillow.

"I can't wake up. I'm dead." Hen sat up, her eyes still shut tight.

"Too bad. Guess you can't come with me to Cuba."

Hen's eyes flew open at that. "Cuba? You're going to Cuba?"

"Papa's sending Andre to Havana on a business trip. He wants to send us too."

Hen bit her lip. "I don't know if Mother will go for that. She's always said Havana is just gangsters and . . . ladies of the evening."

"Oh, Hen, she's not here. You can say *hooker*." Kitty stood up. "And we're not going anywhere shady. We're staying at the Hotel Nacional."

Hen balked. "That's exactly where the gangsters stay."

"And presidents. And movie stars. If it's good enough for Gary Cooper, it ought to be good enough for you."

"I really do have to ask Mother. But if it's only for a couple of days . . . and if we're staying in a nice area . . ." Hen swallowed. "When are we leaving?"

"Good girl." Kitty nodded. "We're leaving next Thursday. That gives us plenty of time to shop for some of those tight skirts like Marcela wears." *And the trip will give us some time away from Charles's phone calls*, she thought.

Kitty left Hen's room so she could take Loco out and get dressed for the day. As she applied her makeup, she thought of Max. The trip meant that she wouldn't be able to see him for a few days, but that wouldn't be such a bad thing. He might even be a little jealous at the idea of her running off to an exotic locale with Andre. Still, she wanted to be the one to tell Max about Havana. His reaction would give her a sense of just how far gone he really was.

She snuck down to the club to see if he might be practicing with the band. No luck. The only people in the club were wait staff preparing for the evening. She needed a reliable way to be able to talk to him in private. She already had the spot outside Andre's office all picked out. Why not use it? She could catch up with him after the band played that night and instruct him to meet her there.

Kitty was surprised by a knock at the door of the suite late that afternoon. Hen was in her room getting ready for dinner, so Kitty opened the door for their guest. A grinning Andre waited on the other side.

"I've got a special treat for you tonight," he said, stepping into the entryway. "You've been wanting to go to the Park Avenue Restaurant? Well, I talked to Wingy Grober today, and he's guaranteed us the best table in the house."

Go figure. Andre finally suggested an interesting outing, and Kitty wanted to be in the hotel. "For dinner? Oh, how nice," she said.

He scratched his temple. "I thought you'd want to go for the whole evening."

"I do," she said quickly. "I just thought we could get Sebastian's take on Cuba. We'll be so busy with packing over the next few days."

"How long does it take you to pack?" he asked.

"Plenty long," she said. "I'm sure men can toss a shirt in a suitcase and go, but it's a lot more work for ladies."

Andre snorted. "I'll take your word for it. But you don't want to go to Sebastian's part of Cuba, believe me."

"I thought he was from Havana."

"Don't worry, I've got you covered," Andre said. "What do you want to know?"

"It's not that I don't trust your guidance, but the first night Sebastian was here, he took us to a great party," she said. "It was nice, meeting his friends. I don't want to go to Havana if all I get to see is the same thing I can see right here in Miami." She was grateful Hen was in her room, where she couldn't contradict Kitty's professed enjoyment of Marcela's party.

"Suit yourself," Andre said. "You know I've got to be in the casinos and meetings, though. It's not a long trip. I can't promise I can take you to see any of his friends like he could."

"I'd like to ask, that's all. Even if it's just for recommendations of nightlife tourists might not know about. I don't want to end up at Sloppy Joe's with a bunch of Americans."

"Then you can ask. I'll make sure we're back before the band finishes up here, all right?"

"Thank you," Kitty said.

She agreed to bring Hen with her to the lobby in an hour to take the car to the Park Avenue. Kitty dressed, then went to knock on Hen's door. After a long pause, Hen called out, "Yes?"

"It's me, goofy. I hope you're dressed; we need to meet Andre in fifteen minutes."

"I'm dressed," Hen said through the door, "but I don't know if I'm in any state to go down."

The door swung open to reveal a red-faced, puffy-eyed Hen. Kitty gasped.

"What on earth happened? Was it your mother?" Kitty grabbed

Hen's hand. "Look, don't sweat it, it's such a fast trip. Tell her anything you want, she'll never know—"

"Not Mother. She didn't care once I told her we were staying at the Hotel Nacional. Said she'd wanted to see that place herself. I didn't have much to worry about there." Hen dabbed at her eyes. "It's Charles."

Kitty's eyes narrowed. *That bastard.* "What happened?"

Hen walked over to sit on the couch. "He was awful, Kitty. I had to call, I had to tell him we were going to Havana. He said he knew I'd been up to no good. That he had proof. What kind of proof?" She held out her hands, helpless. "There's nothing to have proof of! I was having such a good time, and now he's wrecked it. He wrecks everything." She let out a choked sob and hugged a pillow to her chest. "I know I put on a brave face, and I don't dare go against Mother when it comes to him. But, oh, Kitty. This trip, being away from him . . . it's the most cheerful I've been in ages. I know that. And it's all because he's not here."

Kitty's heart ached. While Charles was berating Hen for perfectly innocent fun, he was probably in bed with half the socialites in Manhattan. She wanted to spill out everything, but if Hen changed her mind about him again, she'd hate Kitty for her scheming. And Hen always changed her mind when it came to Charles. Kitty settled for being comforting.

"Listen to me. If the phone rings over the next couple of days, let me get it. I'll keep him at bay for a while. He'll calm down," she said.

Hen sniffled. "There's nothing I can do about it anyway."

Kitty pressed her lips together. "I don't know if that's true, Hen."

"Let's not go down that road again." Hen stood, wiped her cheeks with her hand, and fluffed her hair. "You're right. He'll calm down."

Kitty hesitated. "You don't have to go downstairs if you don't want to."

"I'd like to go. I don't want to stay here and hear the phone ring. Think I can make myself presentable?"

"Sure. Your cheeks aren't even red anymore. All you need is a little powder," Kitty said. "If I'd been crying, my cheeks would be red for a week. You're lucky like that."

Hen smiled faintly and went to her room to powder her face. Kitty shoved down the nagging thought that Hen's sadness was really her fault. *It's all for the greater good*, she reminded herself. *She's sad now, but she'll be as happy as she was last night all the time once he's out of the picture.*

The Park Avenue Restaurant was housed in a concrete building that could have been called nondescript, but for the pastel-pink exterior and the sign on one corner proclaiming it to be WORLD FAMOUS. Otherwise, the square one-story building didn't give any hint of its luminary status. Though the atmosphere was lively and the steak divine, Kitty couldn't appreciate any of it. She recognized the trombone player she'd met at Marcela's party, but the sight of him only served to bring her thoughts around to Max again.

Andre invited Hen to dance. When it was Kitty's turn, she demurred. Hen and Andre headed back out to the dance floor, leaving Kitty to her thoughts. Finally, as the clock's hands crept toward midnight, Andre suggested they return to the Imperium. Kitty eagerly agreed, and they were off.

The Zillionaires were still playing when they arrived. Andre went to check on the kitchen, while the girls claimed a vacant table. As soon as the band played the final notes of the last song, Kitty was on her feet heading for the stage. She waved Max and Sebastian over.

"You came in late tonight," Max said. "Not getting tired of us, are you?"

"No, we went to the Park Avenue. Can't miss all the other Miami attractions just because of you fellas," Kitty said.

"Max, you sound like a jealous boyfriend," Sebastian said. The tips of Max's ears turned pink as he examined the stops on his trumpet.

"I wanted to tell you two that we're going to be gone for a couple of days," she said, the words spilling out.

"Oh?" Max lifted his eyes back to her. "Where are you off to?"

"Havana."

Sebastian's eyes widened. "What part will you go to?"

"We're staying at the Hotel Nacional," she said. "Andre has to scope out some casinos for Papa."

Sebastian's features relaxed. "Ah, well. I think you'll enjoy that."

"How long will you be gone?" Max asked.

"We leave Thursday, and we'll be back on Sunday," Kitty said.

"You know," Max said, turning to Sebastian. "You haven't been home in a while. Why don't you take a long weekend? It's nearly Christmas."

"I . . ." Sebastian looked askance at Max. "Hmm. I hadn't thought about that. It's not a bad idea."

"And I could go with you. I'd love to see your family again," Max added.

A bubble of excitement welled in Kitty's chest. His eagerness could only mean she had him exactly where she wanted him. "What a swell idea! I was going to ask you for recommendations of places to visit. You could just show us yourself."

Now Sebastian's gaze darted from Max to Kitty and back again, his brow furrowing. "Do you really think we could get a weekend off?"

"It's probably the last chance we'll get before the holidays," Max said. "We can have Dave and Roger from the fill-in band take our places."

"My mother would love for me to visit," Sebastian said. He pressed his lips together in thought. "Okay. If we can get Dave and Roger—"

"I'll take care of all of that," Max said. "Let's go talk to Andre." He threw an arm over Sebastian's shoulder and they headed over to where Andre had rejoined Hen at the table. Before Sebastian had a chance to speak, Max spilled out the request. Andre agreed it would be fine, if they could cover their spots in the band.

"And now you've got your local guide," he said to Kitty. Sebastian and Max both looked at her.

"Well, I thought Sebastian might tell us which places we couldn't miss seeing," she explained. "Now he can be the one to take us."

Kitty waited until the others were preoccupied with good nights to slide her clutch purse into the seat of her chair. She tugged on Max's sleeve and gestured to the bag with a flick of her hand. He nodded. She linked her arm in Hen's, and the two girls headed for the elevator.

"Oh, dear," Kitty said when the door dinged. "I've left my bag. You go on up. I'm right behind you."

"Are you sure?" Hen asked.

"Yes. Won't be a moment." Kitty's heels clacked on the floor of the lobby as she strode back toward the club. Max waited around the corner, bag in hand.

"Clever." He held the bag out to her.

"Do you know the patio on the side of the main entrance?" she whispered, concerned that Sebastian or Andre could walk out at any moment and foil her plan.

"Yeah."

"Is it usually empty?"

"At night, sure."

"Good. Meet me there in twenty minutes."

He nodded, and she skipped away again. She went up to the suite to find Hen waiting on the couch in the living room. Kitty waved the purse.

"Found it. Now I've just got to take Loco out one more time before bed."

"Want some company?" Hen asked, stifling a yawn.

"No, you go on to bed. Good night." Kitty clipped the leash on Loco and went back downstairs.

Finding the break in the hedges was a little more difficult in the dark, but Kitty stepped onto the patio to find Max waiting. She let Loco sniff around the trees at the edge of the concrete.

"What did you want to meet here for?" he asked.

"I thought this would be somewhere we could come to talk without everyone around. Easier than leaving my purse behind any time I want to chat."

He smiled. "So what do you want to chat about now?"

"Havana."

"So you like my idea, huh?"

"Couldn't stand the thought of me off in an island paradise without you?" she asked.

"Didn't want to miss a minute of the fun."

"Have you been to Havana?"

"Once. But we went to visit Sebastian's family, and we didn't have the money to go near the Nacional."

Kitty paused. "I'm glad you're going."

"I'm glad to be going."

Loco padded back over and sat at Kitty's feet, looking up expectantly. Kitty clipped the leash back on. "I guess I'd better get to bed. So, this can be our place?"

"Sure," he said. "But I guess the next time we see each other, we'll be in Havana."

"Then I'll see you in Havana."

❈ EIGHTEEN ❈

Kitty couldn't help but notice that Hen fretted more than usual about her packing for the trip, which had started three days before their flight. She'd put a dress in, only to yank it out two minutes later. Bathing suit selection was a protracted agony until Kitty finally recommended packing all three.

"Pack the suitcase all the way," she said, shoving a romper in on top. "Fill it up. Who cares if it's heavy? You won't have to carry it. Pack two suitcases. Take one of mine. But please, let's finish this in time to actually go on the trip."

Hen sat down on the bed and heaved a sigh. "He hasn't called."

Kitty inspected her nail polish, unwilling to look at Hen. "That could be a good sign. Maybe he knows he was wrong to blow up at you, and he's ashamed of how he acted."

"You're sweet to say so, but I'd bet that's not it."

"Well, you didn't want to talk to him anyway, did you?"

"Was that him the other night when the band was here?" Hen blinked up at Kitty. "I heard the phone ring. I didn't want to ask, because . . ."

"It was a wrong number." Kitty held up three fingers. "Scout's honor. Now, can we get excited about this trip? And can we finish your packing so we don't miss our flight?"

"When are Max and Sebastian getting there?" Hen asked. She stood and crossed to her jewelry case to begin sorting what she wanted to take.

"This afternoon. They left yesterday to drive to Key West, and they're taking a ferry from there." Kitty selected a scarf from the drawer and put it in Hen's suitcase.

"That sounds like fun."

"That sounds like a long trip," Kitty said. "Once they get there, they're going to Sebastian's cousin's place in Havana to get Max settled in, and then Sebastian's heading out of the city to visit his mother."

"You know, it sure is funny how eager Max is to come with us." Hen sidled up to Kitty, who kept her eyes on packing.

"You know I'm not interested in some skint musician."

"He is handsome, though."

"Hmm, do you think so?"

"And a good dancer."

"Are you trying to sell him to me?"

"Not at all. But I've seen the way he looks at you sometimes." Hen pulled the lid of the suitcase down. "I think he's got it bad. I'm not going to lecture you. But you should let him down easy, if it comes to that."

"I can't help it if I have a certain effect on men." Even if Hen did think Max was good-looking, there was no way she would approve if she knew how much time Kitty had already given Max. Max liking her was one thing. Returning his affections would be something else entirely. She pressed on the top of the not-quite-closed suitcase, hoping to distract Hen with a more immediate issue. "I think we're going to have to sit on this thing."

Hen hopped onto the suitcase, and Kitty closed the latches. "Leave it on the bed," Kitty continued. "We'll get the bellhop to bring it down."

"Want to do yours?" Hen asked.

"Mine was packed yesterday. Should I call down? Andre wanted us to meet him at eleven, I think." Kitty took a step toward the phone, but Hen caught her arm.

"Tell me the truth," Hen said. "Have you thought about Andre at all?"

Kitty searched Hen's face, which was suddenly tight with worry. "Of course not. He's not my type. The birds and bridge games just confirmed it. But I thought you knew I had a plan for that. You're not worried about me and Papa, are you?"

Hen let go of Kitty. "I was only wondering if anything had changed, even a little bit."

"No, and I doubt anything will change. Now, come on. Let's get downstairs. And maybe we'll get you a cocktail on the plane. You're nervous today."

Kitty called down to the bellhop to get their bags. She made a second call to the maid she'd entrusted with Loco's care. Andre had singled the girl out as particularly trustworthy and kind. Kitty had sweetened the deal with some extra cash—half payment before the trip, half after. She reminded the maid that the money was in the envelope on the television. With that important matter settled, Kitty and Hen were off to Havana.

⇥ ✦ ⇤

The drive from the Rancho Boyeros Airport to the Hotel Nacional seemed to take nearly as long as the flight from Miami to Cuba. Kitty shifted in her seat, unsticking her legs from the vinyl. And she'd thought the Miami temperatures were warm for winter. Beside Kitty, Hen dozed with her head against the window.

They drove through neighborhoods with people on porches and past parks full of children. The ubiquitous pastel stucco did not do much to differentiate the country from Miami at first, but Kitty still sensed a difference she couldn't quite name. At last, when they reached the area the driver called "Habana Vieja," the difference was more acute. This part of Havana simply looked much older than Miami, like the postcards Hen would send Kitty from Europe. She spotted wrought iron and intricate stonework that gave some of the buildings the look of castles. *That must be it,* she thought. *It's that old-world feel. Papa would love this. He ought to have come too.* It would have been the perfect opportunity for them to see each other. Why didn't he come? Why send Andre?

She didn't have long to pursue that line of thought. They turned one corner, and the ocean suddenly appeared on the left side of the car. All along the shore, people sat on a wall, chatting and looking out at the sea. They seemed not to mind the occasional leap of spray that rose up to meet them. Kitty rolled down her window, and a few salty drops carried on the breeze landed on her cheeks.

"That is the Malecón," the driver explained. "And over there, beyond, the *faro*—lighthouse. Very famous."

An enormous ivory building loomed on their right. The structure was topped with what looked like two large crowns, and surrounded by palms and lush greenery. "What is that?" Kitty cried.

The driver laughed. "That is the Nacional."

"That's our hotel," Andre added.

They pulled into the roundabout, which was nestled between the building's two arms. Kitty was out of the car practically before it stopped moving. People bustled through the entrance, all dressed like they were going to a *Harper's Bazaar* cover shoot instead of to lunch. Kitty caught a few words of Spanish, some French . . . was that Italian? She hooked her arm through Hen's and dragged her tired friend inside.

If the outside was stunning and sunny, the inside was pure elegance. Their heels clicked against bronze-colored tiles as they walked along the hallway, which had arches on either side. Dark wooden beams overhead added to a sense of grandeur. As Andre spoke to the clerk at reception, Kitty inspected the brightly colored Spanish tile and a marble statue. After a short conversation, Andre turned around with two keys in his outstretched hand.

"You girls will be neighbors," he said. "Sorry, they didn't have a suite on such short notice. I'll be a floor below."

Kitty took her key. "That's all right. I can't imagine we'll be spending that much time in our rooms."

"It really is beautiful," Hen said. "Reminds me of Spain."

The bellhop stepped out to load their bags onto a cart, and the group followed him to the elevators. Andre got off on his floor, waving off an offer of help with his bags. He slipped a few pesos to the bellhop, and the girls agreed to meet him downstairs in an hour to go to lunch. The man rode up with Kitty and Hen and placed their suitcases in their rooms.

The décor in Kitty's room was far warmer than that in her room in the Imperium, with thick, heavy curtains that she supposed helped to keep the heat out. When she slid them aside, she discovered that her room looked out over the Havana Harbor, complete with the lighthouse the cabbie had pointed out. Kitty rushed to change, so she could catch Hen before she got tempted to lie down for a nap. The cocktail on the flight had relaxed Hen a little too much, and Kitty didn't want to waste a second of their time in Havana.

An hour later, they were back in the sumptuous lobby, ready for a late lunch. Andre led them down the street to an outdoor café, where they sat in the shade of a massive umbrella. In halting Spanish, Andre ordered daiquiris for the girls and, for himself, a beer that came out in a bottle the size of his head.

"Guess you're supposed to share this, huh?" he said, accepting a glass from the waiter.

Kitty lit a cigarette and craned her neck to read the menu from a hand-painted sign. "Do you think they speak English here?" she whispered to Hen. "I can't tell what's what."

"Have you decided what you'd like to eat?" the waiter said.

"That settles that," Hen whispered to Kitty.

"We've heard the seafood is good here. What do you have today?" Andre asked.

"Our specialty is the *camarones enchilados*," the waiter said.

"Then bring us that." Andre smiled at the girls.

Kitty pursed her lips but waited until the server had walked away to say, "That shows a lot of confidence. Do you even know what that means? It could be fried rat."

"Rat isn't a seafood, Kitty," he said dryly, taking a sip of beer.

Camarones enchilados turned out to be a seafood stew that Kitty enjoyed so much, she sopped up the last drops with the crusty bread that came on the side. It was served with something that looked like banana slices, but when Kitty tasted them they were salty and much richer than any banana. The waiter pronounced it carefully for her, assuring her that they could be found in most restaurants in Havana.

"I have to have them again," Kitty said. "Tos-ton-es."

"Very good," the waiter said, collecting her plates.

"Well, Spanish isn't so hard after all," she said.

"Learning one word rarely is," Hen said.

"I know more than one word." Kitty pointed to Andre's beer bottle. "*Cerveza. Daiquiri.* I'm pretty sure that's all I need."

"You won't go thirsty, I guess," Hen said.

Andre stood. "Time for me to get to work. Ready to go back to the hotel?"

"We aren't going to the casinos with you?" Kitty asked.

"I've got a meeting right now—nothing that would interest you. I'll take you around tomorrow. Why don't you two go and enjoy the hotel pool? You can rent a cabana." He checked his watch. "Wasn't Sebastian going to call soon anyway to make plans for tonight?"

"Oh, that's right. We'd better hurry." Kitty grabbed her purse, and the group went to the corner to hail a cab.

Back in their rooms, Kitty and Hen put on bathing suits. The phone rang shortly after.

"Miss Tessler? You have a call from a Mr. Armenteros. Will you accept?" a desk clerk asked.

"Yes," Kitty said. A moment later the line lit up with static that crackled over Sebastian's voice.

"Hello," he said, his voice bright. "How do you like Cuba?"

"The first few hours have been swell," Kitty said. "How was your trip?"

"Good, very easy travel."

"Where are you now?"

"At my cousin's apartment. I'm driving to my mother's house tomorrow, but I can go out with you tonight. Max says he would like to stay in Havana, so he will be here all day tomorrow."

"Wonderful. Where should we meet you?"

"Where all Havana meets—at the Malecón. Can you be there at seven o'clock?"

"Sure. We'll see you then."

Kitty and Hen went down to the pool with a stack of brochures from the concierge. Though each brightly colored advertisement promised Cuba's finest entertainments, Kitty could only focus on the Tropicana.

"It's brand new, with huge glass arcs in the ceiling that make it look like you're outside. And they have fruit trees growing indoors." She jabbed the brochure with a finger. "It's air-conditioned."

Hen fanned herself with one of the flyers Kitty had discarded. "That sounds good right about now."

"And look at the costumes. This looks like the real Cuba to me."

"I'm sure Sebastian will take us wherever we want to go," Hen said, idly kicking her feet in the pool's turquoise water.

Kitty set down the brochure. "Are you all right?"

"I wonder if I ought to call Charles. Won't he worry if he doesn't hear from me?" Hen's red cheeks had nothing to do with the heat.

"He can always call your mother if he's worried," Kitty said firmly. "Calling him now would only bring the whole argument up again. Why don't you take this trip to relax and forget about—" She nearly said *him*, but caught herself. "Forget about what he said. Then the next time you two talk, you'll be calmer, and it will calm him down."

"That's sensible," Hen said, her expression already more relaxed.

Kitty nodded. "Now, on to more important business. What do we wear out on our first night in Havana?"

NINETEEN

HAVANA, CUBA

DECEMBER 1953

Kitty and Hen swept out of the hotel that evening dressed to the nines. Even Hen had put in her best effort, with a daring lime-green halter dress. Kitty had opted for what she hoped would be a more local look, wearing a tight yellow skirt and a black ruffled blouse. The warm salt air pulled them toward the Malecón. There were already groups of people gathered in the twilight, some dressed for a night out, others in uniforms that suggested they had come straight from a shift at a nearby hotel or restaurant. Kitty and Hen passed a fruit vendor, who glanced up from his wares to offer a whistle of approval. Hen flinched, but Kitty just laughed.

Her heart began to pound when she saw a familiar figure leaning over the wall for a better look at the waves. He didn't spot them right away, but Sebastian called out. He held out a hand as Kitty came near.

"Welcome to Havana," Sebastian said. Max jumped beside him, and his face lit up when his eyes met Kitty's.

"We already love it," Kitty said. Sebastian took her hand, and she gave his fingers a little squeeze before slipping her hand out of his. She wanted to reach out for Max's hand, but she mentally slapped her own wrist.

"You two look beautiful," Max said. "Where would you like to go?"

"How about the Tropicana?" Kitty asked. Sebastian's face fell for a split second before he regained his sunny expression.

"Yes, if you would like to go there. I hear the show is excellent," he said. "But I left my car at my cousin's. We'll have to go and get it, or we'll need to take a taxi . . ."

"Oh, don't worry about that," Kitty said. "Hen and I will pay."

Max and Sebastian glanced at each other. "We can't let you do that," Max said.

"I insist. It's the least we can do, since you're escorting us around."

Max thought for a moment. "Let's not waste any more time, then."

Though Hen and Sebastian chatted in the taxi, an odd cloud hung over the group. Kitty brushed it off. Max and Sebastian couldn't be sore for long about her paying, she reasoned. It might hurt their pride to have a girl pay their way, but surely an empty wallet would prove more painful.

The sign over the door read TROPICANA in the same funny, wobbly letters that the brochure had used. At the entrance, Sebastian turned to them.

"We can go to the outdoor stage or the indoor. Under the arches," he explained. "The outdoor show is the big one, but inside is nice too."

"Let's go to the indoor stage," Hen said. "I think Kitty was excited about the crystal arches."

"And you were excited about the air-conditioning," Kitty teased.

"Indoors it is," Max said.

As they walked into the cabaret, Kitty stifled a gasp. She thought Sebastian's English must have failed him. There was no other explanation for him using the word *nice* to describe what lay before them. The huge room's ceiling was a series of ever-widening glass arches, letting in the twinkle of the night sky. A few colorful stage lights lit up the concrete sections between the glass, giving everything a sultry glow. And, as advertised, trees sprang up between the tables right from the floor, adding a woody freshness to the mingling of perfume, cologne, and spicy food.

The host led them to a round table on the second level of the room, farther from the stage than Kitty would have liked. Still, she was pleased to find that the club made good on its promise in the brochure that there were no bad seats; she could see the entire stage perfectly well. A waiter delivered the glasses of rum that were complimentary with their ticket purchase, as well as a few small bowls of snacks. Hen saw that one of the bowls contained *tostones* and nudged it toward Kitty.

"Kitty has found her new favorite food," Hen explained to Max and Sebastian.

Sebastian laughed. "I'm glad you like them. You will eat a lot of them while you are here."

Kitty extracted a slice with the tiny wooden fork. "But how will I get them once I'm back in the States?"

"That will be harder," Sebastian agreed. He seemed to be about to continue, when he looked across the room and froze. His jaw tightened, and he turned his attention to the drink in front of him. Kitty scanned the room until she saw the waitress a few tables away staring at Sebastian. The girl had lovely pale green eyes but was otherwise unremarkable. Kitty couldn't read her expression, but she could tell the encounter had made Sebastian uncomfortable. Perhaps she was a scorned lover. Kitty sensed it would be wiser not to ask.

She was about to reach for her glass when she felt something light hit the napkin in her lap. Max shot her a look, and she slid her fingers around without looking until she located the folded piece of paper he'd put there. She gripped it in her palm and stood.

"I think I'll powder my nose one more time before the show starts," she said.

"I'll come with you," Hen said. Sebastian pointed out where the restrooms were, and the girls weaved through the tables toward them. Once inside, Kitty ducked into a stall and unfolded the scrap of paper Max had given her. The penciled note read:

If you can get away, meet me in front of the hotel an
hour after we drop you off tonight.

Her stomach fluttered. With shaking hands, she refolded the note
and put it in her purse. She had hoped to get some time on her own
with Max, but she thought she'd have to be the one to engineer it.
Clearly, he was as eager to see her as she was to see him.

When they rejoined Max and Sebastian at the table, Kitty waited
until Hen and Sebastian were chatting to bump her knee against Max's
under the table. He glanced at her, and she nodded slightly. The meeting was set.

A roll of African drums that led to blaring music announced the
start of the show as costumed dancers took the stage. Kitty had never
seen anything like it. Women in what looked like glittering bathing
suits shook and shimmied, and the long feathers in their hair swayed
along with their hips. A second group of dancers wore costumes with
such elaborate detail that Kitty couldn't take it all in, except to note
that those getups were no less revealing than the first set. Strips of
glittering fabric wound up the dancers' arms and down their legs but
left their midriffs mostly uncovered. Kitty didn't understand any of
the Spanish lyrics to the songs, but the driving beat would have been
exciting in any language. The show was too loud to permit conversation, but the way Hen kept covering her mouth with her hand and
letting out the occasional squeal said volumes about her own experience.

The grand finale featured additional performers on the terraced
roof, visible through the crystal arches. However great the outdoor
show might have been, Kitty couldn't imagine it would be any better
than the one they'd seen. The girls practically bounced on the seat of
the taxi carrying them all back to the hotel.

"And the woman in the divine dress with the gold ruffles? With the
flowers in her hair?" Hen said as they compared notes.

"That one fella in the dark suit could give Sebastian a run for his money," Kitty said, playfully tapping Sebastian's arm. "Was that a love song he was singing?"

"It was. But are you saying I am not your favorite singer anymore?" Sebastian asked with a sidelong smile.

She faltered, thinking of Max joining in on "The Best Thing for You" back in Miami. "Of course you're my favorite," she said, maintaining her composure. "You're the best singer I know."

As she studied his profile in the moonlight, she thought of the shadow that had passed over his face when he saw the young woman in the Tropicana. She wondered again what had passed between them. Whatever it was, he must have been glad to leave it behind in Cuba.

The taxi pulled up to the front of the Hotel Nacional, and the group piled out. Max motioned for the driver to wait.

"Thank you both for a swell evening," Hen said. "I don't know how we're going to ever top that. And we still have two nights left."

"I'm glad you had a good time, and don't worry. Havana has much more to enjoy," Sebastian said. He kissed each girl on the cheek.

Max stuffed his hands in his pockets. "That's how Cubans say good night, I guess. Mind if I stick with words?"

"Not at all," Hen said. "Good night, you two."

As they stepped into the lobby, Kitty faked a yawn in case Hen had any aspirations of continuing the evening at the hotel bar. Fortunately, Hen seemed to actually be as tired as Kitty was pretending to be. All of her excitement in the cab had drained away, and she leaned on the wall of the elevator. She said a foggy "good night" as she unlocked her door. Still, to be safe, Kitty waited for the full hour before going back down.

As promised, Max stood outside the front entrance. "You are trouble," he said, taking a few slow steps her way. "Look at you, sneaking out."

"I've got a bad influence," she said.

He held out a hand. "Come on. There's a bar this way I want you to try."

After a split second of hesitation, she took his hand. They started down the street. "Where's Sebastian?"

"He decided to go ahead to his mother's. She won't care what time he gets in, and he didn't want to lose part of the day tomorrow driving."

"I'd like to meet his family while we're here. How far away is his mother's place?" she asked.

"I don't think that will work out."

"Why not?" She squeezed his hand. "Is he ashamed of us?"

But Max's face remained serious. "His family is all fishermen. Their home is . . . small."

"I don't mind that," Kitty said. "What does that matter?"

"It's not just small. It's basically a shack, and from your reaction to Marcela's place, I think you'd mind a lot."

Kitty tried to picture worse living conditions than the houses in Riverside. Not that Marcela's place was a dump. It was clean, well cared for. But the ramshackle condition of some of the buildings gave her a clearer image of what Sebastian's family home must look like, and it didn't fit with her impression of him.

Max let go of her hand and pointed to a red awning with CLUB RUIZ painted on it in white letters. "This is it. Hope you weren't expecting another Tropicana."

The crowded bar, packed with unpainted wooden tables and chairs, couldn't have been more different from the Tropicana. Its one extravagance was a jukebox in the corner that could barely be heard over the boisterous conversation. Max led Kitty through the open door on the back wall, which led to an equally crowded patio. They managed to pull two chairs together, out of the way of the impromptu dancing that had taken up one corner of the outdoor space. Max got them drinks at the bar, while Kitty lit a cigarette and studied the crowd. The group reminded her of the one assembled at Marcela's house, an eclectic mix of skin tones that she was still unused to.

"Sebastian has nothing to be ashamed of, no matter where he comes from," she said, plowing back into the topic despite Max's cringe. "I mean, look at him. He works hard, has a swell car, and he's so handsome. Though I guess that last part gets him in trouble from time to time." When Max gave her a sidelong glance, she nodded. "He admitted as much to me in New York. And don't think I didn't notice how oddly he behaved in the Tropicana when he saw that pretty girl."

Max sighed. "I'll admit he's broken a few hearts, but that wasn't the problem in the Tropicana."

"Oh no?"

"No. That girl is a friend of his. Just a friend."

"I don't believe that for a second."

"It's complex." Max turned his gaze to the crowd of dancers.

"So I'm right. There was a romance."

He sighed. "I can't be the one to tell you Sebastian's story, Kitty."

"You still don't think I'd understand, do you? You never really believed I'm clever enough." She crossed her arms on her chest. "Any minute now we'll be arguing about books again."

"I never thought you weren't smart, honestly. That wasn't why I picked on you. Which I'll admit I did." He glanced at her. "Do you want to know the truth? What really bothered me?"

She waved a hand. "Why not?"

"It was what you said about your maid that first night that we visited your place. We were going to take our glasses into the kitchen, but you said to leave them out."

Kitty glared at him. "That's Paula's job. We pay her well for it."

"It saves her a little extra work, though, doesn't it? If we take them into the kitchen? Look, I know you better now. I know you're not so shallow as I thought you were. But when you said that . . . it didn't sound like you thought about her as a person. She was just the help. A pair of hands to pick up dirty glasses the next day. That girl in the Tropicana was the help. I'm sure that's how Sebastian thought you'd see it."

Kitty stubbed out her cigarette without looking at him. "Paula is more than a pair of hands to me. She's worked for our family for years."

"Sure. I'm sure that's true. But I didn't know that. I was going off a first impression."

"You don't want to hear my first impression of you," she said with a sniff.

He raised an eyebrow. "Was it that you were sore that I was giving Hen more attention than you?"

"No," she cried, cursing him for reading her so well, even then.

"I'm only bringing it up to say . . . you already have a lot that most people don't, you know? I still don't understand. What are you going to get out of the top that you don't have now? Do you really think they're better than you?"

She stared at him for a moment. "I don't think they're better than me. *They* think they're better than me."

"And why is that?"

"My primary crime is being Russian. Granddaughter of immigrants. And we're new money to boot."

"Aren't you proud of that? Proud of your pop for everything he's done?"

"Of course I am."

"You have money, so who cares what they think?"

"What they think changes things." The words came out more forcefully than Kitty meant them to. Max sat in silence, waiting for her to continue. She did so slowly, unable to stop the confession that no one else had heard. Somehow, she could make him understand. She wanted him to understand. "I was little when my mother died. Three years old. I think I remember her, but sometimes I think I'm only remembering the photographs my father has shown me." Kitty swallowed, but her tone remained matter-of-fact. "I do remember when she got sick, so sick she couldn't come out of the bedroom. My father called the doctor, but his office said he couldn't come. 'Out of town,' they said. Papa put my coat on me, and we got into the car to the pharmacy to get some more of the medicine that wasn't helping. I think it was all Papa could think to do. And that was when I saw him. As we were driving past. That doctor with his big black bag, going into one of the best addresses in town." She let out a bitter laugh. "A house call for someone more important. And my mother died. That's the difference. You can have all the money in the world, but if they don't respect you, you still lose."

Max offered her a hand, and she gripped it. "I'm so sorry," he said.

"I didn't know her well enough to miss her," Kitty said. "And Papa loved me enough for a thousand parents. But I'll never forget that feeling. I know why that doctor passed us over. I'm not going to let anything like that happen to me again. Status protects people. That's why I need it."

Max leaned forward. "This may not come as a shock, but those people don't think much of me either. I don't have to meet them to know it. I'm way worse in their eyes than some new-money Russian, you can bet on that. Those hotels we walked past in Miami? Some of them still have signs in the windows that say *Select Clientele*. My pop told me that when he was my age, they said it even plainer: 'Always a view, never a Jew.' And it's worse for guys like Sebastian. He can work in a lot of those places, but every one of them would toss him out if he tried to walk in the front door instead of the side. Hell, even Louis Armstrong can't get a room on your side of the Causeway, not even when he plays there."

Kitty shifted in her seat. "It's not *my* side."

"Yeah, but you can stay there. You've got that, at least." Max took a sip of his drink. "I saw Louis Armstrong play at the Lyric. I hadn't been playing music long, but after I heard him, I knew I wanted to play like he did. That trumpet was an extension of his voice, his body. And you know what else? I saw a little bit of gold, right here." He tapped his chest above his breastbone. "My pop told me it was a Star of David. Armstrong was raised by a Jewish family. He never forgot what they went through, how they all had their own troubles."

"I never knew that," Kitty said.

"I'm telling you all this so you'll know that I'm proud of who I am, no matter what doors close on me because of it. That doctor did that to your family not because you should've been someone better, but because *he* should have been. Do you know what I mean?"

Kitty blinked hard. Never in all her years of planning and maneuvering to make her way to the highest circles of society had she questioned what that really meant. Someone would always be locked out. Someone would always lose. Who would she have to help keep out once she was there? If it was someone like Max, someone who listened to her and challenged her, did she really want that? For the first time, her conviction wavered. The uncertainty settled like a brick in her stomach.

When she didn't answer, Max said, "This ended up being heavier cocktail talk than I meant it to be. I know you're here to enjoy yourself. I'm sorry."

"It's all right. Really." She ran a thumb over his rough fingers. It was true. Despite the way the conversation had unnerved her, it had felt good. She wasn't exactly sure why.

"What are your plans for tomorrow night?"

"We're going out with Andre, but Hen never stays up this late. I'm sure she'll want to go back to her room, and I can come out again. If you'd like."

"Sneak out," he corrected, with a glint in his eye. "Same time? Two o'clock?"

Kitty agreed. They finished their drinks, and Max led the way back toward the hotel. Despite the hour, the streets were filled with revelers in all manner of dress, from tuxedos and diamonds to linen pants and cotton blouses. The brochures Kitty had read mentioned start times as late as three a.m. for some shows, so the lively streets were hardly surprising. Even old men and women, who would have been dozing by the fire in New York, were bouncing and swaying to the music that poured out of open doorways. Max paused at an intersection and glanced down each street.

"This way is quicker," he said. Kitty could see the spires of the Nacional ahead of them, lit up with huge floodlights. She and Max fell into an easy pace, and she suspected that he was in no hurry to drop her off.

She was about to comment on one of the groups passing by when a little girl appeared in a doorway near them. Kitty gasped. The child's clothes were rags, and she was barefoot. The girl's shoulders were hard knobs at the top of wilted, skinny arms. Her eyelashes were matted together at the corners of her eyes. Kitty's stomach turned. The girl cried out to her in words Kitty couldn't understand. Behind her, in the darkness of the entryway, a woman sat echoing the girl's cries.

The child grabbed Kitty's hand, and Kitty stiffened. The little fingers on hers felt like they had wires under the skin, and they were cold despite the warm evening air. Kitty wanted to pull her hand away but couldn't move. Max walked toward the girl and held out some coins. The girl released Kitty and snatched the money from his hand. Her shouts had alerted some of the nearby pedestrians, who hastened away, heads down. When Kitty looked back to the doorway, the girl had disappeared into the darkness once more. Her mother still sat, barely visible in the shadows, watching them.

Max slid an arm around Kitty's waist, and she was grateful for the support. Her hands trembled, and she barely saw the buildings as they passed. When they were in sight of the entrance to the Nacional, he spoke quietly in her ear.

"Are you all right?"

"It was just a little girl." She forced a shaky laugh.

"You're pretty worked up." He took her hand. "It's okay, you know. It was a shock. You weren't expecting it."

She met his gaze. Suddenly he seemed so strong. So solid. She wrapped her arms around his waist and buried her face in his shoulder. He rubbed her back lightly.

"Should we go back?" she asked, her voice thin. "Maybe we could help her."

He exhaled. "You can't help all of them."

"But it was only one. And her mother."

His hand sat still on her back. "You know it's more than just one."

Kitty closed her eyes, but she could still see the girl's knotty shoulders.

How old must she have been? Five, perhaps six. What would Kitty have been doing at that age, around this time of year? A little over a week until Christmas. She would have been trudging through wet snow with her father, her hands warm in a fur muff. Papa always took her to see Santa, so she could register her gift requests. She tried to recall what she might have asked for, but her eyes stung with tears as she recognized that she would certainly have been asking for far more than a handful of coins. She sucked in a deep breath and stepped out of Max's grip.

"Thank goodness New York isn't like that," she said.

His brow furrowed. "Some parts of it are."

"I've been all over New York, and I've never seen anything like that."

He hesitated, and she regretted her words. Her head ached, and all she wanted was for Max to hold her again.

"I'm sorry the evening took this turn. I really meant to show you a good time," he said. "Do you still want to come out tomorrow?"

Without thinking, she placed a hand on his jaw and kissed him. His lips were warm, despite the cool of the ocean air brushing lightly on her skin. Max wrapped his arms around Kitty's waist and pulled her so close that she could feel his heart beating through the fabric of their shirts. When she pulled away, she was dazed from the whirl of emotions.

"Tomorrow night," she whispered into his ear, "I want to talk about poetry." Her heels clicked on the sidewalk as she left him. "Good night, Max."

He exhaled hard. "Good night, Kitty."

As she lay on her bed, gazing out of the window at the starry Havana sky, she struggled to slow the tumult in her mind. The girl's face would appear, and then Kitty would see Max's hand offering coins. She'd feel the warmth and steadiness of his embrace, as if he were beside her again. The comfort his arms provided raised questions she wasn't yet ready to answer.

Kitty knew what romance felt like. Romance was the temporary pleasure of roses that would be in the waste bin three days later. Fun to enjoy, easy to cast aside. This new feeling spread roots in her mind, growing and strengthening. She reminded herself that soon enough a thousand miles would separate them, and she could go back to the business of her life. The most important thing would be ensuring that she could let go of him when the time came. But as she fell asleep with the memory of him stroking her back, she wondered if letting him go was still something she wanted to do.

❋ TWENTY ❋

On their second day in Cuba, Andre called up to Kitty's room to offer to take her and Hen to a street market. Kitty accepted, certain Hen would be happy to spend the day somewhere other than the pool.

"Oh, and did you ladies bring nice evening wear?" he asked.

"Of course we did."

"What would you think of going to a casino opening? There's a new one going in not too far from the Tropicana. They're having a real high-society shindig tomorrow night. Might be some celebrities there. What do you say?"

I'd say if it's high society, then they're probably not calling it a shindig. Kitty kept that thought to herself. "We'd love to go. We'll plan on it," she said. At least Andre was finally suggesting more appealing outings than Fancy Pigeon Island.

They met Andre in the lobby and walked out into another balmy day that made it hard for Kitty to believe it was December. Andre stopped in his tracks and pointed at Kitty's feet.

"Look at you, wearing Keds. I wouldn't have guessed you'd own a pair of shoes without high heels."

"If they're good enough for Marilyn, they're good enough for me." She spotted Hen's smirk out of the corner of her eye. "Besides, this is a walking tour, isn't it? Didn't want to turn my ankle on the cobblestones. Let's go."

As they walked down the streets, Kitty glanced into every doorway, hoping each would be empty. She jumped at a cat running out of one but soon realized most were unoccupied. In the market, children rushed past them, but they were kicking soccer balls, their round cheeks gleaming with exertion. Kitty could almost doubt that she'd even seen the poor girl from the night before. Even though she knew she had, she relaxed, feeling more certain with each step that she wouldn't have a similar encounter here. *Just one unfortunate girl*, she thought.

They passed carts loaded with unrecognizable fruits and vegetables, some spiny and brightly colored, some still caked with earth. In between carts, men played dominoes on rickety folding tables and women gossiped on stoops. Artisans called to Kitty and Hen, enticing them to get a better view of their array of carved wooden figurines. One man delighted the girls by making two of his statuettes dance together by manipulating their movable joints. Hen refused to walk too close to a whole pig turning on a spit near one café.

"His eyes." She shuddered. "He still had his eyes."

Kitty wanted a few souvenirs for her father, and Andre pointed out after her first purchase that most vendors expected customers to negotiate the price. Though some of the vendors spoke very little English, she found that she was adept at making her meaning clear with a few well-timed facial expressions.

"I'm going to have to try that at Macy's," she said, counting out centavos into the hand of an especially frustrated vendor. "This is the most fun I've had yet."

"We'd better get Kitty out of here," Hen said to Andre. "She'll buy the whole market just so she can haggle."

The warm sun spurred Kitty's final purchase, a vivid green drink called *guarapo*. As much as she liked sweet drinks, she couldn't finish it. She offered a taste to Hen.

"Ooh, that is sweet," Hen said, declining a second sip.

"Maybe it needs a little vodka," Kitty said.

After the market, they returned to the hotel to shower and dress for their casino tour. Andre had gotten recommendations in his meeting the night before, so they could avoid the less reputable places. They met downstairs to eat dinner in the hotel, and then they were off for a full evening.

Kitty quickly realized at the first venue that casinos were not her preferred entertainment. Gambling required insufficient strategy for her taste, so she watched Hen and Andre place a few bets but did not participate. As they moved from place to place, her thoughts increasingly strayed to Max. She couldn't find a clock anywhere she went, so she relied on sneaking looks at the Rolexes and Heuers on the wrists nearest her. The luxury casinos drew in an elegant crowd, sporting diamonds and silk, but they became a blur of flashing lights and cigar smoke that had to be endured before she could see Max.

At last, Hen announced that she was tired, and the three took a taxi back to the Nacional. Once she was certain Hen was settled in her room, Kitty raced back downstairs. Max was waiting as expected in view of the entrance. She couldn't help running to him and kissing him, inhaling the cedar scent of his pomade.

"That's quite a greeting," he said, pulling away but not letting go of her waist.

"Why, thank you," she said. "I like to think that's one of my talents."

"You go around greeting every guy like that?"

"Only the bad influences." She stepped away. "Where are we going tonight?"

"I thought you might want to go to see some rumba dancing."

"Sounds great."

He led her to the left, turning down a side street. "I'm treating tonight."

"Whatever you say, high roller." She took his hand, and his shoulders relaxed.

The club wasn't nearly as full as the bar from the previous night, and Max steered Kitty to a table in the corner that still had a view of the tiny concrete stage. Though the couple dancing didn't have the flashy costumes that the Tropicana's performers did, they made up for it with the sheer energy of their routine. Their limbs glistened as they swayed and swung around the stage, almost making Kitty dizzy as she tried to follow them with her gaze. After several songs, they took a break, and Max ordered another round of drinks.

"So? Are you ever going to tell me about that poem of yours, or not?" She flicked ash off her cigarette. "I've been waiting to hear about that thing since New York."

He lifted his chin. "You mean to tell me you haven't already looked it up and figured it all out yourself? That's what I would have guessed."

"Come on, what's it about?"

Max paused, more serious now. "That's hard to say. It's complicated. And long, so it's really about a lot of things." He sucked in a breath. "Part of it is this guy, and he's walking around Little Gidding— near the church. And he runs into this other guy, who seems to be all these different poets from the past."

"That is complicated."

"It's mostly about history. How we live with history, why it's important. That sort of thing." He set down his drink and pulled the same shabby journal from his pocket that he'd had in the penthouse in New York, opening to a page filled with blocky handwriting.

"I like this part." He pointed to a section that had been underlined in red pencil.

Kitty leaned over to read:

> We shall not cease from exploration
> And the end of all our exploring
> Will be to arrive where we started
> And know the place for the first time.

He tapped the page with a finger. "That's why I was telling you I want to explore, to see the world. That's why I said New York isn't enough. Miami isn't enough. Not for me."

"There's plenty to see in New York. And plenty of poems that tell you about it."

"But if you don't go anywhere else, you're not truly seeing New York at all. Come on, haven't you learned something new from being in Havana?"

"I've learned that I like *tostones.*" Her confident tone faltered. As soon as the words were out of her mouth, she wished she could pull them back in. Max watched her for a moment, then rubbed his jaw. He must have sensed the off note too.

"A girl as sharp as you, I'm sure you can get the count up to two things before you leave," he said.

Her heart sank. The dancers reappeared to begin their next set before Kitty could answer, and she and Max sat together in silence watching the show. At the end of the set, he offered to walk her back to the hotel. She agreed, not knowing what else to say.

They walked through the streets to the Malecón, Kitty a step or two ahead. At that hour, only couples lingered, embracing along the wall's edge. Kitty kept her eyes trained on the lights of the Nacional, desperate for something to say that would break the tension.

She felt a cool spray on her arm from a wave crashing over the wall. She didn't even bother to brush it off, but Max yelped beside her. Grateful for the opportunity, she turned to tease him for being afraid of a little water. Instead, she gaped when she saw that the wave that had sprinkled her had drenched him. They stood wordless, staring at each other. Kitty thought he might get angry, but instead, he leaned his head back. Beating his chest, he let out a Johnny Weissmuller Tarzan yell. She burst out laughing.

"Oh, is this funny?" Max said, with an exaggerated gesture at his soaked shirt.

"Yes. Yes, it is." She made a great show of wiping the droplets off her arm.

"Would it be as funny if you were the one who got soaked?" His eyes gleamed.

"Oh. No, no. Max, don't you dare." She started to run in the direction of the hotel, but he blocked her path and pulled her into his arms. The seawater from his shirt saturated her dress. But, in that precise moment, she didn't care that he was getting her dress wet. She didn't care that his now-dripping fringe was unfashionable. She didn't even care that he might have changed everything. All she cared about was that he had his arms around her, and she was laughing. The feeling was similar to the one she'd had when the plane had taken off from New York. Her stomach dipped, and the world shifted.

"I'm sorry about . . ." She pressed her lips together. The words wouldn't come. She couldn't think of any way to explain what she was apologizing for that would make sense.

"Look," he said, "I like you. You know?"

Kitty smiled. Easy enough. "I like you, too."

"We don't have to be serious all the time. I shouldn't have reacted like that."

She looked out at the ocean. "I hate that I have to leave soon. Miami, I mean."

"We still have time."

"But I'll miss you."

He placed a hand on her jaw. "I could go to New York, you know. They need musicians."

"There's always music in New York," she agreed.

He kissed her deeply, until another light spray of water hit them. "We'd better move," he said.

"What's the matter? I don't think you can get any wetter," she said.

He walked with her to the hotel entrance but held her hand tight, as if reluctant to let go. "You sure you need sleep?" he asked.

"I'm sure you need to change out of those wet clothes," she said.

"See you tomorrow?"

"We're going to a casino opening with Andre," she said. "I don't know how late he'll want to stay."

Max's face fell. "Ah."

"You don't have a jacket and tie with you, do you? He could prob-ably get invitations for you and Sebastian, too."

"No, we didn't bring anything like that. I don't know if I even own a jacket nice enough for one of those things."

"Why don't you bring Sebastian to meet us at about midnight? I'm not crazy about casinos, as it turns out. It would be a good excuse to put a time limit on it."

"Perfect. I know Sebastian had one more club he wanted to take you all to."

"I'll talk to Andre."

At last, he let go of her hand and they parted. She went up to her room, not caring if she ever slept again. In her distraction, she closed the door a little harder than she meant to.

She had only made it halfway across the room when she heard the knock.

❋ TWENTY-ONE ❋

Kitty cracked the hotel door. On the other side, Hen stood bleary-eyed, with her hair in rollers. Cursing herself for not changing out of her dress first, Kitty opened the door wider.

"Good morning, beautiful," she said. "Need to borrow a cup of sugar?"

Hen frowned. "Where have you been? Why were you out so late?"

Kitty sighed and waved Hen in. Once they were both seated on the edge of the bed, Kitty said, "I was out exploring."

"By yourself?" Hen's eyes were clear now. "That is so dangerous, I can't believe—"

"No. Not by myself." Kitty traced the pattern on the bedspread. "With Max."

Hen gasped. "Is this the first time?"

"We were out last night, too." Kitty braced herself for an avalanche of disapproval. Surely Hen would have plenty to say. But Hen grinned.

"I think that's wonderful," Hen said.

"Let's not make a big thing of it—"

Hen held up a hand. "He's obviously not an acceptable choice for anything serious. That's not what I'm saying. But you know, I think this is the first time I've seen you go out with someone purely for fun. It's nice. I think you should enjoy it."

"I would've thought you'd be more worried about me running around with . . . someone like him, serious or not."

"It's not ideal, of course." Hen paused. "I don't know. Max is different, isn't he? I mean, he's not like what you hear about them. Knowing him . . . it's not as much of a problem. I'm starting to think—" She caught herself. "Never mind. It's late, and I'm just glad you're safe. I'm going back to bed."

After Hen left, Kitty crawled into bed. In the darkness, the faces of boys she'd been interested in over the years went through her mind. There was Phil, whom she let go when he gave up on aspirations of being a banker in favor of becoming a professor. No professor could launch Kitty into the world she meant to be a part of. At least he had the right pedigree, unlike Stephen. Stephen had seemed like such a good choice: handsome, debonair, sophisticated. Turned out his grandfather was nothing better than a first-generation immigrant, an Irish cop in the Bronx. The grandson of an Irish cop would never get an invitation to join the polo club, no matter how nicely he dressed. As she went back further in her history, she realized that she'd never, not even in her most romantic moments, chosen a boy simply because she liked him. What was more, she couldn't recall anything about their hopes or passions. Phil became a professor, but of what? What kind of music had Stephen liked? What she remembered of them was more like a dossier than the memory of a boyfriend she'd once cared for. She'd always chosen a guy because of how he might elevate her status, not how he made her feel. And she never thought about them much when they weren't around.

Max, on the other hand, was always on her mind. She could picture the subtle changes on his face when he played a song he really liked, the way he leaned back to let the music flow. The thought of his laugh was enough to make her smile. As the echo of it rang in her ears, she heard an insistent voice. Not some prophetic voice from on high. This voice was her own.

This is it, it whispered. *This is the guy for you.*

Her last thought before she drifted off to sleep was how glad she was that her own voice was the one she could most easily ignore.

The next morning, Hen woke Kitty a little earlier than she would have preferred. "Why don't we go exploring?" Hen said.

The image of the beggar girl flashed in Kitty's mind. "I don't know if we should go on our own, without Andre. Let's get a cabana at the pool."

"There's a pool at the Imperium." Hen sat on the bed. "Don't you want to see as much as you can while we're here?"

Kitty scrambled for a counterpoint. "We don't speak Spanish. What if we get lost?"

"Hmm. Good point."

"We're going out tonight. Let's just relax this afternoon." Kitty picked up a stack of magazines from the bedside table. "We need to talk about the fashion show anyway. It's only a couple of days after we get back to Miami."

After they changed into bathing suits, they made their way down to the pool. They took their place at the rented cabana, flipping through magazines and munching on sandwiches delivered by the concierge staff. Kitty pointed out dress and skirt styles she wanted to look for at the fashion show. When the sun began to sink, Hen suggested that they go back to get ready for their big night out. Sebastian called as Kitty was pinning her hair, and she gave him the casino's address so he and Max could meet them.

A few hours later, the elevator doors opened and Kitty and Hen stepped out into the hotel lobby. Heads around them turned as they strode toward where Andre stood, checking his watch.

"I hope we're not late," Kitty teased.

He looked up and his eyes widened. Kitty had helped Hen dress up a long, ivory gown with a pink silk scarf draped around her neck and trailing down her back. For herself, Kitty had chosen a sleeveless black dress with a lacy bodice and a long, snug skirt. Both girls sported sparkling earrings that caught the soft yellow light in the lobby.

"No, no," Andre said. "Wow, you two look gorgeous."

Hen bit her lip. "You think so?"

"Couldn't be prouder to have you on my arm." He offered each girl an elbow. "Let's go."

Andre ushered them out to the waiting car. The trip was a quick one, and before they were too far from the hotel they saw spotlights sweeping the sky, announcing their destination. They pulled up to a beautiful older building that had clearly been freshened up with new paint and a burgundy awning.

"It looks like a Hollywood premiere," Hen whispered to Kitty. "A red carpet and everything."

The trio strolled down the carpet to the entrance, where a man in a tuxedo shook Andre's hand. "Mr. Polzer, so glad you could make it. Welcome to the Diamant. And please, tell Mr. Tessler I'd love to buy him dinner when I'm in New York."

"Sure, of course." Andre led Hen and Kitty into the building, then leaned in to them confidentially. "Mr. Tessler wouldn't do business with that man in a million years. He's probably in Meyer Lansky's pocket. Most of these guys work for the mob. But we can enjoy his hospitality, can't we?"

Kitty cast a glance over her shoulder. The pudgy man with the thick Bowery accent was already greeting his next guests. "Maybe your mother was right," she whispered to Hen. "Maybe it *is* nothing but mobsters."

They passed the coat check and headed for the gaming room. The cavernous space had a domed ceiling painted midnight blue, with shimmering gold stars. Tables featured the usual games—chemin de fer, roulette, and chuck-a-luck—with bleach-blond bombshells and men counting bills off rolls of cash surrounding each one. Waiters passed carrying trays of drinks. Kitty accepted one and noted that the swizzle stick bore the name of the new casino emblazoned on a plastic diamond.

Once again, Kitty quickly tired of the gaming. She amused herself by guessing which blonde would be the first to pop out of her strapless gown by leaping with joy at a win. When that didn't happen, she strolled around the room with Hen, trying to discern fake jewels from the real thing.

"What time do you think it is?" Hen finally asked. "Aren't Max and Sebastian meeting us here?"

Kitty snuck a peek at the wristwatch of a man nearby. "It's nearly midnight. Let's get Andre."

They located Andre at a roulette table, and he agreed that they could go. He said good-bye to the man who had greeted them, and they went out into the cool night air. Cars were still arriving with guests for the opening, even as others milled outside the front doors, waiting for their drivers.

"Perfect timing," Hen said, pointing to where Max and Sebastian stood on the other side of the street. Kitty waved, and the boys waved back. She started to cross, but a car roared up the road toward her. Andre gripped her arm and pulled both Kitty and Hen out of the way.

The car screeched to a stop in front of the entrance, nearly ramming into a limo letting out guests. A few people leapt out, screaming in Spanish. One of them fired a gun into the Diamant's neon sign, causing it to go dark. The casino guests who'd been at the entrance cried out and ran for cover.

Kitty wanted to run, but her feet froze to the sidewalk. Andre dragged her into the shadows, where Hen cowered against the building. He stood in front of the two of them, blocking Kitty's view. She searched across the street for Max and Sebastian but could no longer see them. Her heart pounded. Where were they?

The person who'd fired the gun continued to yell, gesturing violently at the casino. A shock went through Kitty as she realized it was a woman. Not just any woman, but the woman she'd seen serving at the Tropicana. The one with the pale green eyes. Sebastian's friend. Kitty only recognized one word out of what the woman was saying: *mafia*. Sirens in the distance finally silenced the woman, and she rushed back into the car with her compatriots. As they drove off, someone in the backseat threw out a stack of pamphlets, which fluttered in their wake.

Everyone who remained on the sidewalk stood quiet for a moment. A woman wailed, breaking the spell. Kitty took a shaky step forward, picking up one of the pamphlets. It was plain white, with large words in red capital letters on the front. LA HISTORIA ME ABSOLVERA. DR. FIDEL CASTRO. Before Kitty could open it, a hand tore it from her grip.

"Put that down." Sebastian tossed the pamphlet to the ground. "You can get arrested for having that. Come on." He offered Kitty a hand. Max stood behind him, his face ashen.

"What the hell is going on?" Andre said. "They're firing guns. I don't want Hen and Kitty out here."

"My car is around the corner," Sebastian said. "I will drive you back to the hotel. And then I need a drink."

Kitty grabbed Hen's hand and they followed Sebastian to his car. The five of them climbed in without a word. Hen's shoulders shook, and Kitty placed an arm around her.

"What was that?" Andre asked.

Sebastian's knuckles were white on the steering wheel. "People are unhappy."

"Hell, I get unhappy sometimes too. I don't go around shooting up casinos."

"There is a lot of trouble here. The casinos and hotels have money, the government has money, but the people are starving."

Andre sighed. "Oh. President Batista."

Sebastian flinched. "I wouldn't blame him for that outside this car.

Unless you want real trouble from the police. Seems like someone's always listening these days."

Kitty didn't dare mention the woman from the Tropicana. She wondered if Sebastian had even seen her in all the confusion. He turned to pull the car into the Nacional's roundabout, but Andre waved a hand.

"Park. Come inside. I'll buy you a drink," he said.

All Kitty wanted to do was hide in her room, but at least she felt safer inside the hotel. She and the others crowded around a table in the narrow bar area. Max caught Kitty's eye and mouthed, *You okay?* She couldn't think of anything to do but nod.

They sipped their drinks for a while in silence. Sebastian was the first to speak.

"She never would have shot at a person," he said.

Kitty lifted her head. So he had seen the woman. But Hen didn't seem to catch on. Of course, she had no idea the woman was Sebastian's friend.

"Horrible, just horrible. I'm glad we're leaving in the morning," she said.

"It's not always like that." Sebastian picked at the label on his beer. "It's a beautiful country, with wonderful people. I hope that you saw that while you were here. They only wanted to make a—a . . ."

". . . statement," Max finished.

"Yes, a statement. They don't like the mafia." He lowered his voice to a hush. "The government takes advantage of its people. The money goes into the pockets of American criminals and our president. Now there is a group prepared to change things, but change is not always pretty. Those who have tried to help are arrested, while criminals walk our streets freely. Now they feel they must do more. You understand that? This is our home."

Hen's lips pinched together in regret. "Of course I do. I'm sorry. I think I'm just overwhelmed." She stood. "I ought to get some rest."

Andre stood beside her. "Would you like me to walk you up?"

"Yes, thank you. Kitty, are you coming?"

"I'm going to finish my drink. I can make it up by myself, don't worry about me."

Hen glanced from Kitty to Max, then said her good nights and left.

Kitty spoke quietly. "She was your friend, wasn't she? The woman with the gun?"

Sebastian did not take his eyes off his beer. "She is my friend."

"I understand loyalty, but come on." Kitty shuddered. "What she did, that was dangerous. Someone could have been hurt."

Now he looked up, as Max shifted in his seat. "And you think someone could do that if they were not desperate?" Sebastian said. "She is a good person. And there are bad things happening." He took a breath, as if to steady himself. His voice was calmer when he continued. "I know you don't understand. It's different for people like you."

"What does that mean? Aren't we all people?"

He thought for a moment. "When we go to the Tropicana, who am I?"

"I don't understand what you mean."

"Am I your friend, or am I at work?"

Kitty stiffened, intensely aware of Max's presence. "We are friends. I want to be."

"Okay. Here we are friends. And what about in Miami?"

She clamped her lips together. He was right. In Cuba, where races mixed more freely, they could be friends. Sebastian could sit at the table at the Tropicana or drink at the hotel bar with Kitty, and no one would bat an eye. In Miami, even in New York, his place was on the payroll. She thought again about what Max had said about the hotels. About how they treated people like him. About Louis Armstrong.

"In Miami, too. In New York. Everywhere." Kitty knew the words were a promise, but she wasn't sure it was a promise she could keep. Under the table, she felt Max's fingers slide over hers.

They finished their drinks in weary silence. Max and Sebastian walked Kitty to the elevator and said their good-byes. As she waited for the elevator, she couldn't help but picture the girl's face twisting in anger as she fired her gun. What could possibly connect someone like Sebastian to someone like that? How could Sebastian defend her? Kitty had to at least ask. She ran back through the lobby.

Sebastian and Max were still close enough to the entrance to hear her calling out. They started back toward her.

"Sebastian," she said. "Can I ask you something? Privately?"

He turned to Max, who nodded and took a few steps to the car. Kitty laid a hand on Sebastian's arm and spoke in a low voice.

"I have to know. How did you get mixed up with a girl like that? I'm sorry, I know it's personal, but . . . I want to understand."

His shoulders sagged. "Her name is Alma. We were neighbors, classmates. She is a smart girl, and we talked about everything together. We both saw what was happening to our country, but we saw the solution through different eyes. She wanted to stay and fight. I—I had to go." His face flushed. "I was a singer. What could I do? I wanted more than the fishing boats and cane fields. I want better for Cuba, yes, but my family comes first. I knew I could make money in Miami that would help them now. She was angry with me for leaving."

"And she joined the revolutionaries?" Kitty kept her voice low, mindful of Sebastian's earlier nervousness.

"Not until her brother disappeared last summer. He helped attack an army base. No one knows how many died and how many were captured." Sebastian winced. "I want to be at home, with my family. But I see that something bad is coming. I don't know if things will really be better, even if the side Alma has chosen wins. I still hope to bring my mother to Miami one day. Give her a better life. But it means I have to be far from home now."

"I can't imagine how hard that must be," Kitty said.

"Alma believes that I am a coward because I do not fight for all Cubans. She doesn't want to talk to me. It was hard to lose her, but I had to leave."

Kitty tried to envision leaving New York for good. Leaving her father and Hen and the life she knew behind. "I think you made a brave choice, even though it wasn't the same choice Alma made."

He blinked back tears as he stared out at the Malecón. "I only hope it was the right one. Good night, Kitty."

As he walked toward the car, she considered how grateful she was that she would soon return to a place where life was far less complicated. If such a place existed anymore.

TWENTY-TWO

MIAMI, FLORIDA

DECEMBER 1953

Kitty had only been back in Miami for a couple of hours when she got the feeling she had left something in Cuba. Loco bounded around her feet as Kitty dug through her purse, relieved to find her passport and favorite lipstick. Her sunglasses had been on the coffee table in the living room, where she'd dropped them as soon as she'd arrived in the suite at the Imperium. She rifled through her suitcase even though she wasn't entirely sure what she thought might be lost. The knot in her chest unraveled as she recognized she hadn't left anything behind. She was simply missing Max.

She had a little laugh at her own expense. After all, she'd seen him the night before. Not that their parting had been ideal. The tension from the events at the casino and the conversation after had left everyone weary. Hen had recovered well once the plane landed, but Kitty had more trouble shaking her discomfort about their trip.

The phone rang, a happy distraction from her qualms. She sat on the bed, still clutching the last shoe she'd pulled from her suitcase. "Hello?"

"Hello, Kitty," her father said. "How was the trip?"

She forced sunshine into her voice. "Oh, Papa, it was wonderful. Havana is so beautiful and lively. How are you?"

"I'm fine, just fine." His voice sounded muffled and slow. She frowned. "Are you all right?"

"Of course. I caught a catnap. Had a late night last night at the club covering closing. We had a couple of bigwig guests, and they didn't want the party to end."

Kitty glanced at the clock. Six in the evening. Not an unusual time for him to drift off in his chair, listening to the news on the radio on his dinner break. "Don't you have anyone else who can do that for you? I don't want you working too hard."

Her father chuckled. "You just tell Andre I'll be glad when he's back and can cover closing for me."

"I'll do that." She tugged on the phone cord. "Have you made any progress on getting down here for Christmas? It's only a few days away."

He cleared his throat. "That's not going to work out. I'm sorry I won't see you, but we'll be together soon."

She drooped. "Oh."

"I have a lot more to do without Andre around. I'm going to be too busy to leave."

"I understand," she said.

"I'll take you out to a nice restaurant when you get back, all right? Just the two of us." Her father's eager tone meant he didn't want to end the call until she perked up. Kitty forced brightness into her voice once more.

"That sounds swell. You take care. No more late nights, if you can help it."

"If I can help it. Love you," he said.

"Love you, too." She hung up the phone, feeling awful. She knew Andre would have taken the Miami trip whether she went or not, but she couldn't shake the guilt over her father having to manage everything on his own. And she wasn't even there to cheer him up with Christmas celebrations.

The phone rang again, and she picked it up quickly. Maybe her father had had a change of heart about traveling after talking to her.

"Hello." It wasn't her father but Charles, and he sounded relieved to have gotten her instead of Hen. "How was the trip?"

"Havana was swell. You ought to go some time. You'd love the casinos."

He paused, and his voice was taut when he spoke again. "Kitty, I'm afraid I really mucked it up with Hen. I'm sure she told you our last conversation was unpleasant."

"What are you talking about?" Kitty's heart raced. Of course Charles would pick this exact time to develop a conscience.

"I had gotten the impression that Hen was—well, having more fun in Miami than she should have. But that's ridiculous, that's not our Hen. I spoke harshly to her, and now she hasn't called. Could you convince her to call me? Tell her I want to apologize."

Kitty gripped the shoe. She had to get things back on track. She should say something that would enrage him again. Some wild story about their time in Havana. That would do it. She finally said, "Sure. I'll tell her to call."

"Tell her how sorry I am. I know only you can convince her."

"I will." She laid the receiver in the cradle and stared at it awhile. She could have taken full advantage of that moment, and she hadn't. Surely hastening Charles's breakup with Hen would be a good thing. Only it would mean that the first part of the plan would be complete, and she would have to take steps toward the second part. The part where she stood at his side, not Hen. The mental image, which once looked like victory, now made her sick.

Since Andre had to get right back to work on their return, Kitty and Hen went on their own to dinner. They didn't want to go too far without someone to escort them, so they chose a barbecue restaurant called Embers that was in easy walking distance.

"I have to say," Hen said as they strolled, "I wouldn't have thought you'd agree to a barbecue place."

"Well, Max says travel changes the way people think. Maybe I'm expanding my horizons."

"All the way to barbecue. That's quite an expansion."

Kitty fanned herself. "I can't believe it's still so hot here. It makes all these Christmas decorations look so strange." She waved her hand to indicate the tinsel and garland looped around the street signs.

"And I suppose when we get back to New York, all the decorations will be taken down." Hen paused. "I know I've been complaining about the heat, but I don't know if I'm ready to go back to the snow, to tell you the truth."

Kitty glanced at her out of the corner of her eye. She waited until they were settled at a table in the restaurant before addressing the comment.

"Hen, I don't know if it's the snow you're really dreading," she said in a firm tone.

Hen sighed and set her menu down. "You may be right about that."

"Are you going to call him?" Kitty asked.

"I suppose I should. Maybe he's calmed down. Except . . ." Hen toyed with the straw in her drink. "Except I don't know if I care anymore. I don't know if I want to talk to him, even if he is sorry."

Kitty fought to hide the excitement that was bubbling up inside. "What are you thinking?"

"Well, there's always Mother to contend with. And, after all he's done, a few shouting matches on the phone seems like a silly thing to end it over." She shook her head. "I knew, Kitty. Before what happened with Bebe. Of course I knew. Every time I'd hear he went out with someone, I had to pretend." Hen dropped the straw and met Kitty's gaze. "But it's not just the shouting phone calls. I know that, too. It's that, after everything he did, he didn't trust *me*. He didn't respect me.

And now . . ." She bit her lip and looked down at her lap. "Well, let's just say I have a different perspective."

"You're absolutely right, Hen. And you know—"

Hen jerked her head up. "I'm not saying I'm definitely ending it. It's Mother I'm really worried about. She'll put me out on the street. She'll be on the phone with her lawyer making sure I'm cut out of any and every will I might be mentioned in. And that's just for starters."

"You don't know that she'll do any of that. You've never stood up to her before." Kitty nearly pointed out everything that Bebe had gotten away with over the years in spite of Mrs. Bancroft's bluster but sensed that wouldn't help matters. Instead, she grabbed Hen's hand. "And if she does throw you out, you'll come live with Papa and me. We'll find you a better fiancé, someone who actually deserves you."

"That's very sweet." Hen smiled ruefully. "I can't risk losing my family, but I don't want to be with someone who makes me this unhappy. I need to think. And I'm glad we have more time here, so that I can do that."

The waiter delivered their cocktails, and Kitty raised hers high in a mock toast. "Take all the time you need," she said. Even if Charles's anger had cooled off, it now seemed Hen was the one on the cusp of ending their relationship. And whoever needed the push over the edge, Kitty was prepared to do the shoving, especially if it meant Kitty could get Hen to the right place by counseling bravery instead of lying behind her back.

❖ TWENTY-THREE ❖

To pay back the guys who had filled in for them in Havana, Max and Sebastian had to play on the nights they usually had off. On Monday, Kitty gave a little wave with her purse when she and Hen were leaving the club, hoping Max would remember their signal to meet. He nodded and winked.

As the band played, she and Hen debated which version of "Harbor Lights" they liked better. Kitty noticed Max's eyes widen at something behind her. She leaned out of the booth to look and saw two people plowing through the crowd toward her. One was a short, stout woman with a small white hat perched atop black ringlets. The other was a slim man with a graying beard, whose resemblance to Max left no doubt as to their familial connection. The two stopped in front of the booth.

"Are you Kitty Tessler? We asked the maître d', but it was hard to tell who he was pointing to," the woman said.

"I am," she said, a bit hesitant.

The woman beamed. "I'm Gail Zillman. This is my husband, Ben." She gestured to the man, who offered a wave. "We're Max's aunt and uncle."

Kitty stepped out of the booth. "It's so nice to meet you! This is my friend, Henrietta Bancroft."

"Everyone calls me Hen," Hen said, shaking Ben's hand, then Gail's.

Gail turned to the stage. "I'm so excited that Max is playing tonight. It's so hard for us to come see him any other night, because of Ben's work schedule."

"Why don't you sit with us?" Kitty said. She glanced up to the stage to find that Max's whole face was now broadcasting panic. She frowned at him. *Does he think I can't make a good impression or something?* she thought, sliding into the booth once the others had taken their seats.

"And how wonderful that we get to meet you," Gail continued. "Max didn't say much about you, only that you'd been spending time together, but it was written all over his face." She punctuated this statement with a knowing raise of her eyebrow.

Ben nudged his wife. "He has a type, doesn't he?"

She poked him back. "Stop it, you'll have her thinking he's got girlfriends all over the city." Gail turned to Kitty. "He doesn't, really. There was one girl—blond and pretty, like you—but she broke his heart. I warned him she was no good. Didn't I warn him, Ben? He never listens to me. But you're nothing like her, I can tell. She didn't have your manners."

"Oh. Thank you, Mrs. Zillman," Kitty said, not sure what else to say. She was beginning to suspect that she wasn't the one Max was worried about.

"Please, call me Gail. So Max tells us your father owns this hotel?" Gail asked.

"That's right."

"And one in New York?" Ben said.

"Two, actually."

"That's fantastic. He must be some businessman," Gail said. "Did he always work in hospitality?"

Kitty couldn't fight a smile as she thought of her early conversations with Max. It seemed the third degree was a family tradition. "My grandfather was a tailor who started a clothing store. But Papa had more of a knack for the leisure industry."

The four chatted about New York and the girls' families until Max rushed to the microphone. "We're going to take a quick break, ladies and gentlemen. Back in five." He set down his trumpet and headed for the booth. Gail and Ben jumped to their feet.

"You sound wonderful. So talented," Gail said, hugging him.

"Thanks, Aunt Gail. How's everything going over here?" he asked.

"Swell," Kitty said. "It's so nice to meet your family, Max."

He laughed nervously. "I wish I could sit with you guys."

Ben patted him on the back. "But we came to hear you play. Kitty's doing a great job hosting us."

"Is that a fact?" Max said.

"They're in good hands," Kitty said.

With slight reluctance, Max rejoined the band. Kitty caught the waiter's eye and encouraged Ben and Gail to order something. "On the house," she said.

"I insist on paying," Ben said, reaching for his wallet.

"If you sit at my table, your drinks are my treat," she said.

"That's very kind," Gail said. The two only ordered ginger ales but looked pleased nonetheless.

The four sat back to enjoy the set, occasionally commenting on the song or style. As the Zillionaires signed off, Gail spoke to Kitty under her breath once more. "I hope we didn't say too much, talking about that other girl."

"It didn't bother me, I promise," Kitty said, hoping it sounded true.

She laid a hand on Kitty's. "Just be kind to him. That's all I ask. He's been hurt before, you know?"

"Of course," Kitty said. They went to say their good-byes to Max, and Hen and Kitty left so the family could have a few moments together.

"They sure were sweet," Hen said, as they entered the elevator. "What did Gail say to you before we left?"

"Oh . . . she thanked me again for the drinks. Nice people," Kitty said, not willing to share Max's troubles. It certainly did explain why he'd been so intent on testing her in their early conversations.

She returned downstairs about an hour after closing time with Loco and checked the patio on the side of the hotel. Empty. She decided to wait, hoping the arrival of Max's aunt and uncle hadn't caused him to forget the signal to meet.

It quickly became apparent why the patio was less popular at night. The only light came from the silvery moon and the reflection of a lonely streetlight off the office window. Kitty could barely see Loco sniffing around at the shrubs. She supposed she hadn't noticed last time because her meeting with Max was so quick. Now that she was waiting, her eyes strained in the dark. She had almost given up when a service door opened on the other side of the bank of trees.

"Kitty?" Max stepped between the trees.

"I'm here." She stood, and he wrapped his arms around her waist.

"Sorry it took me a while," he said. "I thought Aunt Gail would never leave."

"It's all right." She kissed him lightly on the lips. "It was nice to meet them."

"They didn't go on and on, did they?"

"They were lovely. And how interesting to know you've been telling your family about me."

He rubbed his cheek. "Only a little."

"Mmm-hmm. So, are you settling back in okay after the trip?"

"Playing Mondays is hard. Now I remember why I hate it. The crowd is so dead." He brushed his lips on her neck. "You smell nice."

She closed her eyes and smiled. "I can't stay too much longer. I told Hen I'm walking the dog." Even though Hen knew about the time Kitty and Max had spent together in Havana, Kitty had preferred to pretend their evening excursions wouldn't continue back in Miami. She didn't want another admonishment from Hen reminding her to let him down easily.

He leaned back. "You don't have much longer here, do you?"

Her smile suddenly felt too tight. "Another two weeks."

"When do you go back, exactly?"

Kitty let go of him and snapped her fingers to get Loco's attention. "On the fourth."

He took a step toward her. "I'm sorry. I didn't know it was a sore subject."

"It's not. I'll be glad to see Papa again." She knelt and fussed with the dog's leash. "And you'll call, won't you? When you can."

"Yeah. Yeah, of course." He rubbed the back of his neck. "And there's plenty of time. Maybe we could ring in the New Year together. I'm playing that night, but we could go out after."

She stood, feeling lighter. "I'd like that."

A light flooded the patio. They both startled, and Kitty accidentally jerked Loco's leash. The dog let out a yelp. Kitty looked into the office window, her heart pounding. But she only saw a man emptying the trash into a wheeled container. He never even looked up.

Max clutched his chest. "Phew. Wasn't expecting that. I thought we were caught."

Kitty nearly gasped. She had almost forgotten that getting caught was the entire purpose of the rendezvous spot. The light in the office went out again, and she waited for her eyes to adjust. She thought uncomfortably of Gail's words: *He's been hurt.* She shoved the thought away.

"Are you okay?" he asked.

"Oh. Oh yes. Just scared me, that's all."

He watched her for a moment. "You better go. Don't want Hen sending out a search party."

Kitty nodded. She kissed him again, this time lingering on the feel of his lips. She broke away flushed and wiggled her fingers in a good-bye. As she started through the hedges, Max called her back.

"Are you going to that fashion show thing tomorrow?" he asked.

"Yes. How did you know about that?"

"I think Marcela wants that singer to go. You know, the one I introduced you to at the house party. Daniela."

Kitty couldn't find a nice way to say that Daniela wouldn't be able to afford the kind of clothing that would be on display. Instead, she said, "Oh? Is she interested in fashion?"

"I think it's more of a 'see and be seen' kind of thing for her. Marcela is trying to get her noticed by some hotshot singer who will be there—she used all her connections to wrangle Daniela an invitation. She hopes Daniela could get her start by singing backup. Or at least meet someone important."

Kitty had to admit that Daniela was gorgeous. She would easily get attention, even at an event like that. "Well, I'll keep a lookout for her."

"Yeah, would you? Just . . . if you see her, will you say hi? I think she'd feel more welcome."

"Sure." She nodded. "Hen and I will say hello when we see her."

"Great." He waved. "Have a nice night."

"You too."

The next morning, Kitty rummaged through Hen's clothes to find the right look for the show. "It needs to be charming but effortless," she said, tossing a dove-gray skirt onto the bed.

"'Effortless' sure requires a lot of work," Hen said.

Kitty wagged a finger. "Don't try to pretend like you don't care. I've seen the way you've done yourself up lately. Admit it. I've been a good influence, haven't I?" She handed Hen a blouse and a blue scarf.

Hen blushed. "I'll go change. We don't want to be late."

"You just can't stand to admit it," Kitty said in a singsong, turning her attentions to Hen's jewelry box. There was no response from the bathroom, which Kitty took to be confirmation.

They took the elevator down to the lobby and entered the ballroom several minutes after the announced start time. As Kitty suspected, the show had not yet started, and many of the attendees were already seated. Since she didn't know anyone important in Miami society, she and Hen weren't able to secure chairs in the front row. But they were at least able to glide in past those who had already arrived and make an attempt at a grand entrance.

The folding chairs had been arranged in a semicircle around the short, V-shaped runway. On the right side of the room, screens hid the models and the racks of clothing from view. Kitty scanned the room, hoping to see Daniela. She recalled the girl having striking good looks, but that description fit many women in the audience. Hen elbowed Kitty to get her attention.

"I'm starting to think we're underdressed," Hen said, gesturing to the entrance.

Kitty nearly jumped out of her seat. Daniela strode in, wearing a strapless teal dress with a draped skirt that hit just above the knee. A short train fanned off the back hem, giving the dress a dramatic flair normally unsuitable for the day but ideal for turning heads at a fashion show. Daniela's ink-black hair was swept into a high bun, and a coral necklace and earrings made her pale skin glow.

"She looks familiar," Hen continued.

"We met her at Marcela's, remember? Let's go say hello." Kitty stood, but Hen grabbed her arm.

"At Marcela's? And she's here?" Hen hesitated. "Should she be here?"

"She has an invitation, doesn't she? Look." Kitty pointed at the ivory rectangle poking out of the side of Daniela's clutch. A flicker of uncertainty passed over Daniela's face as she paused to look for an open chair in the back, but the expression was gone so quickly, Kitty thought she might have imagined it.

"Where do you think she got an invitation?" Hen asked.

"The same place we got ours. Come on." Kitty made her way toward Daniela, intent on keeping her promise to Max. She worried Daniela might not remember her, but the concern vanished when the girl's face lit up.

"You're Kitty, right?" Daniela said.

"That's right." Kitty wasn't sure why she'd thought Daniela had an accent. Her English was as unaccented as Kitty's own. "It's so nice to see you."

Daniela looked over Kitty's shoulder. "And that's your friend Hen?"

Hen walked up a bit warily. "Hello. Good to see you again."

Light music came from a speaker in the corner, and a woman fiddled with the microphone stand.

"It looks like they're about to start," Kitty said. "We should probably take our seats."

Daniela smiled. "Yes. But let's talk afterward, all right?"

"We can compare notes," Kitty agreed. "I love your dress, by the way."

"Thank you." Daniela settled into her seat, and Kitty and Hen returned to theirs.

Hen leaned in to Kitty. "Where do you think she got a dress like that?"

"I think she made it. I haven't seen anything like it."

"It is something else." Hen craned her neck to get another view.

The woman adjusting the microphone stopped when someone came up to whisper in her ear. She nodded and disappeared back behind the screen. Kitty checked the front rows. Sure enough, several of those seats were still vacant. She rolled her eyes. Some VIP must be holding up the process. They wouldn't start and risk having someone waltz in and steal attention from the clothes on display.

Whispers swept the crowd as a stunning redhead entered the ballroom, flanked by two friends. Kitty didn't recognize her, but it was clear this was who the Miami set had been waiting for. *She must be the singer Marcela is hoping will notice Daniela*, Kitty concluded. *Miami famous—too bad*. Kitty had been hoping for a real celebrity sighting. And she wasn't sure how the woman was supposed to notice Daniela

when the poor girl was stuck in the back. Maybe that was why Daniela
was hoping to linger a bit after the show.

A sudden commotion at the door stole everyone's attention from the
redhead. The man who had checked Kitty's invitation was blocking the
door as a woman waved a piece of paper at him. Kitty caught a glimpse
of the woman's face when the man moved his shoulder.

"I think that's Marcela," she said.

"Are all of Sebastian's friends coming to this thing?" Hen asked.

"I don't know. It looks like they won't let her in."

Again, Marcela's face popped into view. This time, she spotted
Kitty. She gestured violently. The man pointed at the spot where Kitty
sat, then turned and stomped toward the chairs. Marcela stayed in
place at the door.

As he came nearer, his face relaxed from its grimace. "Ma'am, I'm
sorry to bother you," he said in a low voice to Kitty. "There's a woman
at the door who says she knows you."

"She does. I mean, I do know her." Kitty kept her eyes on the man's
wristwatch. She couldn't look at Marcela.

"She has an invitation, but . . . ma'am, she can't come in here."

"Why not? If she has an invitation, she should be able to come in."

"I don't know where she found that thing. It's real. But she can't
come in here."

Kitty's face burned. People around her were now staring. She
looked the man in the eye. "Why can't she come in?"

He huffed. "You know why. What, is she your maid?"

Select Clientele. Always a view, never a Jew. Marcela might be allowed to clean this room once everyone left, but she was not welcome
to sit beside Kitty. A flare went through Kitty's chest. This heavy-
lidded bully was standing beside her, asking her to tell a woman who
had welcomed Kitty into her home to leave Kitty's hotel. She stood and
marched across the ballroom.

"Hello, Marcela," she said, trying to breathe normally. "How are
you?"

"I'm . . . I'm okay," Marcela said. Her brow wrinkled as she studied Kitty's expression.

"Good. Will you please wait here for me? I need to talk to someone."

Marcela agreed. The man returned to the doorway, ready to escort Marcela out, but Kitty held up a gloved hand.

"You wait too," she said, her tone far icier. He took a step back and nodded. She stormed into the lobby, heading down the hallway toward the offices. Andre's door was open.

"I need your help," she said, not bothering to knock.

He didn't look up from his paperwork. "Kitty, I'm sorry, I'm in the middle of something."

"A guy—I suppose he works here—is trying to kick my friend out." She folded her arms over her chest.

"Who? Hen?"

"A woman we met through Max and Sebastian."

At this, Andre looked up. "Your friend, huh?" He sighed heavily and pushed his chair away from the desk. "Let me see."

He followed her to the ballroom, where Marcela and the man stood waiting in the hall. The door to the ballroom was now closed, and the muffled sounds coming from inside indicated that the show had started. When the man saw Andre, he straightened his tie.

"Hello," Andre said, shaking the man's hand. "I'm Andre Polzer."

The man's face was red. "Steve McLaughlin."

"I'm the manager here. What's going on?"

"I'm sorry, sir, I can't let this woman in," Steve said.

"She has an invitation," Kitty cried. "If she has an invitation, she can come in."

Andre took Kitty's arm and pulled her aside. "This guy doesn't work for me. He works for whoever organized the show. They make the rules about who comes in and who doesn't."

"But it's our hotel."

"I know that. What, was she causing trouble or something?"

"No. She just wanted to come in."

Andre looked from Kitty to Marcela, then back again. He turned to Steve. "Hey, buddy, I know you've got your orders. But this girl's father owns the hotel. If she wants this lady to come in, I gotta make sure that happens." When Steve hesitated, Andre shot him a conciliatory smile. "She won't make a scene. If she does, I'll answer for it. All right?"

Steve thought for a minute, then opened the door to the ballroom. Marcela walked in, head held high, but stayed to the shadows and took a seat in the back.

"Is that all?" Andre asked Kitty.

"Tell me the truth. Is that our hotel's policy, or is it theirs?" she asked.

"It's not policy," Andre said. "It's just Miami."

"And what about New York?"

Andre shook his head. "Don't worry about it, Kitty."

She pinched her lips together, unsure what else to ask or say. She gave him a halting nod, then entered the ballroom herself. Careful not to draw attention, she crept around to her seat beside Hen.

"What in the world was that about?" Hen whispered.

"I'll tell you later." Kitty wasn't even sure she could articulate what had taken place. She knew why Marcela wasn't admitted, but it wasn't the sort of thing one talked openly about. Worse, she wasn't sure Hen would see the problem. The thing that stymied Kitty most was that Marcela had been stopped, but Daniela had walked right in.

Then it hit her. Those who couldn't hide being Cuban, or Dominican, or Jewish, didn't. They had to live with the restrictions or face consequences. Those who could hide, on the other hand, had to choose to bury part of themselves to be accepted. It was more than pretending to be part of the elite. It was pretending to be someone you weren't. Disowning and disavowing your memories, your home, your family.

I'm proud of who I am, no matter what doors close on me because of it.

Kitty missed all the elegant dresses, all the playful rompers, and all the daring bathing suits as Max's words echoed in her head. After the show, she noticed that Daniela and Marcela didn't speak. Instead, Daniela fell into conversation with the redheaded chanteuse after bumping into her in a way that seemed accidental but was likely carefully choreographed. Marcela watched from the edge of the room, a satisfied smile on her face. Had she come merely to make sure the fruits of her effort paid off? Did she come prepared to engineer another avenue toward meeting if the first gambit didn't work? What had she had to do to get the invitations to the show in the first place? Kitty would never know. Marcela caught Kitty's eye, mouthed a silent *thank you*, then slipped out of the ballroom.

TWENTY-FOUR

The evening after the fashion show, Kitty flagged Max down with her purse at the end of the show. He nodded. An hour later, they met on the outdoor patio.

"Where's Loco?" he asked, pulling Kitty into his arms.

"No need for a ruse," she said. "Hen was falling asleep walking in the door."

He drew back, studying her face in the low light. "Marcela told me about the fashion show."

"Oh." Kitty dropped her gaze to the concrete beneath her feet.

"That was great, what you did."

"Don't sound so surprised."

"I'm serious." He cupped her chin in his hand. "She said you stuck up for her."

"She had an invitation. I don't know what all the fuss was about."

"Yes, you do." He kissed her. "Thank you."

Kitty smiled. "Well, did she see anything she liked?"

"Nah, that stuff is not her style. But she did want me to tell you that Daniela got a tryout with Rose Wilson's group. Rose really liked her."

"That's the redhead?"

"Yep."

"Daniela must have made a big impression."

"I'm sure she did. But, as it turns out, Rose is really Rosa. Guess she wants to give Daniela a break."

He said it with a chuckle, but Kitty couldn't laugh. How long would it be before Daniela was Danielle?

"So what did you want to meet about?" he continued. Kitty was relieved at the change of topic.

"Only this." She wrapped her arms tighter around his waist.

"Hey, I wanted to ask you something." He cast his gaze downward. "My aunt was at my mom's house today, and she said she hoped she hadn't said too much to you. What did you talk about, exactly?"

"It's nothing to worry about," Kitty said.

"I knew it. She told you about Joan, didn't she?" He slid his arms from hers and ran a hand through his hair.

"I didn't catch a name. But yes, she mentioned—a girl." Kitty couldn't bring herself to say *girlfriend*. "If you're thinking it upsets me to know that you existed before we met, it doesn't. I assumed I wasn't your first kiss."

"I wish Aunt Gail hadn't brought it up."

"I know it's none of my business. But are you still . . . do you ever . . ." Kitty picked at a fingernail.

Max stepped closer once more. "No. I've let Joan go, I promise."

"Well. I think she made a mistake, personally." Kitty's face burned.

"It wasn't—" He caught himself. "We don't have to talk about her if you don't want to."

"Are you sure *you* want to?"

"It might help to explain things. The way I've acted, especially when you and I first met." He took Kitty's hand. "It wasn't her. Her family didn't approve of me. They're rich, so I guess they've got appearances to maintain. She told me she didn't care, but . . . they wore her down, I guess. She just stopped calling. Stopped coming to see me. She never even said good-bye."

Kitty stopped herself from asking if the issue was money. Of course it wasn't. "You deserved better."

He let out a half laugh. "I didn't plan to tell you all that. I'm worse than Aunt Gail."

She squeezed his hand. "We should go dancing again."

"Everything is closed Christmas Day, and I'm playing all weekend. But we could go Monday."

"Perfect." She could think of something to tell Hen later. Or maybe she could tell Hen the truth. Kitty was more comfortable every day with the idea of Max, while growing less comfortable with the idea of letting him go.

❄❄

The next day was Christmas Eve. Kitty tried calling her father twice, but there was no answer in their suite at the Vanguard all morning. When the phone rang early in the afternoon, she was pleased to finally hear his voice.

"Hello, darling," he said.

"Papa! How are you?" She settled on the couch, Loco by her side.

"I'm well, how are you?"

"Fine," she said. "But I don't think this is a very good connection. You sound so far away."

"Must be a bad line. So, are you going to midnight mass?"

She sat up, concerned now. "What's that beeping in the background? Where are you?"

"It's nothing. Probably the switchboard. Now, if you need help finding a church—"

"Papa, I don't believe you're at work on Christmas Eve. You never work Christmas Eve." Her fingers trembled on the receiver. "Are you in the hospital?"

"Katarina, do you really think I wouldn't tell you if I was in the hospital?" He sounded as if he was about to laugh. "I'm at work. You're not here, so there was no reason for me to take the day off."

Kitty took a deep breath, hoping to slow her frantic heart. He was at work. Her father would never fail to tell her if he'd had an emergency; she knew that. The first time he went, they'd called her as he was leaving his doctor's office to go to the hospital. She couldn't remember the exact words the doctor had used to describe what had happened— some fancy medical term. Then he'd said "heart attack." He may have said "minor." But how could a thing like that ever be minor if it was happening to the one family member someone had left?

"Did you hear me?" Her father's voice interrupted the memory. "I'm at work, that's all."

"Yes, Papa, I heard you. Sorry. I was just wondering if you would be going to mass yourself."

"I will be, and I'll be thinking of you." He chuckled. "But I know what's really important to my girl. Don't worry. We'll do presents when you get back from Miami, okay? I'm just glad you're spending Christmas with Andre. I bet he got you something good."

The knot in Kitty's throat tightened. He was still counting on her coming home attached to Andre. She tried to keep her tone light. "Nothing he could get me would be better than time with you."

"Don't start with the flattery," he said, amusement in his voice. "I know that means you expect something especially shiny under the tree."

"You know me too well."

"Now, tell me. Have you and Andre made things official yet? Or do I need to have a word with him about dragging his feet?"

Kitty gripped the receiver until her fingertips were numb. The last thing she wanted was for her father to force Andre to make his move, but there was no way to answer the question without making him do exactly that. "I-I'll talk to him," she said at last.

"I know he'd never string my daughter along. Sometimes a man needs a little extra encouragement, you know? I'll have a word with him."

"No," she said, with more force than she intended. "It will look like you're meddling, Papa. I'll talk to him, I promise."

"Good. The only thing I want for Christmas is to see my daughter settled down."

After that declaration, Kitty steered the conversation back to midnight mass and presents, then promised to call first thing the next morning. She flopped back onto the bed. Though she'd never entertained the Andre idea with any seriousness, she now recognized that the idea of substituting Charles was equally ridiculous to her. Hen was so close to calling it quits with Charles, and Kitty was still committed to making sure Hen got free. But now, the future she could see with such clarity before was obscured by fog. She understood better that the standing in society she had wanted for so long would mean breaking off bits and pieces of her own identity. Not only that, she would be expected to exclude people who didn't fit the required mold. Max had shown her that.

Max. She sat up. Max had mentioned meeting her father. He must have seen something he liked in him to make Max the bandleader, to trust him with the show every night in a club he couldn't directly oversee. Perhaps they'd talked about the piano, about her father's love of music. Her papa was a self-made man. Maybe he would understand. No, of course he would. She'd talked him into enrolling her in Alastair Prep. She could convince him to let her follow her heart. After all . . . after all . . .

She laughed a little to herself. *You might as well admit it to yourself,* she thought. *You're going to have to tell Papa.* Kitty was falling in love. And now, more than anything, she wanted to tell her father the truth and give a relationship with Max a real chance. But first she had to tell Max himself. And no more plans. No more trickery. This time, she was going to do things the right way. She was going to tell the truth.

Christmas Day went so slowly, Kitty was convinced the hands on the clock actually moved backward at some points. She and Hen had arranged to have dinner in the suite with Andre so that he wouldn't have to spend the day alone. While they waited for him, they exchanged presents and sang along to Christmas music on the radio. But Kitty masked her distraction poorly.

"Tell me what's going on," Hen said, interrupting Nat King Cole's version of "The Christmas Song."

"Nothing," Kitty said.

"I'd ask you if you're missing your father, but you don't seem gloomy. You seem agitated."

Kitty sighed. If she was planning to tell the whole truth, she might as well practice now. "You know how I had a plan to get rid of Andre?"

"You're not reconsidering, are you?" Hen's voice was uncharacteristically shrill.

"No, no. If anything this trip has shown me how wrong for me he really is."

"Then what's going on?"

"The plan may have changed. Because I think I found someone who is right for me."

Hen's eyebrows shot up. "Max?"

"Max."

Hen sat still for a moment, her mouth a tight line.

"I know what you think," Kitty began, but Hen put a hand on Kitty's knee.

"There are certainly obstacles. It's not the easiest choice. But I think you should try to be with whoever makes you happy." Hen leaned in. "Does he make you happy?"

Excitement bubbled up in Kitty's chest. "He does. I don't know what comes next. Maybe Papa can move him to the New York band, if he wants to move. I don't know. I haven't talked to him yet."

"You better tell him soon," Hen said with a laugh. "We'll be leaving before you know it."

"I was planning to talk to him tomorrow."

"Well, I hope he has the good sense to see that he shouldn't let you go."

Kitty hugged Hen tightly. "And I hope you have the good sense to see that you deserve to be happy too."

Hen pulled away, waving Kitty off. "Let's not talk about that right now. Only pleasant things today. Come on, let's pick up this wrapping paper. Andre will be up soon."

❈

When Kitty went down to the patio the following night, there was no need for pretense. Hen sent her off like a proud mother. Kitty arrived downstairs to find Max already waiting for her. She wrapped her arms around his shoulders, kissing him before he could speak.

"You're certainly in a good mood tonight," he said when she finally let him go. "I guess you got what you wanted for Christmas this year?"

"You could say that. And how was your day off?"

"Good. Sebastian and I went to Marcela's. She had a huge dinner."

"That sounds like fun."

"It was." He gestured to the chairs. "Do you want to sit down?"

"I want to stay just like this. Which is what I wanted to talk to you about."

"Oh, yeah?"

"Yeah." She lifted her hand to his jaw. "You know how I said this all had to be secret? I don't think I want it to be anymore."

He hesitated. "So what would that mean?"

"I like you. Really like you. And I don't want to leave Miami and have to forget about you."

"I like you too," he said in a low voice. "More than I thought I would."

"I want to tell my father that I'm not going to be with Andre. Because . . . because I'm interested in someone else."

"Are you sure? Do you really want to risk making your pop sore? We've only known each other a couple of weeks. And I like you. But I don't want to be the reason you get in trouble."

"Don't worry about that. I know how to handle Papa. And I know you love Miami—I'm not asking you to leave or anything like that. But you could visit New York more often, don't you think?"

"Yes. Yes!" He lifted her and spun her around, both of them laughing. When he set her back down, she kissed him again. Neither of them noticed at first that the office light had flooded the patio. Max turned his head, but Kitty brought her lips back to his.

"It's the janitor," she said, as he tried to turn again.

"No. It's not."

She turned to see. Instead of the janitor, she saw Andre staring back. Kitty leapt away from Max, only to immediately regret the move. Max's eyes narrowed.

"What's this all about?" he asked, his words measured and slow.

"No. Oh, Max, no." A chill crept up her spine.

He took a step away from her. "You said . . . you told Hen you had a plan for 'the Andre thing.' You said it. Is that—is that what I was?" He lifted a hand to his head. "You picked this place out. You knew it was his office."

Kitty drew in a few deep breaths, determined to get this right. A lie would easily solve her problem, but she couldn't lie to him. Not after she had promised herself to do better. "Let me explain."

"It's true?"

"It's—it's not what you think."

He barked out a bitter laugh. "I think that's all the explanation I need. Why in the world would your pop ever agree to you dating me? Why would I believe that?"

"Listen to me. You've got it all wrong."

He winced. "I can't believe I thought you were better than that. I knew I had you right the first time. Stupid. So stupid."

"Max—"

He tore through the line of trees and was gone. Her knees wobbled, and she stumbled to the wall to brace herself. She wished she had lied to him. He might have stayed if she had lied. But he wasn't wrong. She had chosen that place for that exact purpose and had confirmed the worst of his beliefs about her. She had gotten what she wanted. Andre had spotted them. She couldn't think, couldn't silence the chatter in her mind. *Back to the suite*, she thought. *Go back.*

She raced around the side of the hotel and back into the lobby. Halfway to the elevator, Andre called to her. He jogged to catch up. His face didn't show that he had seen a breakup. On the contrary, his eyes were wrinkled with amusement.

"You two couldn't pick a better place to do that?" he asked.

"What were you doing in there?" The words rushed out of her.

"It's my office. What I don't get is why you were out there."

Her lips went numb as she studied Andre's cheerful expression. She felt like she'd swallowed lead. Andre could not have cared less that he caught her kissing Max.

She had been so sure. Andre had obviously wanted her to come to Miami. He'd taken time off work and come up with those ridiculous outings. There were the kisses on the cheek, the sly looks. But his expression could not be misread. His face betrayed no hint of jealousy. He didn't like her, not in that way.

"I don't know why I was out there," she said, her voice barely above a whisper.

"Wait, what's the matter?"

Her throat tightened. "I need to go to bed. I'm sorry. Good night."

Andre's cheerful demeanor evaporated into confusion, but he let her go. She wanted to crumple to the elevator floor, but she managed to stay upright. She had fallen in love for the first time in her life, and she had lost him to her own scheming. If only he would listen to her explanation. But as she heard the justification in her head, it sounded indefensible. He had been right to try to protect himself from her. She *had* set him up. Even if that wasn't her intention that night, it was the plan all along.

By the time she stood in front of the door to the suite, her thoughts were a confused jumble. She had lost Max. Why had she let herself become convinced she wanted him in the first place? Kitty knew what she needed. What she deserved. Her flailing mind cast about until it landed on the truth that had guided her for so long. She wouldn't let her future be in jeopardy again.

❖ TWENTY-FIVE ❖

Kitty entered the suite, relieved to find the living area empty. The crack under Hen's door was dark. She hadn't waited for Kitty. *Good*, Kitty thought. She didn't want to answer any questions. She wasn't even sure if she could. Her mind was such a mess, she was hardly aware of what she was doing until she had the phone in her hand.

"Hello?"

"Charles?"

"This is he. Kitty, is that you?"

When had she dialed Charles? Now she couldn't hang up. "Yes. It's me," she managed to say.

"It's awfully late. Is Hen all right?"

Kitty gaped at the phone. In her moment of desperation, she had called Charles, of all people. But of course she had. She could still save Hen and prove she wasn't the horrible person Max thought she was. And Hen being free would open up Kitty's own opportunities again. She could salvage her plan for her future. If she had to live with a broken heart, at least she could live well. Kitty straightened her back, preparing. The only surprise was how hard it was to force the lie out. "It's all true, Charles. Everything. I had to tell you."

"Do you know what time it is? What in the hell is going on?"

"You thought Hen was . . . seeing other men here in Miami. Didn't you? You said as much to her on the phone."

His voice hardened. "Yes, and she denied it."

"I can't let her deceive you anymore. You deserve to know the whole truth. Ever since she stepped off the plane, she's been a different person. At first it seemed so innocent, but now? Well, you were right, and that's all there is to it." Kitty exhaled shakily. She couldn't say any more terrible things about Hen.

"I want to talk to her." His voice blared in Kitty's ear. "Put her on the phone right now."

"I can't. She's not here."

He groaned. "I want to talk to her as soon as she gets in, do you hear me? Tie her to the chair and hold the phone to her ear if you have to."

"I will. I promise you."

"Thank you." He paused. "I'm so glad I can trust you."

Her throat stung as she said good-bye. She wrapped her arms around her waist, squeezing herself tightly. *This is the right thing. You're doing the right thing*, she assured herself. *This will all be over soon, and everyone will be happier.* She ignored the nagging *Except Max* that followed.

She heard a rustle and looked up. The flame in her throat seared down to her chest when she saw Hen standing in the doorway. But Hen's face was smooth and serene. When she spoke, her voice was level, but dangerously low.

"There is no possible way to defend what I just overheard," Hen began. "But why don't you try anyway?"

Kitty stared up at Hen. No words would come at first. Finally, she said, "I thought you were in bed."

"Is that the best you can do? That you thought I wouldn't hear you?" Hen asked. "I waited up for you, of course I did. I was just changing into my pajamas. I heard you say 'Charles,' though I have to admit, I never thought you'd be calling him to say that."

"It was for you. To help you."

"So many people tried to warn me over the years." Hen blinked hard.

"I did," Kitty said, a hopeful lilt in her voice. "I tried to warn you about him."

"Not about him. About you. They saw what I guess I couldn't see in you. But they were right."

Kitty stood, reaching out for Hen's arm, but Hen recoiled. "No, I did this for you. I swear," Kitty said.

Hen tilted her head and looked at Kitty through misty eyes. "I saw you do it to other people. I knew who you were. I never thought you could do it to me."

"No, just listen." Kitty's pulse throbbed in her temples. Unlike any explanation she could have offered Max, her reasoning here was justified. "He never deserved you. You wouldn't ditch him, so I was helping—"

"Don't pretend you were helping me. How does this help me? What I can't figure out is how it helps you, but I'm sure there's something cooked up in your head." Hen's cool demeanor broke as her face crumpled. "Now I'm heading back to a broken engagement and a furious mother. I'll be a laughingstock. Never mind that if Charles starts spreading the word that I'm that kind of girl, no decent man is going to want anything to do with me." She dropped her gaze to the floor. "I know you wanted me to end it with him, and I know he's done some terrible things." She looked back up at Kitty, her lower lip wobbling. "Why couldn't you believe that I know what's best for me?"

Kitty shook her head. "It was your mother, not you. You didn't want to be with him—you said as much."

"What I didn't want was to start the husband hunt over again at twenty-five. I didn't want to have a tainted reputation. I didn't want my friend—" Hen's voice cracked on the word. "I didn't want you in charge of my life any more than I wanted my mother telling me what to do."

Kitty's eyes widened. She was nothing like Hen's mother. Kitty wanted what was best for Hen. She had to make Hen see that. "Let's sit down," she said. "Let's talk. If you'll only listen, you'll understand."

"I heard everything I needed to a few minutes ago. I don't want to hear any more from you."

Hen turned and walked out. Kitty's nails dug into her palms. Why wouldn't Hen just listen? If she would hear Kitty out, she'd realize that the whole plan—well, most of it—was for her benefit. If Hen stopped to think for even a moment, she'd recognize that her life would be better without Charles, no matter what her mother might say. Was Hen's only concern having a fiancé? Kitty could find her ten of those. Hen herself knew plenty of eligible bachelors who she seemed to feel were worth pursuing, since she was constantly trying to set Kitty up with them. So why did it have to be good-for-nothing Charles? A small whisper at the back of Kitty's mind suggested that she really had made a mistake this time.

No. She was right. She had to be right. Hen couldn't stay angry at Kitty. Eventually she would hear Kitty out, and everything would be all right.

But what if she doesn't?

What if Hen is gone for good?

The touch of a cold, wet nose on her ankle interrupted her thoughts and alerted her to Loco's presence. As she looked into the dog's warm, brown eyes, she doubled over with sudden sobs that racked her body. Despite all her conviction that she was right in proceeding with the plan, she'd never felt so wrong in her life.

Kitty did not leave her room the next day except to take Loco out. She sprawled on the bed, not even bothering to change out of her dress. Doors in the suite opened and closed, and Kitty hoped Hen might poke her head in at some point, ready to talk. Or that Max might call. But Hen did not come in. The phone did not ring.

Loco's whimpering roused Kitty again at sunset. She changed clothes, brushed her hair, and took the dog downstairs. Loco had, at least, provided her with some inspiration in her sleepless night. Kitty could avoid the flight with Andre and Hen and head back to New York by train, thanks to the fact that the dog couldn't accompany her on the plane. There was no way she could ask for the dog to ride with the New York band members now. Once back in the suite, Kitty called her father to request a train ticket. She made up an excuse about not wanting to subject Loco to another long trip on the bus.

"What about Hen? Don't you want some company?" her father asked.

"I think she needs to get back on time. Something her mother has planned."

Her father agreed to arrange for the ticket. That meant she had to find some way to tell Hen about the change of plans, but there was no way Hen was going to speak to her. The last person Kitty wanted to discuss her current situation with was Andre, but he was the only choice. Compounding her embarrassment was the fact that he'd actually been present for the debacle with Max. She consoled herself that she only had to deliver this one piece of information, and then she could go back to wallowing.

After hanging up with her father, she called Andre's room.

"Sounds like you blew it with Hen," he said.

Kitty was taken aback. "She told you?"

"She had to have lunch with someone. We made conversation. She didn't tell me much, but she seems awful mad."

"Well, she won't have to worry about seeing me much longer. Papa is going to get me a train ticket. I have to get Loco back somehow, and I don't want her riding on the bus again. Do you mind being Hen's escort back to New York?"

"No, I don't mind," he said. "But does she know about this?"

"Will you please tell her? She sure doesn't want to hear anything from me right now."

"Okay." He paused. "Sorry you'll be on your own."

"Thanks, Andre." She hung up the phone. The words *on your own* echoed in her head. She worried she'd be on her own for much longer than a train trip.

TWENTY-SIX

NEW YORK CITY

JANUARY 1954

Kitty had never been so relieved to leave Hen as she was when she walked out of the Imperium for the last time. They'd spent the time until Kitty's departure avoiding one another in the silent suite. She could only assume Hen had continued dining with Andre, because he'd tried to rally Kitty into coming downstairs. He'd said something nonsensical about "patching things up," which meant that Hen still hadn't shared the details of their falling out. Since going to the club meant seeing both Max and Hen, she declined. Andre hadn't offered again. Kitty had ordered room service.

The train ride took her through rolling hills and quaint towns all along the Eastern Seaboard. Loco kept Kitty company as she flipped through magazines she wasn't really reading or stared out the window at views she wasn't seeing. Mostly she occupied herself replaying the final days in Miami over and over again. How had her perfect plan gone so wrong? She was near Virginia when the answer surfaced: Max. If he hadn't come along, everything would have worked out. Everything had always worked out before he entered the picture. He'd turned her head around, clouded her judgment. She'd thought he respected her, admired her mind. If he really had, he would never have convinced her to question things she knew to be true.

Virginia passed by the window, and the answer seemed less certain. After all, Max wasn't to blame for Hen's disappointment. Nor was he responsible for Kitty's complete failure to realize that Andre was never a serious threat to her lifestyle, since it appeared that all the interest her father had ascribed to him had been imagined. Max had done nothing wrong. Finally, painfully, she had to admit that despite his innocence, he had ended up hurt too. As New York drew closer, she could not escape the answer. She had devised the scheme. She had put the plan into motion. She had ignored all warning signs. No one had forced her hand.

Kitty was to blame.

For so long, her main point of pride was her perfect, clear-eyed assessment of the world. She had been so sure she knew everything about Hen, about Andre, even about Max. In reality, she knew nothing. Hen wasn't grateful for Kitty's interference. As it happened, she was secretly wary of her oldest friend. Andre had no interest in Kitty at all. And Max . . . the worst part was, she'd known deep down exactly how upset Max would be to discover he'd been used. Hadn't he said he worried Kitty would be "the wrong kind of smart"? He'd shown greater understanding in that one statement than Kitty had shown in her whole friendship with Hen. Of course he'd be happier walking away from Kitty. She wasn't worth the trouble she caused.

The recognition opened all the wounds afresh, and she welcomed the pain of each one. Using Max the way she had set out to do was cruel enough, but Kitty at last accepted that what she'd done to her best friend was unpardonable. She stroked Loco's soft fur. *If you knew what I've done*, she thought, *you'd hate me too.*

Her father met her at the train station, and his excited smile fell at the sight of her face. "Kitty, are you ill? What happened?"

She opened her mouth to speak, but threw herself into his arms and burst into tears instead.

Kitty spent the next couple of weeks holed up in the suite at the top of the Vanguard, except for the short walks she took with Loco. Most of her day was spent listening to a recording of "Habanera." Each time the song ended, she would lift the arm of the record player and set it down to start the song over. After a few hours, she could hit the exact moment the song began. *And if I love you, take guard yourself.*

The saving grace was that Kitty could be sure that once Hen had explained everything to Charles, he wouldn't want to break the engagement. Hen could keep her fiancé and avoid her mother's wrath. Kitty had even written a letter, explaining her part in the scheme, and sent it to Hen to present as evidence to Charles of Kitty's wrongdoing. There was no response, but Kitty hadn't expected one. She tortured herself thinking about how Hen had been so close to letting go of Charles on her own, and Kitty had pushed her friend back into his arms with no way out. It was small comfort to think that, with the letter as proof, Hen could have him back and wouldn't be ruined socially.

The upside to her new exile from her former society was that in the evenings she had more time to spend with her father. They resumed their weekly dinners out, always at places carefully selected by Kitty to be least likely spots to run into one of Hen's crowd. Kitty hadn't been able to bring herself to tell her father the whole story. No sense having him angry with her too. All she could manage was that she and Hen had a fight, and she wouldn't be coming around anymore. She was grateful that her obvious distress kept him from even mentioning Andre.

Since she didn't have much to say, she listened a great deal. To fill the silence, her father began explaining parts of his business in more detail than he ever had before. Kitty found herself fascinated by the negotiations required in the building of an empire, and surprised herself by having suggestions on how her father could finesse difficult deals. More surprising was how receptive he was to her ideas. He shared more and more of his plans, and she offered advice that he took seriously.

One evening, as they sat in a booth at Keens, her father described a complaint he'd received from a guest renting a banquet room. As soon as he said the name, Kitty inhaled sharply.

"Dr. Stone?" She set her fork down beside her plate.

"Yes, why?"

"Not the same one who was supposed to come for Mama?"

He thought for a moment as he searched his memory then shook his head. "I don't know who you mean."

"When Mama was sick, right before she died. You called for the doctor, and I know his name was Stone. I'll never forget it. I'm surprised you don't remember."

Her father's tone was tender. "We called for a lot of doctors. I don't remember all their names. Though I'm sure Stone was likely one of them. He's one of the best."

"But he's the one who wouldn't come. His office said he was out of state, but I saw him. When we drove to that one special pharmacy, I saw him walking into a hoity-toity high-rise that same day."

There was a long pause. "I think you're remembering it wrong. Every doctor, every specialist I called came to see her. It was just that none of them could do anything."

"I know this happened. I know it."

"You were very little, Katarina. I think you're mistaken."

Her father moved on to a new topic, and Kitty tried to listen. She picked at her food, but her mouth was too dry to eat any more. The sight of the doctor entering the building repeated in her head, along with her father's assertion. She must have confused the order of events at the time. How would she have even recognized Dr. Stone if she hadn't already seen him with that same black bag in their home? She must have built the narrative in her mind later around what she believed, not what she'd actually seen. As with so much lately, she'd been wrong. Without the certainty of that vision to guide her, what would she do with herself?

Her pleasant hours with her father were too few, and she would always find herself back in the suite, ruminating on what a total mess she'd made of her life. A few times, she attempted letters to Max, unsure what else to do. Each one started with:

> *Dear Max,*
> *I know what you must think of me*

And each one ended up in the wastebasket. She could not defend herself, and he would not want to hear it anyway. Unable to write to him, she made up her mind to forget him, but that proved impossible. Thoughts of him popped up constantly. Sometimes it was images, like the sight of him drenched on the Malecón. Other times, it was sensations on her skin, like his fingertips pressing on hers as he helped her play the piano. Mostly, though, it was the echo of his words in her ears.

If you don't go anywhere else, you're not truly seeing New York at all.

That was the phrase that finally got Kitty out of the building for something other than dinner with her father. She searched her memory, but she couldn't recall the exact wording of the poem that had inspired those sentiments in him, not even the part he'd shown her. He'd said he'd assumed that once she'd heard of it, she'd run out and read and interpret it for herself. The urge to do so needled her, so she hauled herself down to the bookstore to find the stupid thing.

Normally, she'd go down to Book Row on Fourth Avenue and browse store after store, chatting with clerks about her next selection. But since she knew exactly what she wanted, she only made one stop, at the Strand Bookstore. A dark-haired young woman Kitty recognized greeted her cheerily.

"Welcome back," the girl said. "Haven't seen you in a while. Did you ever get around to reading *The Robe*?"

"I didn't," Kitty said.

"I know you don't go in much for current books, but it's that classics style you like."

"Thanks, but today I'm looking for a book of poetry."

The girl's eyes widened. "That's new."

"I'm trying new things these days," Kitty said with a smile. "I'm afraid I don't know the title of the collection, but the poem is 'Little Gidding.' It's by T. S. Eliot."

"Oh, that's over here. That one is in *Four Quartets*." The girl motioned for Kitty to follow her down the cramped aisle. "It's a good thing you caught me working today and not Ralph. I'm an English major at NYU. Poor Ralph would have taken forever to find it. He's strictly a Louis L'Amour type of guy." The girl pulled an unassuming black-and-white volume from the shelf. "This is it. What else can I help you find?"

"This is all for today, thank you." Kitty ignored the girl's attempt at hiding her surprise and followed her back to the register to pay.

Back home, Kitty scoured the poem. She wondered how Max could have made heads or tails of it. It had five sections, each so different from the last she couldn't believe they were all part of the same work. The lengthy poem seemed to wander aimlessly, much like the speaker in the second section. And very little of it made sense to Kitty. She found the excerpt Max had shown her, about searching and exploring, but just before it were a few lines that caught her attention:

> *What we call the beginning is often the end*
> *And to make an end is to make a beginning.*
> *The end is where we start from.*

The simplicity of the lines' truth startled her. She was at an end; it certainly felt like an ending. She'd lost her best friend and the man she was falling in love with, and the future stretched empty before her. But that emptiness was not a permanent hole that her life had fallen into. It had the possibility to be blank pages for a new chapter. If she acknowledged the ending, she could face a new beginning. Max's suggestion that she had never really seen New York seemed like a good enough place to start. She needed to walk out into the city and explore.

And walk she did. She also took the subway, buses, and sometimes taxis, something she'd avoided before in favor of riding with her father's driver. She listened to folk singers in Washington Square and jazz singers in Harlem. She tried food from the pushcarts on Arthur Avenue and from vendors in cramped storefronts in Chinatown. Mostly, she walked the streets and watched. She met people and really listened to them. Sometimes she viewed New York through the same eyes she'd seen Havana with, and then suddenly the scene would flip and become her home again. She would feel lost one moment and found the next.

In expanding her view of the city, Kitty began to see what Max was talking about. She hadn't known her world as well as she'd thought. She saw injustices small and large, things she never would have noticed before. A certain group prohibited from this building. A muttered word to that person. If those were the things she could see, how much more was hidden? And the penthouses of Manhattan always towered high above it all, far away from the realities on the ground. But as she went out into the city each day, pieces of it began to seep into her. She took bits of her experiences with her, and they began to reshape the map of her home in her mind. She was newly arrived in a different world.

One afternoon, about three weeks after her return, the phone rang. Hoping her father was calling to say he was free that evening, Kitty picked up.

"Kitty? It's Charles," said the voice on the line.

Her shock prevented her from answering right away. She concluded that he was calling to berate her, and she started composing apologies in her head. "Charles, hello," she said in the calmest tone she could muster.

"How are you?"

Just dandy. He wanted to go through all the pleasantries first. "I'm fine, and you?"

"Fine." The word came out in a short burst. "I suppose you've heard."

This was a sharp left turn she hadn't expected. Why wasn't he screaming at her? *Get it over with.* "Heard what?"

"I would have thought you'd be the first to hear. You mean you really don't know why I'm calling?"

"I have an idea, but why don't you just tell me," she said.

He heaved a sigh. "Hen and I—well, we split up."

The street could have cracked open, swallowing the whole hotel, and Kitty still wouldn't have been more stunned than she was at that statement. Hen hadn't actually done anything wrong. And Kitty had been so sure her letter would be enough to mend things between Hen and Charles. But, then, she'd been right about very little lately. She couldn't speak, so he continued.

"I was calling to see if I can take you to dinner on Saturday," he said. "I think we need to talk."

Her jaw clenched. So, he'd heard everything and still wanted to leave Hen. Maybe he thought Hen and Kitty cooked up the plan together. Now he wanted to read her the riot act to her face. She guessed he deserved his chance to tell her off. He was every bit as affected by her scheming, if likely nowhere near as hurt. She could explain once again that it was all her fault, maybe convince him where Hen and the letter had not. If Hen really wanted to be with this guy, she could at least try one more time to help with that.

"Okay," she said. "Where were you thinking of going?"

"How about the Palm? Eight thirty. We can meet there."

Kitty rolled her eyes. Of course Charles would choose the most high-profile place he could think of as the best place to chew her out. "I'll be there."

✦ TWENTY-SEVEN ✦

On Saturday, Kitty lay in the bed when she first woke up, checking herself for any sign of illness. None appeared. No fever, no scratchy throat, no headache. No excuses. She would have to go to the Palm and face the music. The thought that Kitty might be able to take the full blame and at least get Hen back in Charles's good graces was the only thing that could get her out of bed.

Most of the day was occupied in choosing the proper outfit. She hadn't really mined her closet since she'd gotten home. There had been few opportunities to dress up. After much deliberation, she decided the demure look was best. She chose a white blouse with a slim black-and-white plaid skirt she'd gotten in Miami. The black ribbon in her hair was purely for the other Palm patrons. She couldn't look as though she'd given up entirely.

As the car pulled up to the curb in front of the Palm, she twisted the strap of her handbag. She considered telling the driver to turn around, but he was already opening the door for her. She had no choice.

When she walked in, the maître d' explained that the rest of the party was already seated and led her to the table. Charles stood when he spotted Kitty and kissed her on the cheek.

"Kitty, good to see you," he said. "Sit down, please."

Good to see you? She sat, and the waiter spread a napkin on her lap. "Hello, Charles," she said, accepting the menu. She guessed that, whatever her transgressions, she still merited a sleazy kiss.

Charles already had a martini, so Kitty ordered a drink. The second the waiter stepped away from the table, Charles grabbed Kitty's hand. She nearly dropped the menu.

"What's going on?" She blurted the words out without thinking.

He cocked his head. "I would have thought it was obvious."

"I can't say I was expecting a warm reception, that's all." She withdrew her hand from his on the pretense of smoothing the napkin in her lap.

"Don't be silly. You and I have known each other almost as long as Hen and I have. Why can't we still be friends, even if Hen and I aren't together?" He smiled. "More than friends?"

She took a moment to collect herself. "Why don't you tell me exactly what happened?"

"Hasn't Hen already told you?"

Curiouser and curiouser, she thought. "I'd like to hear it from your perspective," she said smoothly.

The waiter came over with Kitty's drink, and Charles lowered his voice. "Well, you told me yourself Hen was . . . indiscreet in Miami. When she came back, I was ready to forgive her."

Kitty pursed her lips involuntarily, but covered it with the first sip of her vodka pineapple. "That's very big of you."

He nodded. "The way I see it, she may have indulged herself too much, but that's no reason to throw away everything we have. She kept dodging me when she got back, so I assumed she was ashamed of how she'd behaved." Charles threw his hands in the air. "That wasn't it at all. She wasn't the least bit sorry. She said she didn't regret a thing."

Kitty struggled with this information. Hen had nothing to regret— why would she put it that way? "That's . . . odd," Kitty said.

"I thought so too. But nothing was odder than what she told me next. She said not only was she leaving me, there's someone else." His mouth twisted in a sneer. "Leaving me! For him."

Kitty abandoned all pretense of knowledge. "I have to admit, Charles. This is the first I've heard about any of this. Hen and I had a disagreement before coming back home. We haven't spoken."

"I'd have thought her little affair would have been obvious. She said it was no one's fault, just that they'd been thrown together so much and had fallen in love. What kind of life is that guy going to give her, I ask you?"

"What guy?" The words came out before she could stop them. Had Hen invented some man from the trip to get out of her engagement? The more Charles said, the less the conversation made sense.

Charles looked no less confused. "You were with her the whole time. You were the one who told me. Are you saying you didn't notice her with Andre?"

Kitty sat, dumbfounded. The bridge game, the trip to the bird sanctuary. The glances Kitty had brushed aside, the touches on the arm she had written off as friendly, the sweet compliments she'd assumed were for both of them. Hen had even asked Kitty point-blank if Kitty was interested in Andre. Now that question revealed an entirely different intent, one that really hurt. Hen wouldn't have been willing to consider Andre a romantic possibility if Kitty had designs on him. No doubt the final days in Miami and the flight home without her had provided the final push Andre and Hen needed. Yet Kitty hadn't seen what now seemed so clear.

Charles took advantage of the silence to grasp Kitty's hand again. She couldn't even flinch.

"None of that really matters now," he said. "If she wants to attach herself to that boor, then she can live with the consequences. But the fact is, I need a woman by my side who will represent me well. A woman who will value the life I can give her. Kitty, I can't believe I was so blind."

"Blind," she echoed, still lost in the whirlwind of her thoughts.

"You're the one for me. Hen and I were never right together, I see that now. None of it ever made sense. It was what our parents wanted." He waited for her to respond, but all she could manage was a nod. He took that as permission to continue. "Just look at how glamorous you are. Hen could never pull that off. Well, I guess with her new *friend*, she won't have to worry about that." He grimaced but caught himself and went back into romance mode. "But you. You're gorgeous. You'll make me look good."

And there it was. Charles saw her as a well-dressed paper doll who would display the right clothes at his parties and clubs. The corners of his mouth ticked up as he failed spectacularly at looking humble, but his eyes flickered with impatience. "What do you say, Kitty?"

She jolted out of her reverie. Everything had seemed to go wrong, but here she sat, being offered exactly what she'd wanted in the first place. Hen had found a worthier man, and Kitty had a one-way ticket to the elite class she'd dreamed of. All she had to do was say yes, and the brass ring was hers. Really more like a platinum ring. But she couldn't move her mouth. She couldn't even loosen her hand from his grip. The only sensation she could concentrate on was a sour taste at the back of her throat that meant the vodka pineapple she'd swallowed was about to make a swift return. She sputtered out a few incoherent syllables, and Charles chuckled.

"I know, it's sudden," he said. "No need to say anything. I'm just sorry I wasted so much of what could have been our time together. Of course, we'll have to announce it as soon as possible. That way we can get your application for the athletic club in the works. I don't know what they'll think of your father. Though I'm sure *my* father can convince them to look past that." He snapped his fingers in the air, looking around. A waiter passed by, and Charles snapped again. "Boy! We'll have a bottle of your best champagne. And don't dally."

The waiter, who didn't look a day under fifty years old, stopped. "Of course, sir."

"Well, don't stand there staring at me. Go." Charles turned his attention to Kitty, massaging her shoulder. "It's not just how lovely you are," he said. "You're smart. I know you'd never so much as look at a fella like that Andre, would you? Some low-class hotel manager. No. You want something better." He slid his arm over her shoulders. "And now you've got it."

She shrugged his arm off under the guise of reaching for her drink. Charles, better than Andre? But Andre was friendly, hardworking, solid. What would Charles think of Max? Max had said the same words to her—*you're smart*—but they sounded so different coming out of Charles's mouth. She realized she ought to offer some response, but nothing came to her. Then she realized that Charles hadn't seemed to notice that she wasn't answering him. He didn't care. Sure enough, he continued, oblivious to her reticence.

"When we finish here, perhaps we should go back to my apartment. I have some good champagne there, not the swill they serve here. Then we can really celebrate." He drew out the last word, and Kitty was convinced she would retch this time. Thankfully, the waiter returned, glistening champagne bottle in hand. Charles sat back in his chair as the waiter began opening the bottle.

"What was your mother's name, by the way? Her last name, I mean," Charles said, watching the waiter pour.

"Oh . . . um, Orel."

"We can probably pass that off as Scottish. Not ideal, but it will be all right."

An electric shock ran up Kitty's spine as she looked at Charles's smarmy expression. Every instinct in her fought against the possibility of becoming like him. Someone who shouted at waiters to prove some kind of flimsy importance and assigned rank based on last name. Her future with Charles wouldn't be spent making him sorry for the way he'd treated Hen. Their union would be lonely nights covering for his infidelity, ignoring his idiotic remarks, and looking the other way as he berated those he considered beneath him.

Of course she couldn't accept him. She could barely look at him.

Her thoughts returned to Hen's mother's comments at the hotel months ago, when Kitty had listened for the millionth time to the way those people talked about her. Hen's mother and her friend had enumerated Kitty's many supposed faults. Surely Charles had thought of her the same way, until she had proven to be a convenient accessory. She was now a beautiful bauble to wear on his arm and nothing more.

Even though she'd understood Max's meaning when he'd said that the doctor ought to have been better, not her, now the full weight of his words settled on her. She had the chance to be better than them. Not higher on the social ladder, or decked in more jewels, or living in the most expensive high-rise. No, she could follow behind them, opening every door they were determined to close. She was struck by a sudden feeling of pride in every aspect of her that separated her from *them*.

Kitty reached for her purse. "I'm sorry, Charles. I'm afraid the answer is no."

"I don't understand," he said, his eyes widening.

"Then don't try too hard. First time and all, don't want you to strain anything." She stood, pulling a crisp ten-dollar bill from her purse and placing it in the waiter's jacket pocket. "This is just in case you have to put up with this jackass for any longer."

"Now wait just a damn minute—" Charles began. Kitty had already turned her back on him. She walked out of the restaurant and into what seemed like a new city. She gazed up at the twinkling lights atop the buildings around her. How many people did they conceal from the streets below? The thoughts that had been taking shape in her mind now solidified, and at last she saw clearly what Max had seen from the beginning. Those people lived at the top not because of some inherent importance or superiority, but because they were hiding. Sheltering themselves from the changes that were happening on the sidewalks. She wanted to be part of the new world that was taking shape. Not a monochrome statue to the glories of the past, but a patchwork quilt of the people of the present. Those who would shatter the old order, not pay reverence to it. In that world, she could be proud of her heritage, not ashamed. Her own future now felt inextricably tied to the future of the city and all the people in it. She thought of a fragment of Max's poem: *We cannot follow . . . an antique drum.* She primed her ear for the new rhythms around her.

⋇ TWENTY-EIGHT ⋇

Kitty woke up the morning after leaving Charles at the Palm refreshed in a way that she hadn't been for weeks. After dressing and walking Loco, she sat down on the living room couch with a notebook and pen. A better outlook called for a better plan.

Unlike the letters to Max that Kitty had been unable to finish, her words to Hen flowed easily. She knew exactly what she needed to say and she said it, plainly and without her usual flourish. The pages filled as she explained herself without asking for anything more than the possibility of offering an apology. As she neared the end, she realized she could only imagine saying the words to Hen's face, if Hen would agree to listen. She turned to a blank sheet and wrote: *#1 Speak to Hen*.

The rest of the list came easily, too. A picture of herself formed in her mind. The image was foggy and different from any other version of herself she'd ever imagined. Still, this was the image that informed her new plan, and the image would only grow sharper as she enacted it. *#2 Speak to Papa*.

She listed a few more steps, knowing none of them were as certain as the first two. But in order to get the rest of her ideas to take shape, she'd have to cross the first two items off. With that in mind, she lifted the phone to call Hen.

"No," she murmured. She turned to Loco, who sprawled on the couch beside her. "No preamble. Better just to go, don't you think? She can always turn me away if she wants to."

Kitty ruffled the dog's fur and dialed down for the car instead.

As Kitty knocked on the front door of Hen's apartment, a queasy feeling she'd never known before rolled through her. She took a deep breath, exhaling just as the maid opened the door.

"May I help you?" the woman asked.

"I'm here to see Hen. Is she in?"

The maid's expression didn't change. "Let me check."

"No need, Doris," said a voice down the left hall. "Let her in."

Kitty stepped into the doorway to see Hen standing, her arms crossed over her chest.

"I had a feeling you'd show up sooner or later." Hen raised an eyebrow.

"I won't stay long," Kitty said. "Can we talk?"

Hen turned and started toward the library. "I'm sure you mean, can *you* talk."

"Well, yes, I plan to talk. But you can say anything you like back. All I ask is that you listen." Kitty followed Hen into the library, careful to choose a seat with a few feet of distance from the sofa Hen occupied.

"So. What exactly do you want me to listen to?" Hen's tone was airy.

"An apology." Kitty swallowed. "With no excuses."

"Is that so? Not what I expected, actually."

"I know what I did was wrong. Why bother trying to excuse something that can't be excused? I shouldn't have called Charles. I let him believe you were doing things you'd never do. I hurt you, and you were the last person on earth I should have hurt." Tears tingled at the corners of Kitty's eyes. "You were such a good friend to me. Loyal. You cared when no one else did. And I broke our trust. I ruined it."

Hen nodded. "Yes, you did."

"But I'm so happy for you and Andre. What I wanted most was for you to find someone who would be good to you, and he will."

Hen stared at Kitty for a long moment. "And that's it?"

"Well," Kitty said. "Yes. That's it."

"No helpful suggestions or muddling explanations? No reasons why I should forgive you?" Hen twirled a hand in the air. Her ring finger looked so different without a bulbous diamond on it.

"No." Kitty shook her head firmly. "I can't think of any reason why you'd forgive me. I only wanted to apologize."

Hen laughed. "No ulterior motive? That's not like you. What's the scam?"

"I know. You have every right to believe it's a scam, because that's who I have been. And you don't have any reason to believe me, but it's not who I'm going to be. Not anymore."

"I watched you do it so many times to other people. I convinced myself that your plans were always for someone else, never for me." Hen's eyes narrowed. "I want you to tell me the truth right now. Was this the first time I was part of one of your little schemes?"

Kitty looked out the window. "It was."

"You never took advantage of me in any other way?"

Kitty hesitated. She knew the only way to atone for what she'd done was to tell the whole truth about her plan. Hen would hate her, but there was no other way.

"There's more," she said.

"Oh, dear." Hen winced.

Kitty took a shaky breath. "I thought that once you and Charles had broken up, I would be with him."

Hen sat forward, her eyes hard. "Did you? That's low, even for you."

All the explanations that might soften the confession tumbled around in Kitty's head. *I thought I could help you. I wanted to torment him, to pay him back. I wanted connections, I wanted what you have.* But those were all excuses, and she'd promised herself she wouldn't offer any of those. Instead, she said, "You're right."

Hen stood and paced the room. "Well, he's on the market now. You can probably still land him if you want."

"He did ask me out," Kitty admitted. "I turned him down."

Hen stopped but kept her eyes on the floor. "Why did you do that? You ought to at least get something out of this."

"I'd rather be alone than be with someone knowing that it would hurt you."

Hen pondered this for what felt to Kitty like hours. At last, she turned to Kitty. "Thank you for coming. I know how hard this must have been. Especially for you."

Kitty stood. "Thank you for listening." She held Hen's gaze for another moment, then turned to leave. She was at the library door when Hen called to her.

"How are you, Kitty?" she asked, real concern in her voice. "You look tired."

Before, Kitty would have had a clever comeback for a comment like that. Now, she lowered her head. "I've made a lot of mistakes. Setting them right is going to be hard work."

"At least this time your heart was somewhat in the right place," Hen said. "I do believe you thought I'd be better off without Charles. And I am happier now. I ought to at least grant you that. Besides, you wrote that letter to him explaining everything. You tried to come clean."

"I take it you never gave it to him?"

"No reason to. I was finally rid of him."

Kitty turned back and offered a tentative smile. "What did your mother say when you told her about Andre?"

"What didn't she say? You should have heard her." Hen straightened her shoulders. "She tried to throw the book at me. But you predicted it. Turns out she's not quite as fierce when someone calls her bluff. I guess you did teach me to stand up for myself, in the end."

Kitty studied the rug under her feet. "I hope it's not the end."

"It doesn't have to be. Doesn't mean things will be at all the same. But no sense throwing out the good with the bad." Hen bit her lip. "You told me the truth. That counts for something."

"Maybe we could have lunch sometime. I am dying to hear how a 'lumberjack' stole your heart." Kitty regretted the joke when Hen didn't respond right away.

"If we have lunch," Hen said, "you're paying. It only seems fair."

"And you choose the restaurant."

"You're on," Hen said.

Kitty walked out of the apartment feeling lighter than she had in months. *First step complete*, she thought. *Papa is next.*

TWENTY-NINE

"Katarina, you don't have to set an appointment to see me. You can just come down, you know."

Kitty sat in her father's office two days after her visit to Hen, flush with the excitement of her small initial success. "I know that, Papa. But I want to propose something important, and I wanted to set the right tone."

He smiled. "So it's a meeting, then."

"It is." She sat up straighter, fighting the itch to slip off her shoes.

"Well, then, let me hear it. You're looking to buy something more expensive than a dress this time?"

"It's more serious than a dress." She pressed her lips together. "I suppose you've heard about Andre and Hen."

Her father sighed. "Ah, yes. So you want to know if this gets you out of our agreement. I don't know how you managed it—"

"That wasn't my doing. They enjoyed each other's company, and I'm glad they found each other. But it's true. I can't marry Andre if he's with someone else."

"I see. So you want to know if this gets you out of the other part of my plan." He rubbed his chin. "It does. You're free to do what you please. I guess you always were. I knew you'd find some way around me."

"No." She shook her head. "That's not it at all. I don't want out."

Her father gaped. "I'm sorry. I don't think I understand."

"You said it yourself. I know you'll be around for a long time, but I can't expect you to take care of me forever."

"This hotel will take care of you," he said. "All of them. I would have liked to see you with Andre, but I was never serious about my daughter cleaning toilets. I had to think of something that might scare you. You must have known that."

"I thought so, if I'm being honest. But it doesn't mean you were wrong."

He stared at her. "I'm lost. I think you need to explain better, because right now I'm hearing that you want to work in housekeeping."

"I need to be able to take care of myself, Papa. So I want to learn everything. I want to study with you, with Andre, maybe take a couple of college courses. I want to learn the business. The way I see it, if these hotels are meant to take care of me, I need to take care of them."

Her father snorted. "That's absurd. College classes? I never meant for you to have to work. Where did all this come from?"

"It came from a clearer understanding of how the world works. Things are changing, and I want to be part of it. I'm only going to be able to do that if I'm doing more with myself than going to cocktail parties and clubs."

"I did this. I put all this into your head by discussing the business with you these past few weeks." He leaned over the desk. "You don't have to work. This industry is complex and challenging. And I'm not going to let you be a secretary somewhere any more than I'm going to let you clean."

"You think it will be too hard for me? You must not know me that well. Which is a surprise. What does it take? A head for strategy? Persistence? Smarts?" Kitty pointed at him. "I got all that from you, and you know it."

"You're certainly showing your stubborn streak." He sat back in his chair. "Fine. You want to follow us around, you can. Until you get tired of it, and I assure you, you will. Trust me, no hard feelings when you decide to give up."

Kitty stuck out her chin. "All I ask is that you give me a chance. Do you really think I can't do this?"

"What I'm having a hard time understanding is why you want to. Do you hope you'll end up running things? Do you want to take Andre's job when he takes over mine?"

"I don't know what I want in the end," she admitted. "But I know how I want to start. I'm asking you to have faith in me."

"But wouldn't you be happier as someone's wife?"

"I don't think this will prevent me from that kind of happiness too."

"It will if it means that you're always hunched over a calculator in some office," he said. "You'll never meet a nice man."

"I've met plenty of men. This is what I want now."

He studied her for a long moment. "I'll let you try it. That's all I can offer."

"And I promise you, I'll do the best job I can." She stood and held out a hand. Her father rose and shook it. "At least I'm starting with more than a ring in a bar of soap."

"I'll give you this. Twenty-five years, and you've kept me guessing for every one of them." His eyes twinkled. "Tomorrow morning, eight o'clock sharp. Andre will meet you in his office."

"Thanks, Papa." Kitty tilted her head. "We allow Jews in our hotels, right?"

Her father's face changed as his lips flattened into a thin line. "There's no religion test to stay in my hotels. Where is all this coming from?"

She drew in a breath then exhaled slowly. "I've been doing a lot of thinking lately. Walking around the city. I've seen things I don't like. I've talked to people. I don't know what I can do, exactly, but I feel like it starts here. With me. With us. I've also made some mistakes lately, but I'm planning to learn from them."

"That's admirable," her father said. "But what are you going to do if this turns out to be a mistake too?"

"I'll keep learning."

The next morning, Kitty stood in front of Andre's office door five minutes early, her hand poised to knock. Before she could, the door flew open. She and Andre both gasped.

"I was opening the door for you," he said. "I didn't think you'd be down early. I suspected you wouldn't come at all, to tell you the truth."

So she was going to have to prove herself to Andre as well as her father. She stepped into the office, which was far smaller than her father's. Andre had very little furniture, just a desk, two chairs, and a standing lamp in the corner. The desk was covered with papers and had a calculator with printing tape spewing out down to the floor.

"Thank you for meeting with me," she said, taking a seat in the chair nearer the door. "I know how busy you are."

He chuckled. "No need to be so formal. So your pop says you want to learn the business. I'm not sure I understand what that even means, but I'll help you if I can."

"Surely you know what that means. You help run the business."

"But there's an awful lot to it. I don't even know where to begin."

"You must have started somewhere yourself, right?"

"I did. At the front desk. Not back here, in the offices."

Kitty was surprised she hadn't known that. She'd only gotten to know Andre when he started working at her father's side, so she'd never considered the years of work that led up to his current position. The thought was daunting. How long would it take her to learn what Andre had? For the first time, she saw Andre as an expert, not as her father's sidekick.

"Do you think that's where I should start?" she asked. "At the front desk?"

"Is that where you want to start? It helps, but what I do now is so different."

She folded and unfolded the pleat on her skirt, not wanting to admit to any doubt. "How about you do what you normally do, and we'll see how I get on. I'm a quick learner, at least."

"I know that." Andre rubbed his forehead. "Look, your pop says he doesn't understand why you've got this sudden inclination, but if you can really follow through, I'm here to help. Today I'm going through payroll. Want to have a look?"

Kitty pulled her chair around to the side of his desk, grateful that Andre wasn't pushing further. If he sensed her hesitation, he was willing to ignore it and give her a shot. Since hearing about his attachment to Hen, she'd increasingly considered what a stand-up guy he was. No-nonsense, reliable, and apparently more willing to consider her capable even than her father. She could easily see him as a partner in her future work with the hotels.

As the hours passed, Andre worked and Kitty watched. He explained things at every step, and she asked occasional questions. She was so invested that she hadn't noticed the afternoon sneaking up on them.

"Want some lunch?" Andre stood and stretched.

"Sure. What are you having?" she asked.

"I was going to grab a sandwich from the cart outside. That's usually what I get, but you probably want something fancier. I'll get you something from the restaurant if you'd rather."

"I'll have whatever you're having."

He returned with two turkey sandwiches wrapped in wax paper and two bottles of cola. They unwrapped their sandwiches on the desk and ate.

"Are we on lunch break?" Kitty asked between bites.

"Looks that way," Andre said.

"Then we can gossip. Tell me what happened with Hen. How'd you win her heart?"

He laughed. "Come on, isn't that girl talk?"

"I'm a girl, so talk."

Andre shrugged. "Turned out we liked the same things. She charmed my friends at the bridge game, and I'd always thought she was pretty. Guess that's all it takes for a guy like me."

Kitty could have sworn she saw his cheeks redden under his beard. She smiled. "So you've always had a thing for Hen?"

He shifted in his seat. "I knew she was engaged, and it's not right to go after a girl who's got a guy. But when you and Hen had your falling-out in Miami, and she and I had those dinners together, she told me what a bum that guy really is. She said on the plane she was planning on dumping him. I said good riddance. Then, after she broke it off with him, she called me."

"A love story for the ages," Kitty said.

"It might not be Hollywood, but it works for me." Andre balled up the wax paper from his lunch. "I gotta tell you the truth, Kitty. I knew your pop wanted you and me to get together."

She pressed her lips together to keep her jaw from dropping. "You did?"

"Yeah. And I'm sure you felt the same way I did about that."

"What do you mean? Am I not good enough for you?" she huffed.

He gave her a sidelong glance. "I got the impression you thought you were too good for me. And I always thought of you as trouble. Since the day I met you. Even if you had been interested in me, I can't say I would have taken you up on it."

"You're probably right." She nearly winced at the thought of Max when Andre said *trouble*. "I may have been. But that's what all this is about. I'm trying to make a change."

"Yeah, that's what Hen said. And I can see it on you. You look different."

"I'll take that as a compliment," she said. "Let's get back to work."

THIRTY

Kitty and Hen rekindled their friendship slowly, starting with a casual lunch here and there. Kitty didn't have as much time as she used to, thanks to her work at the hotel, but she took Hen up on every invitation. Though Hen was tentative at first with what she shared, the more time they spent together, the more they fell back into their old rhythms. Kitty worked to prove that she could be truthful and trustworthy. Hen's wariness, though not entirely gone, began to melt.

One evening in late February, Hen suggested that they all meet at the Alhambra Club, and Kitty finally had the sense that things were returning to normal. She raced up to the suite after working in the office and dolled up, feeling almost giddy as she rode the elevator back down. Hen and Andre were waiting outside the club entrance for her. Hen's cheeks were straining with her smile.

"You look like you're about to burst," Kitty said, hugging Hen. "What's going on?"

"I have a surprise for you," Hen said.

"Oh, Hen! Are you—"

"Stop right there. We're not engaged. Yet." She elbowed Andre before continuing. "You've seemed so down lately. I thought this might cheer you up. Come on, we'll show you inside."

Kitty followed them but froze as she walked through the doors. What she saw had to be due to the haze of smoke, or the distance. It couldn't be Max standing on that stage. But, sure enough, there he stood beside Sebastian. His trumpet gleamed in the stage light.

When she saw Kitty's expression, Hen's wide smile drooped. Kitty forced herself to brighten.

"What a wonderful surprise," she said, with much false cheer. "Will you ask Jimmy to get our usual booth for us?"

Hen went to the maître d' stand, and Kitty held Andre back.

"Why didn't you tell me they were coming back?" she hissed.

"You'd quit coming to the club," he said under his breath. "I didn't think it mattered."

"You didn't want to tell Hen this was a bad idea?"

He held up his hands. "I thought she knew something I didn't. So I take it you're on the outs with him?"

"Yes."

"Doesn't she know that?" he asked.

"I didn't want to get into it," Kitty said.

"Well, tell her. We can leave."

"No. This is my club. I can tough it out."

Andre shook his head. "Whatever you want."

Hen returned to them. "Jimmy said he's ready when we are. Why don't you go say hi to Max, Kitty?"

"They look so busy," Kitty said. "I'll catch him on a break. Let's go sit down and get a drink."

Hen still looked confused, but she said nothing more. The group followed Jimmy to the booth, and Kitty immediately lit a cigarette. There had been no good time to tell Hen what had happened with Max, given that Hen was only now starting to think of Kitty in a positive light again. Spilling the truth would have brought up the ghosts of Kitty's old crimes, so she'd mostly avoided talking about him. When

Hen had brought him up, Kitty had implied that the distance had cooled things between them. Hen had always dropped it. But now, either Kitty would have to tell Hen the whole story right then and there, or she would have to speak to Max at some point that evening. Neither seemed particularly appealing.

Kitty leaned back to be sure her face was in the shadows the booth offered, but she realized quickly there was no reason to bother. Andre and Hen talked and laughed loudly in full view of the stage. Surely Max would see them and know Kitty was with them. When the band started playing, all she could hear was a clanging racket. Every note jabbed her eardrum. They played song after song, and each passing minute brought them closer to taking a break. Kitty was concerned Hen would start hounding her about saying hello to Max, but it turned out she didn't have to worry about that.

At first, Kitty thought the crowd was just lively, but the increasing noise from two men at a center table began to distract her. They had come in looking swimmy-eyed and had put away drink after drink since then. The more the men drank, the more animated they became. Sebastian was in the middle of the second verse of "Mona Lisa" when one of the men yelled out something Kitty couldn't discern. Whatever it was, it made Sebastian flinch, but he kept going with the song. The second man pounded on the yeller's arm, and they both erupted into laughter. Sebastian closed his eyes and kept singing.

The second man stood, lost his footing, and righted himself by holding on to the edge of the table. At this, Andre stood too.

"Hey," the second man said. "Didn't you hear?" He looked around the room. "They should have one of those signs here. 'No dogs and no Puerto Ricans.'"

When the man returned to his seat, Andre did the same.

"Aren't you going to kick them out?" Kitty said.

"They've been in here before," Andre said. "They're a couple of loudmouths spoiling for a fight. Don't give 'em one, and they'll drink themselves to sleep."

"But you can't let them talk to Sebastian that way."

Andre's eyes darted from the men to Sebastian. "They're friends with the cops. The taller one might be on the force. I'm not sure. I do know they served in the war. If I go over there, I'll have a fight on my hands. We don't need that."

Kitty turned her attention back to the men. The first one was now glaring at Sebastian through bloodshot eyes.

"Hey," he called. "Get your PR ass off the stage and out of our city."

Other patrons looked away as Sebastian stopped singing. The rest of the musicians slowed or stopped their playing in a confused jumble of notes. Max walked to the front of the stage, staring out into the audience. Sebastian leaned into the microphone.

"I'm not Puerto Rican," he said in a low, deliberate voice. "I'm Cuban."

The response was like a boxing bell had rung. The two men raced for the stage, pulling Sebastian off and hitting him with their fists as he scrambled to get away. Andre and Kitty stood at the same time. He grabbed her arm.

"Sit down," he said. "I'll take care of it."

Then Max dove into the fray.

Kitty lurched forward, but Andre held her back. She struggled against his grip, keeping her eyes on Max. A few more people jumped into the fight, but she couldn't see if they were helping or hurting. The only thought in her mind was getting to Max.

"Kitty!" Andre wrapped an arm around her shoulders to hold her in place. "Stop."

Her vision narrowed to a pinprick, until all she could see were the muscles in the arms of the men currently beating her friends. Without a thought, she bit Andre's hand. He howled in pain, but he let her go.

She raced across the dance floor until she could clearly see the back of the first man's head. Desperate, she grabbed a nearby chair. With strength she didn't know she had, she raised it above her head and brought it down hard on the man's back.

He went limp. The people crowding around stepped away, and some ran. Two of the chair's legs had hit the floor after making contact with the victim, and the whole thing had broken to pieces. Kitty still held the splintered half of the chair's back. As the second man stood, she raised the piece of chair over her shoulder like a batter at home plate, ready to take aim at his face. Her chest heaved as she panted.

"You want some of what your friend got?" she asked. "Hold still."

He stood for a split second, evaluating, then ran for the front door. Andre was already waiting to block his path.

Kitty dropped the remains of the chair to the floor. Panting, she turned to where Max and Sebastian lay. A few people now crowded around, trying to help, so she could only see their motionless legs.

The last thing she saw before she blacked out was the slick of blood on the dance floor.

THIRTY-ONE

Kitty woke in her bed, blinking at the alarm clock. Ten o'clock. Someone had put her dressing gown on her, but underneath she still wore the dress she'd had on at the club. A few dark spots on the dress's lapel brought the whole evening rushing back. She fought her way out of the twisted blankets, desperate to see if someone else was in the suite. Someone must know what happened to Max and Sebastian.

To her surprise, Andre waited in the living room. He stood when she walked in.

"How are you feeling?" he asked. "Here, come sit down."

"Are they all right? Max, Sebastian?" She wrung her hands.

Andre took a seat in an armchair. "I won't lie to you. They're not the best they've ever been."

"Where are they?" She perched on the arm of the sofa, dizzy now.

"They went down to the hospital to get checked out. I think they're staying another night."

Kitty leapt to her feet. "I'll change clothes—it will only take a minute. Will you call down for the car?"

Andre reached for her hand and gently pulled her back down to the couch. "I think it might be better to wait, don't you?"

"What do you mean? Are they not . . . ?" She held the back of her hand to her mouth.

"No, nothing like that. They're both awake, alert. Sebastian's still a little fuzzy. He got knocked around good. But your pop sent the best doctor in town to look at them. They'll be back to normal in no time."

"Is Papa mad?"

"Not at you. He wanted me to wait up here for you to wake up, so you wouldn't be alone. He's downstairs working things out."

Her heartbeat pounded in her ears as the faces of the assailants popped into her mind. "And the other guys? What happened to those bastards?"

"You don't have to worry about them."

She shook her head. "I walloped one of them good. I'm sure that won't be the last we hear from them. Oh, I hope I haven't caused too much trouble for Papa."

"I don't know," Andre said. "When the one you cracked with the chair came to, he claimed he had no memory of what had happened. And—here's the interesting part—his buddy didn't either. Which is odd, because his buddy was looking right at you. Seems to me neither one of them wants to admit to their cop pals that they got beat up by a girl."

"But we'll press charges against them, won't we? I mean, they started it."

"You've got to understand. If we push them, they'll push back." Andre's face was taut. "We have to let it go. Nobody is going to lock a couple of vets up because they got drunk and started a bar fight. Not when it's with guys like Max and Sebastian."

Kitty sat still, processing this. She wanted to scream that Andre was being ridiculous, that those guys would get what was coming to them and then some.

"They've agreed to stay away from the club and leave Max and Sebastian alone," Andre continued. "Honestly, with their connections, these guys could make a lot of trouble for the band and for your pop if we start pointing fingers. I think we have to drop it, unless you want Max and Sebastian arrested for assault. Max jumped in pretty quick, and there's no telling what the other witnesses will say about how it started."

"I see," said Kitty, and she thought she did. The patrons of her father's club might not feel any incentive to tell the truth about the sequence of events if the truth favored a Jewish musician and a Cuban singer over two white men, however the white men had behaved.

Kitty and Andre sat in silence for a moment, not looking at each other. Then he patted her hand and said, "We won't let them back in. I promise you that."

"And next time? What if it happens to someone else? I don't want anyone harassed in my father's hotels. In my hotels."

"There won't be a next time." He held up his hand, which had a pink semicircle on the skin. "I don't want to get bitten again."

"Sorry about that," she said, looking away.

"I should have known better than to try to hold you back," he said, his tone kind. "I'll recover."

She nodded. "I'd still like to go see Max and Sebastian."

Andre placed a hand on her arm. "They look pretty bad. And you've had a shock. I think you ought to wait."

"Don't be silly," she said, her voice wavering.

"Kitty . . . are you sure Max will want to see you?"

"I know he was angry. Maybe this changes things."

Andre nodded slowly. "Maybe. I'm sure he appreciates what you did. But it might be better to give him some time. It's your decision."

Tears stung the corners of her eyes. "If I wrote them letters, would you take them over there?"

"Sure. Sure I will." He patted her hand again. "You need anything? Did you want the doctor to come by?"

"No. I'm fine. Where's Hen?"

He chuckled. "She had the good sense not to jump into a bar fight, so she's at home. I promised her I'd call when you woke up."

"I guess you really think I'm trouble now. Glad you found yourself a nice girl who doesn't beat guys up with chairs."

"I think what you did took guts. No matter what happens with Max, he's got to know that." Andre stood, buttoning his jacket. "You call down when you've got those letters, all right? I'll make sure the boys get 'em."

"Thanks, Andre." As she watched him walk out, she considered that while he might not have made for a very good love match, he had all the makings of a good friend. She resolved to start thinking of him as one.

⇥⋇⇤

Kitty had no problem with the letter to Sebastian. She hoped that since that one came so easily, the letter to Max would flow from that promising start. No luck.

> ~~Dear Max,~~
> ~~I hope you understand that I~~
>
> ~~Dear Max,~~
> ~~What happened to you, and what I did~~
>
> ~~Dear Max,~~
> ~~Please forgive me~~

Stuck again. She was in the same place she'd been weeks earlier, writing *Dear Max* on sheet after sheet, and then crumpling each up and discarding it. Still, she couldn't have her letter to Sebastian arrive without one for Max. She jotted down a few earnest wishes for his quick return to health and an apology that didn't scratch the surface of the one she needed to make.

She knew why the right words wouldn't form, and the reason nagged at her. She couldn't write a good letter to Max for the same reason she hadn't been able to write to Hen. Max deserved to hear her voice when she expressed her regrets. He had the right to respond. She had to go to the hospital.

⊰ THIRTY-TWO ⊱

In the car on the way to the hospital, Kitty vowed to herself that she would leave if Max was really in no condition to see her. She didn't want to add any more stress to an already horrible situation. At least she had thought to ask Andre when visiting hours ended, so she wouldn't have to work up the courage to go all the way down there only to be turned away.

A nurse led her down the tiled hallway to Max and Sebastian's room. The smell of disinfectant burned Kitty's nose, and she fidgeted with the handkerchief in her hand.

"Right here," the nurse said, gesturing to the doorway.

"Are they . . ." Kitty hesitated. "They're awake, right?"

The nurse peeked in. "Yes, they're awake." She smiled at them. "You have a very pretty visitor, boys."

Kitty nodded and turned the corner. Max and Sebastian lay on beds separated by a pale green curtain, hooked against the wall so the two could see each other. She stifled a gasp. The faces of both were swollen and covered in purple bruises, and Sebastian had a row of angry black stitches above his eye. Max's left arm was in a sling. He only glanced at her, but Sebastian attempted a smile.

"Hello, Kitty. This is a nice surprise." He pointed at a chair between the beds. "Andre said you might come."

Kitty sat in the chair, gripping the arms to keep her fingers from trembling. "I had to see how you are. Are you feeling all right?"

"Better than the last time you saw us, I'd guess," Max said, his eyes now on the wall.

"They're taking good care of us here," Sebastian added quickly.

Her breath caught in her throat. "I'm so sorry. That never should have happened in our club. Not to you, not to anyone. But I want you to know that I'm going to do everything in my power to make sure nothing like it happens again."

Sebastian closed his eyes briefly and nodded. "I believe you will try."

"I promise I will. And I'll be your friend, if you still want me to be."

"Thank you, Kitty." The corner of his mouth crept up, but his eyes drooped.

She leaned in and gave him a light kiss on the cheek. "I'll just speak to Max, and then I'll go," she whispered. "All right? We'll talk more when you're feeling better."

He nodded again, and she unhooked the curtain to pull it between the two beds. She took a seat in the chair on the other side of Max's bed, by the window.

"Is . . . is it broken?" She gestured to his arm.

"No. Just sprained."

She steeled herself. "I owe you an apology."

He exhaled hard. "I appreciate you coming all the way down here and that you helped us, but I don't know if we should get into all that. I hope you understand."

"I do. But I needed to apologize in person. I won't make you sit through this if you don't feel well enough, but it would mean a lot if you'd hear me out."

He sat in silence for a beat too long. Kitty was sure he was ready to throw her out. Instead, he said, "Okay, sure."

"You have every right to think the worst of me," she said in a low voice. "And you don't have to believe me, but I truly did care about you. I did everything wrong. I hurt you, and I'll never stop being sorry for that. But I'm trying to do better. That poem of yours has changed me."

The mention of the poem must have caught his interest. "Is that right?"

"I'm learning the business from Papa and Andre. I have a real job in the hotel, and I'm earning my own way."

"That's . . . nice." He sounded confused. She had planned her words so carefully, but now she couldn't get them out.

"But I've also been going around New York, places I didn't use to go," she continued. "And, what do you know? You were right. It looks different to me. Some good, some bad. But I see all those familiar places with new eyes. Like the poem says."

"I'm glad to hear it." His voice had softened, and she took that as her opportunity to continue.

"I see my father's work differently too. You talked about doors being closed. I realized I'm in a position to help open those doors. And . . ." She sucked in a breath. "It's not really because of the poem. It's because of you. Because I cared about you. Because I still do."

"I see."

"So I realized that if I was going to be part of a change, I would have to be different on the inside. Better, like you said. That's more important to me now than being at the top."

"Kitty, that's great that you're making a change for yourself, but you're talking about big problems. Bigger than one hotel or one fight in a club. I mean, what can a girl like you do?"

His question was the same one that had rolled around in her mind over and over, taunting her. She offered him the same answer she'd always given herself. "Well . . . she does anything she can, I suppose."

Max's only response was to stare at the blanket on his lap.

"So," she continued, "that's what I wanted to say. To make sure you knew. I'm sorry for what I did. I'm grateful to have known you. And I'll go now."

She stood and hesitated, hoping he might respond. Ask her to stay. When he didn't, she walked to the door.

"Hey, Kitty?"

She turned back. "Yes?"

"Sometime you'll have to tell me, in as much detail as possible, how good it felt to crack that guy over the head with the chair." He finally looked up at her.

"I would love that." She stood and took a few steps toward the door. "Take care, Max."

"Take care."

THIRTY-THREE

NEW YORK CITY

JUNE 1954

Kitty's father walked briskly into her cramped office one hot morning. She spun in her chair, greeting him with a slow smile.

"Why, hello," she said. "And how are you this morning?"

"I'm in need of the itemized invoice from the Miami contractor," he said.

She grabbed a file from the neat stack on her desk. "I've got it, no need to be so short."

He took the papers and started rifling through. "Looks good. Glad I put you on this. Andre's chicken scratch made everything unreadable."

"I'm so glad I could dazzle you with my penmanship," she said, her tone dry.

He squinted at the columns in front of him. "Don't worry. If you keep at it, you'll get more responsibilities. Learning this work takes time." He snapped the file shut and smiled. "But you're quick."

"And you knew that already." She fanned herself with an envelope, wishing her tiny room had a window she could crack. "Are we still going to dinner tonight?"

"Yes. I've got a meeting with the fellows from Los Angeles on

Thursday. I want to pick your brain." He started for the door then paused, looking back at her. "You really think Los Angeles is the way to go?"

Kitty picked up a pen. "We'll talk about it again at dinner. Have a good afternoon."

Her father nodded and walked out. She returned to the figures she'd been entering into the large whirring calculator on her desk. In the past few months, she'd been working as a glorified secretary, but she could feel the incremental progress. Andre, in particular, had been guiding her through what each of her tasks really meant and how her work, even when it might seem trivial, fit into the bigger picture of the office. He encouraged her, and she felt like she was learning. *Small steps*, she reminded herself almost daily.

Her father had only been gone a few minutes when Andre knocked on the open door.

"Hey, Kitty. Have you—"

She picked up a stack of papers and held them out. "All organized. What would you do without me?"

He grinned. "A lot more paperwork. Say, you want a ride to the party on Saturday?"

"You're giving me a ride to your own engagement party?" she asked. "You must really be proud of that new car."

"Got to show it off." His whole face radiated satisfaction.

"I still can't believe Hen's mother is actually throwing an engagement party. Nothing against you, but after everything that happened, you'd think she'd still be sore. You must have made quite an impression."

"Not on her ma, that's for sure. But her pop likes me just fine. Turns out I'm a natural at golf."

"I'd love to ride with you. Thanks, Andre."

"Anytime." He leaned against the door frame. "Hey, you hear that Max is coming back to New York? Sooner than he planned, from how it sounds."

She kept her eyes on the documents she was filing. "Is that right?"

"So you two haven't talked then?"

"Not exactly. I've been writing to him." She had sent him letters, maybe dozens, since their last meeting in the hospital, telling him all about her job and changed perspective. After she'd apologized, it had gotten easier to write to him. Besides, he ought to know how things were going for her, she thought. He'd been a part of her new direction.

"He hasn't written back?"

"No." She gave Andre a sad smile. "But he hasn't told me to stop, either."

"There's always hope. Maybe he'll come around. You never know."

"Thanks, Andre."

The afternoons had been terrifically hot, so the trouble was balancing an elegant look with an outfit that wouldn't have Kitty sweating through it. She chose a daisy-yellow sleeveless sheath dress with a wide white bow at the back. As she styled her hair, she wondered if the platinum color she'd adored so long suited her anymore. Perhaps it was time to go back to her natural black.

Andre arrived at six o'clock. He let out a low whistle when she walked out of the suite.

"Should I take that as a compliment?" she asked.

"I've been seeing you in office wear for so long, I forgot how sharp you can look," he said.

She rolled her eyes as they walked to the elevator. "Don't forget, sweet-talker, you're engaged now."

"Ah, Hen would still be the prettiest girl in the room to me, even if she was wearing a paper bag." He pressed the lobby button.

"You're good for her. Can't think of a better match."

Andre did a double take. "That's . . . that's awfully nice of you."

"Yes, well, I can find it in me to be nice every once in a while."

Out on the sidewalk, Andre led her to his new Buick. He opened the passenger door for her, beaming.

"It's even better than you described it," she said when he sat in the driver's seat. "I love the color."

"Mandarin Red, they call it. I don't know how you tell the difference between Mandarin Red and any other kind, but it looked nice enough to me." He turned the key in the ignition, and the car started with a satisfying purr.

Andre navigated through the streets toward the Upper East Side. Kitty played with the zipper on her bag, opening and closing it. She reminded herself that she was not going for the reasons she had gone in the past, to supplicate and prove herself. She was going to celebrate Hen and Andre. No need for fear of censure from Hen's mother and the rest. And yet her stomach still flipped at the thought of being surrounded by those people again.

Hen's mother stood in the foyer, as always, greeting her guests. "Ah, Andre, welcome," she said, taking his hand. "Hen's already circulating."

"Thanks for throwing this party for us," he said.

Hen's mother leaned in. "Well, there's already a nice stack of envelopes on the table in the hall. I'm sure that's exciting for you, isn't it?"

Andre's forehead creased, and Kitty stepped in. Even if Andre hadn't felt the full meaning of Hen's mother's words, Kitty knew exactly what she was implying.

"Isn't it always nice to see such enthusiastic support for a happy couple?" Kitty said brightly. "So thrilled you invited me, Mrs. Bancroft. We haven't had a chance to see each other for so long."

Hen's mother turned to Kitty, her face stony. "Yes, I believe the last time we spoke was before your trip to Miami. Did I ever thank you properly for taking Hen along? She picked up so many interesting souvenirs."

"Please," Kitty said smoothly. "No thanks needed. I've never seen her enjoy herself more. Well, we don't want to keep you. We'll go find

Hen." She strode away from Mrs. Bancroft with a spring in her step. The pairing of Hen and Andre was better revenge than Kitty and Charles would ever have been.

They entered the living room, and Kitty searched the crowd for Hen. But the first familiar face she saw was Charles's. She stopped short.

"Andre," she said under her breath. "Charles is here."

"Oh, yeah. Hen told me her mother invited his family. Something about how they're all still friends, blah, blah. I think she was trying to make nice, if you ask me."

Kitty hadn't expected that. But it did speak to what she knew of these circles. Preserving the social order was paramount, because every seat at the dining table required the right sort of person in it. Who could step in to fill the holes left by the Remingtons or the Bancrofts? No, the status quo must be maintained. Far better to seethe quietly than to make new friends.

And Charles did seem to be seething. His face was locked in a scowl, and he downed a martini in one gulp. At his side was Patricia, whom Kitty had last seen being pursued by a misled security officer outside the entrance to Macy's. She spotted Kitty before he did, and her eyes narrowed to slits as she whispered something in his ear. Thankfully, Hen walked up to Kitty and Andre at that precise moment.

"Hello," she said, giving Andre a kiss on the cheek.

"Let me say congratulations quickly, because I have about a million questions to ask about Charles and Patricia," Kitty said. "How did you neglect to tell me about that?"

"I just found out about it myself," Hen said. "But they're only dating. Nothing serious yet."

"I never thought I'd say this about Patricia Davenport, but poor girl." Kitty shook her head. "I hope she comes to her senses."

"He's appropriate and she's appropriate," Hen said in a blithe tone. "I think that's all that matters to them. I'm sure their parents threw them together."

Kitty glanced one last time at the icy couple across the room. For so long, Hen had been the one at Charles's side, for no better reason than their mutual suitability. Now, she leaned on the arm of a man devoted to her. That was a true victory, worthy of the celebration Mrs. Bancroft had reluctantly given. Kitty accepted a glass of champagne from a passing waiter. "On to more agreeable subjects. How is decorating going?"

"Slowly," Hen said.

"But it looks great. She has such an eye," Andre said.

Hen glanced around. "I'll miss living here. It was home. But I'll be glad to have a little place that's truly all my own."

"Don't forget about me," Andre said. "I'm planning to live there too."

"Only if we can agree on the curtains," Hen said.

Andre started to laugh, then caught sight of something across the room that stopped him. He reached out for Kitty's arm. "I probably should have told you, but I didn't want you to chicken out and not come."

Kitty scanned the guests. "What are you talking about?"

Hen stepped forward. "We invited someone. Well, it was his first night back in New York, and we didn't want him to be alone . . ."

At that moment, Kitty caught sight of him. Max stood in the doorway, greeting a bemused Mrs. Bancroft.

"I told you he was coming in early," Andre said, a mischievous spark in his eye.

Kitty's fingers and toes tingled. "Are you sure he wants to see me?"

"I think he does," Hen said in a soft tone.

Hen and Andre stepped away as Max approached Kitty. His tentative smile failed to conceal a touch of wariness.

"It's good to see you," she said, her heart pounding.

He fidgeted with a button on his coat. "I got your letters."

"I hope they weren't a bother," she said. "I . . . I had a hard time forgetting about you."

"I read them all."

"You did?"

"Yeah." He held out a hand for hers. "Everyone deserves a fresh start, don't you think?"

She took his hand, relishing the familiar feel of his rough fingers. "I'm glad you think so."

"Why don't I get you a drink? We can talk."

Kitty held up her glass with a smile. "I'm taken care of. Why don't you get something?"

His laugh was still a bit shaky. As he crossed to the bar, Kitty took the opportunity to stroll around. All she heard was the same chatter that filled the room at every party, about summer homes and business meetings. She crossed to the giant windows and looked down at the street below. Even in the fading twilight, she could see people bustling around on the sidewalks. From this height, they hardly looked like people at all. More like dolls.

She sipped her champagne, a private toast to herself. She had made the right choice in letting all this go. Change was slow, a series of tiny steps over a long distance. But it didn't mean that she shouldn't appreciate each inch of progress along the way. And, thanks to the people she loved, Kitty Tessler would not have to walk that road alone.

ABOUT THE AUTHOR

AMBER BROCK teaches British literature at an all-girls school in Atlanta. She holds an MA from the University of Georgia and lives in
Smyrna with her husband, also an English teacher, and their three
rescue dogs.

LADY BE GOOD

Reading Group Guide
for *Lady Be Good*

In order to provide reading groups with the most in-formed and thought-provoking questions possible, it is necessary to reveal important aspects of the plot of this novel—as well as the ending. If you have not fin-ished reading *Lady Be Good,* we respectfully suggest that you wait before reviewing this guide.

1. Kitty claims she desires the "warm, cocooning protection of good breeding" (page 4). What does she mean by this, and what kind of pro-tection is she seeking? What is she seeking protection from?

2. What do you think prompted Kitty's father to urge her to get married or start working? Do you think his offer was unfair?

3. On page 87, Kitty notes that she prefers ro-mance to love. How do you think Kitty defines those terms? How do they differ?

4. Why do you think Max is so interested in Kitty? What about her sends a message that there's more than meets the eye?

5. Max says he likes Kitty best when she's not trying to be anyone else. Who else is she trying to be? Is that person fundamentally different from her true self?

6. Why does Hen care so much about what her mother thinks? Why do you think she can't be honest with her mother about how she really feels about Charles?

7. Does Kitty identify more with the level of privilege people like Hen have or that of people like Max and Sebastian?

8. On page 129, Max says he can't tell if Kitty is the "right" type of smart. What do you think he means by this? What type of smart do you think she is?

9. Is it wrong for Kitty to care about social status? Would she miss any opportunities by being with someone like Max as opposed to someone like Charles?

10. Kitty remembers her mother dying because a class-conscious doctor refused to see her. Her father later clarifies that this wasn't the case.

Why do you think Kitty perceived it that way, and how has that shaped her views?

11. Do you think Hen was right to have forgiven Kitty? Can she trust Kitty after her scheming?

12. Why do you think Kitty becomes so protective of Max and Sebastian?

13. How well do you think Max fits into Kitty's world? How would being a part of it affect his life and Kitty's? Do you think their relationship will continue?

A Conversation with Amber Brock

Q: Your debut, *A Fine Imitation,* is set in the 1920s and follows a fortunate socialite's restless life. *Lady Be Good* tells the story of Kitty Tessler, the mischievous, status-obsessed daughter of a hotel magnate in the 1950s. Why do you choose to build your novels around complicated, privileged women? Is that intentional?

A: Certainly, my choice of creating complex female protagonists is deliberate. I'm often reminded of Jane Austen's line about her titular character Emma: "I am going to take a heroine whom no one but myself will much like." I love Emma, precisely because her character develops so much throughout the novel. The journey is compelling to me—if a character starts the novel without flaws, where does she have to go? Vera and Kitty are both flawed women, but their flaws are realistic. At various times, they are their own worst enemies, but that's a very human struggle. I like the contrast between those internal challenges and the external luxury that these women live in. There are some problems money can't solve and some lessons about ourselves that require trial by fire to learn. I prefer to have a character who feels real, even if that authenticity means she has sharp edges.

Q: Can you tell us a bit about the significance of the title _Lady Be Good_?

A: The title is a reference to a song by George and Ira Gershwin that's now associated with Ella Fitzgerald, thanks to her legendary performance of it. I loved the line, "I am so awfully misunderstood," since that's certainly how Kitty sees herself at the beginning of the novel.

Q: Why did you choose to set _Lady Be Good_ in the 1950s?

A: The 1950s have become a sort of idealized, golden past in the United States, but that wasn't the case for every member of society. There's a nostalgia for the 1950s that ignores some of the realities. The economy was booming, but the full benefits were only available to those who already had a certain level of privilege. It was a decade noted for its conservatism in America, but the groundwork for the major social change that happened in the 1960s was being laid. That undercurrent of change mirrors the changes that happen to Kitty internally as she navigates parts of the world she hasn't encountered before.

Q: _Lady Be Good_ takes place in New York City, Miami, and Havana. Was it always your plan to set the novel in these cities? If so, why? If not, how did that develop?

A: New York City was a natural choice for a hotel magnate to start his empire since the city underwent enormous growth in the early decades of the twentieth century. Kitty's father would have been building his first hotel in the early 1920s, taking full advantage of the first postwar boom. Miami would have been a savvy place to expand to since south Florida became a more accessible tourism destination during those years for a variety of reasons. The choice to send Kitty to Havana came out of the inclusion of Sebastian, the Cuban lead singer at the Miami hotel. As his character developed, I wanted to spend more time with him and reveal more of his personal history in his home. Since the roots of the Cuban Revolution had begun to spread by the early 1950s (though the revolution wouldn't take place until the end of the decade), I wanted to explore how that changed the dynamics for someone like Sebastian, who'd left his home and family behind in so much uncertainty.

Q: Identity is a major theme in *Lady Be Good* as Kitty comes of age, despite herself, once exposed to the world beyond her privileged corner of Manhattan. In your opinion, what are the other major themes in the novel and why?

A: I wanted to dig into what happens when someone really, deeply messes up. How does a mistake like that change how we see ourselves? It's a painful reckoning, but one that I think we all have to face. If we face it with honesty, it can usually make us stronger and smarter. Oftentimes, a mistake like that can impact our closest relationships, just as it does with Kitty and Hen. Kitty does have a romance in the novel, but I think the real love story is the one between the two childhood friends and the lengths Kitty goes to save her friendship when her actions threaten to end it.

Q: You must've done extensive research for this novel. What were some of the more interesting and surprising things you learned?

A: I always have a lot of fun building settings, and I try to use as much from the real world as possible. The internet is a treasure trove of highly specific interests, and it's fascinating what people document. I found an entire website devoted to the golden age of air travel, full of scanned luggage tags, brochures, and menus. I also discovered that people have uploaded their home videos of family trips to YouTube, so I was able to see southern Florida of the era through the eyes of real tourists. I bet no one expected anyone outside of their families to ever watch those! Another fun tidbit: I found photos of the actual menu and place mat from Pickin' Chicken, where Max and Kitty have their first lunch date. They're exactly as described in the book!

I'm also lucky enough to have a librarian in the family, and she was instrumental in helping me find oral histories and archive materials, particularly about Havana and the club scene in the 1950s. Through her, I discovered Irving Fields, a Jewish musician from New York City who set Yiddish standards to Latin rhythms. It led me to information about other Jewish musicians who gravitated toward, and found success in, the Latin music scene of the 1950s and '60s. It was such a unique blend of cultures, and it helped me form Max as a character.

Q: What do you hope readers take away from *Lady Be Good*?

A: I hope readers enjoy following Kitty's growth. It's hard to confront ourselves in those times when we are truly wrong about something, and it's even harder to make a change based on what we discover about ourselves in those moments. Ultimately, Kitty learns to look outside of her own experience, and she takes steps not only to be a better person, but also to make the world a better place in her own way. Those kinds of changes and initiatives are powerful, even when it's just one person.

Q: What are you working on now?

A: I'm dabbling with several potential projects, but I've been spending the most time with a mystery set in Hollywood's studio system era. More strong, complicated women!

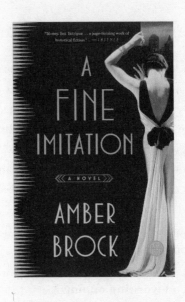

If she had to guess, Vera Longacre would say that most of the girls at Vassar College knew her name and could pick her out of a crowd, even if she could not do the same for them. Her peculiar brand of celebrity came without any effort on her part, much like the money, the houses, and appearances on the society page. Very few of her fellow students could claim to know her personally, and a still smaller group would be able to identify her favorite foods or pastimes or which room in the dormitory was hers. But almost everyone knew Vera's face well enough to whisper and nod discreetly in her direction as she glided past them on the quad. She sometimes felt like a walking magazine cover, with her name above her head in place of a title.

Not that she didn't have a social group. In her first two years, she had selected a couple of girls of adequate means and manners, with whom she ate dinner and studied from time to time. The classroom, however, was a sacred space for her. When the instructor lectured, she preferred to be out of danger of distraction. She found the third row of the classroom the perfect compromise. Freshman year she had made the mistake of choosing a seat too close to the professor's podium, and sophomore year had taught her the back of the room made it difficult to hear over the whispers of less inspired classmates. Now, as a senior, she had found the perfect balance. Close enough to hear well, not so close that the professor would expect her to answer every question.

Vera liked to arrive a few minutes early. On that morning, she walked into the classroom in the Main Building to find only three other girls giggling in the back row. The auditorium-style seating sloped down to a lectern and desk at the front of the room, and three large windows at the back provided far more light than the new electric bulbs overhead. Once she had chosen her third-row seat, she opened her textbook to the assigned reading. She skimmed back over the paragraphs, then found her attention drifting to the plates, which showed richly colored prints of a set of neoclassical paintings. Who could read endless pages of dry description when the paintings were right there to be devoured?

A satchel thunked down beside Vera, but she did not bother to look up. Her two closest friends did not share any of her classes, and she didn't care for small talk. She flipped the page to a new painting as the girl in the neighboring seat let out a huff.

"If you ask me, the problem with the neoclassicists is all the lounging," the girl said.

Vera looked up to find a pretty girl with hair as black as her own, though her eyes were blue instead of Vera's brown. A playful smile lit up the girl's round face.

"I mean, look," the girl continued, gesturing at the plate on the page. "Every single figure here is draped against a marble wall or slumped against a column. Surely one of those painters must have known the ancient Romans or Greeks could stand and sit like normal people, don't you think? Just look at how this woman is flopping around."

"I . . . suppose." Vera could not think of a better answer to such an absurd observation. "It is part of the style, though."

The girl tapped the paper. "Oh, it's always part of the style. Anytime they're doing something silly-looking it's part of the style."

"How would you have done it, then?"

The girl pulled the book from Vera's desk and inspected it. She waved her hand again, dismissing the painting in front of her. "I don't know. Wouldn't it be much nicer if it looked like real life? If it had real detail?"

"Like a photograph?"

A grin spread on the girl's pink-cheeked face. "Exactly. See? You understand. With their eyes all rolled to the gods like that, it looks like they're having fits. The worst thing is how lazy it is on the artist's part. Making a person look real is far more of a challenge."

Vera stared at the girl. At least she wasn't talking about the weather. "I'm sorry, have we met before?"

"I don't think so, why?"

Before she could prepare a more polite answer, Vera said, "Because most people introduce themselves before barging up to complain about women in neoclassical paintings having fits."

The girl's eyes widened. Vera thought for a moment she would get up and leave, but instead she laughed. "Then I'd better introduce my-self. I'm Bea Stillman. Please, never, ever call me Beatrice."

Vera's brows shot up. "Stillman? I'm surprised we haven't met be-fore now. I didn't know there were any Stillmans here."

Bea shook her head. "Not those Stillmans. Related, though. He's my father's cousin. We left for Georgia before he left Texas." She sat up straighter. "We're the Atlanta Stillmans."

The mention of Georgia explained Bea's breathy cadence and drawn-out vowels. "I must say I'm surprised," Vera said. "Why come so far north?"

The girl toyed with her bracelet. "I was at Agnes Scott, in Decatur, but my parents decided the New York set would be a good influence for me. Fewer pearls, more diamonds. Though I don't know how good your manners are after all." At Vera's frown, Bea leaned forward. "You haven't introduced yourself yet."

"Oh." Her stern look relaxed. "Right. I'm Vera Longacre."

"Of course I knew there was a Longacre among us," Bea said with a wry tone.

Vera turned to fuss in her bag. "Yes, that's me."

Bea paused at Vera's tightened expression. "Oh, now, don't be that way. That's not the first time you've gotten that reaction, is it, Rockefeller?" Her softened pronunciation of the final *r* made it sound closer to "fella."

Vera's features loosened into a smile. She adopted the tone her mother and her friends used to speak to the wait staff at the club. "We are not the Rockefellers, goodness."

Bea played along, lifting her nose into the air. "Don't like the comparison?"

"Certainly not, darling." Vera leaned in, lowering her voice to a hush. "New money."

The girls laughed. The room had filled as they were talking, and now most of the rows were occupied. The instructor walked in, set her briefcase on the desk, and turned on the slide projector. The slight, gray-haired woman's voice bounced around the oak-paneled room for about five minutes before Bea started scribbling on a scrap of paper. She passed the note to Vera.

Are you a senior?

Vera wrote *yes* and passed it back. After further scratching on Bea's part, the scrap returned.

I'm a junior. I live in Josselyn. You?

Ignoring the note for a moment, Vera put on a firm listening-to-the-teacher face. When she felt her point was made, she wrote *Strong Building.*

Bea didn't write back for a good while. At last, the paper returned to Vera, with a new line.

You ought to get moved to Josselyn. We have showers.

Vera wrote back, *Josselyn wasn't built when I started here.*

Bad luck. Do you have a beau?

This question took Vera by surprise, and she missed most of the discussion about the sculptor Canova as she chose an answer. Finally, she put *yes* on the paper and slid it back down the long desk.

Bea glanced at the paper and pursed her lips dramatically.

a shot of affection through her. Perhaps it was that carelessness that drew her to Bea. There was none of the social posturing Vera was so accustomed to. The girls she typically socialized with were so afraid of saying the wrong thing, they hardly spoke at all. Bea wasn't a breath of fresh air, she was a balmy gust.

"If we must be friends, then I guess we ought to go to lunch together," Vera said. "Would you like to?"

Bea nodded, and the two headed off, trailing paper all the way.

That took a while to write.

I didn't want to miss any more of the lecture.

But you sure didn't look like you were listening. Who is he? Is it forbidden? I simply love forbidden romance.

It's not forbidden.

You can tell me. I'm good at keeping secrets.

Not now.

Vera thought for a moment after this and added: *It's not a secret.*

When the professor dismissed the class, Bea stood and exhaled hard. "I must say, you have me in suspense, Vera Longacre. Why don't you come with me and tell me all about your scandalous love affair?"

Vera laughed. "It's not a scandal. It's the exact opposite of a scandal, as a matter of fact."

Bea scooped up her books, papers, and pen in one messy jumble with one hand and hooked her elbow through Vera's. "Well, come with me and tell me your deadly dull story anyway." She shot a look out of the corner of her eye. "I may as well say it. I wasn't planning to like you."

"Oh, no?"

"That's why I started talking to you." Bea led Vera down the stairs to the exit.

"You started talking to me because you thought you wouldn't like me?" Vera asked.

"That's right. I like to pick a serious-looking girl and say a few shocking things, to see how fast she moves to another desk."

Vera nudged Bea with her shoulder. "That's horrible."

"It is, but I'm starved for entertainment." She rolled her eyes and drawled out the word *starved*. "Anyway, you didn't move desks. You sat right there and said something clever." Bea released Vera's arm as they entered the hallway. "I'm afraid this means we have no choice. We simply must be friends."

Vera studied the odd, lively girl beaming in front of her. Papers dripped from the clumsy stack in her arms. Bea's careless stance sent